About the Author

Adam Dickson is a novelist and screenwriter. His novels are *The Butterfly Collector* (2012), *Drowning by Numbers* (2014), and *Billy Riley* (2020). He has also co-written three non-fiction books in the sports genre, and a book on mental health, *Surfing the Edge: a survivor's guide to bipolar disorder.*

His screenplays include adaptations of both novels, and a pilot for TV. In February 2020, he appeared as an expert in the CBS Reality crime series *Murder by the Sea.* The episode titled *Neville Heath, the Lady Killer* documents the real-life case of ex-RAF pilot Neville Heath, who was hanged at Pentonville Prison in 1946.

www.adamdickson.co.uk

INDIGO BLUE

BY

ADAM DICKSON

Castra publishing

ACT I

THE SEA

She found the journal in a cabin locker, a handwritten inscription on the inside cover. Diary entries made up to July 3, then nothing, blank pages. Reading back inspired a morbid interest – the thoughts and observations of someone no longer around; in one sense these people had never existed, except as a distraction, an irritation. But here it was, all laid out in such a neat hand. All those rich and meaningful conversations of yesterday; dancing and champagne in Beverley Hills; sailing trips along the coast with the Hollywood elite. Privileged lives that had never known hardship of any kind, never been beaten or abused in any way. How quickly those lives had been ended. Cut short in the most desperate of ways.

Johnny was still on deck, working the sails. He looked up as she came through the companionway, that same teasing half-smile that contained all their secrets.

'Wind's picked up,' he said. 'We're making good headway.'

She held up the journal. 'I found this.'

Ignoring her, he hauled at the mainsail. 'Why don't you make us something to eat?'

'I ain't hungry.'

'Gotta eat, honey. Keep your strength up. Can't expect me to do all this on my own.' His look silenced her, a reminder that out here he was the boss and he gave the orders. It paid her to let him think that way, to keep the uneasy balance between them – at least until they got to Mexico. His moods could change, set off by the slightest thing. Then everything would be her fault again. Laura-Mae Ellis, the girl from Hicksville. When she was around, bad things happened. That was the way it was and always had been.

The last speck of grey headland fell behind. Every nautical mile brought them closer to safety, beyond the jurisdiction of the authorities on the mainland, and whoever else might come looking for them. Johnny said if they could make it to Mexico things would improve. They'd find a hotel with room service and hot water. His friend, the Colonel, would be able to help them get the papers they needed, maybe even a loan from the bank to start a business.

Indigo carried them off into the night, the sleek yacht both their means of escape and a kind of prison. She couldn't get used to the narrow confines below deck, everything compressed into small, stowaway niches. The master cabin, with its leopard-print cover on the wide double berth and brass adornments on the walls. A few personal items stored in a drawer under the bunk. Johnny knew all about her, having sailed the coastline with the previous owners many times; where she was built and the details of her construction, from the mahogany planking to the teak handrails fitted to the cabin roof. Seeing her slip through the waves, it was hard not to admire her beauty and craftsmanship. But now she was here purely to facilitate their escape, to put distance between them and their would-be pursuers.

Rocked by the motion of the waves against the hull, Laura-Mae breathed in the cabin's musty air and tried to acclimatise. Still it didn't feel right. An essence of the previous owners remained, like the scent of an animal left behind to ward off intruders. Finding the journal had made her inquisitive. She wanted to know more about them, who they were and where they came from. What Johnny had told her wasn't enough, and maybe she didn't believe

him anyway. Johnny liked to tell stories. And sometimes the stories seemed like pure inventions from all the crazy things he carried round in his head.

An old copy of Photoplay lay on the side. On the cover, the face of the great actress, Margot Katz, captured in a serene, almost ethereal light. Inside, details of her long career in the movies, the famous contract that had guaranteed her $10,000 a week and the front cover of all the trade magazines. The huge star, who once strolled into hotel lobbies, flashing that enigmatic smile, as the press hounds swarmed around to snap shots and write up copy. Now a has-been, left to grow old and die behind the walls of her big old house.

Funny to think they'd sat around her living room, smoking her imported cigarettes and drinking English tea. The way she would touch Johnny's arm in a gesture of affection, as if the two of them had known each other a long time By then her star was fading, but the aura around her remained untouched. Memories left in the photo portraits that lined the walls, stories she liked to tell in that exquisite voice. The Hollywood of old. Such wonderful times that would never be recaptured.

Next to the magazine, lay a hat. She put it on, seeking out the vanity mirror to see how it looked. The wide rim would protect her from the sun, but it gave her something else, a kind of veiled innocence that radiated outward. Her eyes shone with a melancholy lustre. 'Pools of sorrow,' Barthez once said, without doubt her best feature. Why, in a certain light she even resembled the great actress herself, whose elegance she so admired. One of the reasons Barthez had promised to sign her in the first place, create a special role for her that would break her in the movies and get her a start. She'd get to wear the fancy gowns and the expensive jewellery, sign autographs for the waiters and bellhops on Sunset Boulevard. But none of that ever happened. All because of Johnny.

He looked up to find her posing in the companionway.

'What do you think?' she said.

'I don't think much at all.'

'Don't you like me in the hat?'

'Sure, honey, but right now you need to be up here with me. Weather might change and we need to be vigilant. You know what that means?'

She took off the hat, deflated.

'Gotta be prepared at all times,' he said. 'No telling what's gonna happen out here.'

The night closed in around them, wave tips like beacons far out. Out here there were no distractions, no parties to go to and no jazz bands playing to take her mind off things. No intimations of the place they'd just left, with its strange mix of inhabitants all looking for the same thing.

'Don't it make you feel lonesome?' she said.

'Why would I feel lonesome when I got you?'

She smiled, distant and sorrowful. Johnny Boy. The only one in the world for her, and she for him. They were good together. She did what he told her to do without thinking too much about the consequences, and that's the way it had been since they'd first met. 'You're my favourite corner of the universe,' he told her one night, and she believed him, gave herself to him completely from that moment on. And when the darkness came over him and he withdrew into that awful place that shut everything out, she let him know she would always be there waiting for him. Together they would take over the world. Nothing could stop them.

*

Sunrise came in a wash of brilliant colour. *Indigo* cut through the water, rolling in the troughs. The choppy motion gave her a sense of exhilaration, that now they were really underway. Right from a child she had that feeling – the journey itself always better than any destination. Somehow, when you got to where you were going it always seemed a disappointment – just a bunch of houses and people doing the same old thing. Even in California, where people lived out the weirdest dreams. Out here, alone and surrounded by the vastness of the sea, the past no longer existed, carried away by the wind and the tide.

The ocean rose in angry peaks that passed beneath them and rose up again in surges that took the breath away. Easy to see why human characteristics had been applied to it over the centuries: angry and cruel; harsh and unforgiving. Yet here they were on the loneliest place on earth and somehow she felt freer than she'd ever felt before.

'How long before we get to Mission Bay?' she said.

'Keep heading due south, should be there in a day or so. Pick up a few supplies and head on out again.'

'Won't they come looking for us?'

'Why should they? Everybody thinks we're still in LA.'

The first time she saw the ocean she wept tears of joy, far enough away from the dust bowl of her previous existence to feel a sense of gratitude and belonging. How could anyone fail to be seduced by a place where oranges grew in abundance, and people talked excitedly about all the golden opportunities there. Finding work in the studios. Being near the big stars, like Margot, who lived in mansions on Wiltshire Boulevard and were chauffeured around in limousines. Even the most outlandish dreams were made possible if you knew the right people.

'You think we'll ever go back?' she said.

'Don't you think we got enough troubles?'

'I'm just saying. '

'What you wanna go back for anyhow? We got a new life waiting for us in Mexico.'

But there were things she would miss. A ride along Mulholland Drive in the open top Buick – through the electronic gates of Barthez's big house and over the gravel towards the pool. The crunch of the stones beneath the tyres, and the grinding of the gates as they clanged shut; the energy-sapping heat as she stepped out. Recollections so vivid and so real. Yet somehow she'd given up the right to call them hers.

Death changed everything. One person's loss always another's gain. Like the journal, now a possession of hers. A useless artefact to go with all the other things she'd found in the cramped cabin space. Johnny said they had to forget what had happened, that it had all been a mistake. But she couldn't get it out of her head. The events of the Fourth of July changed everything.

She cooked chicken and rice on the galley stove. The supplies wouldn't last longer than a few days. Hopefully, by then they'd have dropped anchor and found a hotel, met with the Colonel. Best to be frugal just in case – ensure they didn't run out ahead of time. Johnny said he knew where they were and where they were going, but she wasn't convinced. Pride would stop him admitting he might be wrong. And if she challenged him he might erupt, throw a mean fit with one of his terrible tempers.

Taking the food up, she sat with him. He coughed, hard, and put a hand to his mouth, his eyes watering.

'You OK, baby?' she said.

'I'm fine.'

'Maybe we can find a doctor when we get to Mexico.'

'I don't need a doctor – how many times I gotta tell you that?' He gripped the helm, watching the dip of the bow and the plunge into the next trough. Once again, she admired his resilience, his courage. The supreme effort it must have taken to get them this far with his constitution, this weakness he tried to keep hidden.

They ate in silence. She tried to keep her thoughts pure and wholesome, but the worries crept back in. Now and then she felt the need to talk, to discuss what had happened, but he cut her off. That was all dead and gone and the people inconsequential. Best they didn't talk about it at all.

'Remember that song?' she said. 'St Louis Blues? Always makes me think of that night we drove to Encino.'

He nodded, lost in his thoughts.

'Will there be places like that in Mexico?'

'Sure there will, honey. Lots of places.'

'And we'll have a house by the sea, like you said?'

'That's right – just like I said.'

He'd become insular again, at times forgetting she was even there. Even the physical changes seemed to hint at an inner transformation. The sunburned face and the windblown hair, no longer plastered back across his scalp with brilliantine. How strange it was to love someone so unconditionally, and yet at times to hate them when they wouldn't respond the way you wanted them to. And yet she couldn't be without him. Like the fortune teller on Sunset Strip said, their souls had merged and become one. They did everything together. Even the bad things they couldn't talk about. And just maybe, if you pushed those things so far back in your mind it would seem like they hadn't happened at all.

*

Day Two, and still no sign of the stop-off at Mission Bay. She sank again into sad reflection, her mood, encased as it were by the totality of the sea. Thoughts of childhood: a one-room shack in the shadow of a mountain range; freezing winters and burning hot summers. A sense of impermanence about everything, except the poverty, the one thing that was always unchanging.

Distant wave-tips aroused more memories; a picture-book ending at odds with reality. What if she hadn't met Johnny? What if she'd listened to Barthez's warnings instead and stayed well away. 'He ruins everything he comes into contact with, Laura-Mae. Allow him close enough and he'll ruin you too.' But she hadn't listened, seduced by Johnny's aura, that hint of vulnerability he tried to hide behind a nonchalant front. She fell in love with him, promising to look after him and make him happy. Now they were out here, the two of them alone together with nothing else to get in the way. She would honour that commitment. Get him the help he needed.

There were other things to consider. Tasks of a more practical nature she hadn't been ready to face until now. And whether he liked it or not, they were going to have to deal with it sooner or later.

'What we gonna do with their things?' she said.

'Leave 'em for now, I guess.'

'Is that a good idea?'

'What do you suggest – dump it all over the side and have

some fishing boat pick it up in the nets?'

'No, but – '

'Just leave it, OK? I'll work it out when I'm good and ready.'

Death didn't look so tidy up close. Not like it did in the movies when the actor clutched his chest and dropped to his knees when the gunshot rang out. The actor's performance was theatrical, contrived, and always with the certainty that he would get up when the director yelled 'Cut!' Then, when the scene was wrapped, they would all go home and the whole thing would be forgotten. But not in this instance. The reality left an imprint, a slow-motion playback every time she thought about it.

The spirits of the dead were here. She could hear their voices, pitched high above the wind. A sad and mournful lament that carried an unmistakeable note of accusation.

'If something happened out here nobody would find us,' she said.

He looked up sharply. 'Nothing's gonna happen. Why you gotta keep talking like that?'

'Please don't be angry with me, Johnny.'

'I ain't angry with you. I just don't wanna hear all that. It ain't fortuitous.'

The horizon line merged with the sea. She had that same feeling of insignificance, somehow comforting and unnerving at the same time. Out there, an expanse of black ocean, completely indifferent to them or their needs.

What would become of her when they got to Mexico? Maybe she'd be expected to cook and wash the dishes like a good little housewife – the worse thing she could think of after all she'd been through. To end up as someone's possession, a chattel, like the womenfolk back home. How long could she go without the habits she'd become accustomed to? The music and the dancing. The select band of actors and actresses she'd joined who welcomed her as one of their own.

California, a safe haven for the generation who wanted to escape drudgery and find a new life in the sun. The six months they spent in Ventura seemed like forever, like she'd found her

spiritual home. Such good friends they made there: the artists and the poets at the Pierpont Inn; the hard-drinking men from the Union Oil Company that Johnny fell in with. How they'd all meet and talk about the future, everyone drinking in the spirit of optimism, the belief that things would work out if they all pulled together. Even the talk of a coming war in Europe didn't seem to trouble them none, they were all having such a good time.

After Ventura, wherever they ended up always seemed like a stopover, a brief hideaway from the authorities or whoever else they were running from. One exotic location replaced by another – but always with the unspoken agreement they would have to keep moving. And the further they travelled, the harder it would be to maintain their disguise.

The first time she saw their pictures in the newspaper she couldn't believe it was them. Johnny thought it was truly something, said now they were famous like Bonnie and Clyde. She didn't think it was funny at all. They were fugitives, forced to keep on running. Always a chance someone might recognise them and turn them over to the law.

'Why don't you get some sleep?' she said. 'I'll take over here.'

'I don't need sleep, I need to stay vigilant.' He raised an arm and beckoned her over. 'Here – come and sit next to me.'

She shifted her butt along the seat, felt the warmth of his body against hers. The sea looked almost peaceful, the white tips of each swell illuminated under the moonlit sky. Staring into the swell, she felt a sense of calm, that nothing could touch them. Close as they might be to the coast, this was still a wilderness, and they were nothing but a speck upon it.

Johnny smiled down at her. 'You look beautiful, you know that?'

'I don't think so, my hair's a mess.'

'Looks pretty good to me.'

She touched the stiff ends of her bob, self-consciously. 'I wouldn't want anyone else to see me looking like this.'

'Ain't much chance of that happening out here, honey. It's just you and me.' He smiled, that way he had of imparting confidence to her when she was needy and anxious. She smiled back, but something nagged at the back of her mind, gave her an uneasy feeling every time she thought about it.

'You never told me who she was.'

He stared at her, blankly. 'Huh?'

'The girl from Encino. The one in the car that night.'

'What the hell made you think of that?'

'I don't know. I just did.'

Detectives came to the house – two bozos with shirtsleeves rolled up and mean, almost comical faces. They showed her the photograph of a crashed automobile, twisted beyond recognition. The girl in the passenger seat had been killed instantly, they said. Now they were looking for the owner of the vehicle – did she know where he was? It couldn't have been Johnny, she told them. He'd been with her at the time they said it happened. All that with her face stained with tears, and a hankie to dab at her cheek. They must have believed her because they let it go. The first time she'd lied to someone in authority.

'Don't matter who she was,' Johnny said.

'Why can't you just tell me? It don't matter none seeing as she's dead anyway?'

He grimaced, stared out into the darkness.

'We was all drinking. I passed out on the couch early in the morning. When I woke, someone said she'd taken my keys and drove off in my car.'

'Is that the truth?'

'True as I'm sitting here, honey.'

There were things Johnny didn't know about her, too. But she could always work them out in her own mind. Find a reason. Justification for what was better left unsaid. But the girl from Encino left a bitter taste, like a poison she had to swallow.

*

Sickness came upon her by stealth. Bent over the guard wire, she pitched the contents of her stomach into the sea until there was nothing left. Most unladylike, Johnny said, and she had to agree. He didn't seem to suffer the same way, or maybe he'd gotten used to it from all those trips along the coast and around the islands.

'How do you feel?' he said, as she groped her way back.

'Terrible.'

'Well don't go messing up my nice clean saloon, you hear?'

'Thanks for the sympathy!'

Sinking back in the cockpit, she watched him work on deck. Even with the sickness it was hard not to feel a sense of admiration. After all they'd been through, he could still take care of 'business' and stay focussed. And yet still it was hard to trust him in other ways.

Sometimes it was hard to know when he was telling the truth. She was reminded of her mother's admonition when she was a child: tell one lie and you had to tell a whole lot more to cover up the first. How many lies had Johnny told her since they'd met? And how many times had she chosen to believe him because it was convenient, because the excitement of being with him outweighed the negatives?

'How you feeling now?' he said.

'Like my insides have been sucked out and there's nothing left.'

'Won't be long now, honey. We'll be on dry land and everything'll work out just fine.' He massaged her shoulders, just how she liked it, working his fingers into the soft, fleshy part of her neck. She tried to be optimistic. If they could make it to Mexico his health would improve. The climate in California had made a difference, and any hot, dry country would help his ongoing treatment. The rest would be down to her and how pleasant she could make the conditions for him.

But the nursemaid act got tiresome after a while. Out here on the ocean she couldn't afford for him to take to his bed. Selfish of him to even think such a thing after all they'd been through.

Indigo's bow rose and fell, a sense of strength and durability in her solid timbers. But the security she offered was illusory. She'd witnessed all the things they'd done and knew all their secrets.

Laura-Mae checked herself, having broken the unwritten rule.

Not to think about what had happened. To put it out of her mind. Johnny gazed out over the water saying nothing.

She stood, light-headed from fatigue and the effects of the sun. 'I'm going below.'

He looked up, distracted. 'I'll come wake you in a few hours. You can take over.'

Sleep came in fits. She kept waking to the rolling of the yacht and the occasional lurch as a wave broke against the bow. In her dreamlike state she saw the faces of the townsfolk she'd left behind, considering all the evidence against her. I didn't do it! she yelled, but they wouldn't listen. She was bad through and through. Laura-Mae Ellis. Guilty of everything, right from a child.

Later, she heard movement from the galley; a cupboard door opened and closed. Johnny Boy's familiar hacking cough, like a retort in the confined space.

The cabin door opened, and he peered in.

'You still awake?' he said.

'Kind of.'

He sat on the bunk, and slipped off his shoes. 'Take a turn at the helm if you like, it ain't as rough out there now.'

She sat up, and hugged herself, oppressed by the gloom, the absence of choices.

'What's up?' he said.

'I had a nightmare. Folks back home were standing over me whispering things. It was horrible.'

'Just a dream, honey, that's all.'

She got up, and edged past him. He took hold of her wrist, his gaze lingering over her, playful but intense. 'Don't you go getting soft on me now, you hear?'

'I ain't getting soft on no one.'

Pulling her down beside him, he kissed her neck. She closed her eyes, tired and unable to respond. But his need was greater, so she went through the pretence to comfort him, hoping it would be over quick. How that side of things had changed between them. He didn't bother with the niceties anymore; the light touch and the affectionate smile to make her feel good. The ugliness in him came more quickly now, a desperate need he couldn't suppress.

After, empty and drained of her ability to give, she went up on deck, relieved to be alone. But any separation could only be temporary. Wherever she went, he would always be there, watching her, demanding and expecting her love and loyalty. And if she ever withdrew that part of herself from him intentionally he would make her suffer. He told her that, right from the beginning.

*

With the yacht on course, all they could do was sit back and wait for conditions to change, a fundamental truth for life on the ocean. Nothing stayed the same for long, not even the rhythmic slap of water against the hull, or the wind in the sails. In spite of her sickness early on, she'd come to enjoy the thrill of being on board, the tremendous isolation and occasional moments of danger. The feeling of being truly alive.

A gannet flew over and circled the masthead. Wherever they went they were never short of company. Along with the gannets was the ever-present marine life: the school of fish that appeared when they left the island; the dolphins that stayed with them for what seemed like hours, diving beneath the hull and leaping above the surface in spectacular formation. No signs of human traffic; no yachts or cargo boats. Nothing but the white tips of the waves and the endless sea. For every hour they sailed away from California the likelihood of their being apprehended faded. They were free, just the two of them against the elements, the whole world behind them at last.

'I found the lifejackets,' she said. 'I hope we ain't gonna need 'em.'

'Chances are we will, honey. Forecast says there's a storm coming in.'

'Will we be OK?'

'Sure we will. Didn't I tell you that already?'

In spite of Johnny's confidence she had to think in terms of survival. They might drift off course, or run out of fuel. If the storm was bad enough, they might capsize, or get washed overboard. The desire for sanctuary grew stronger – the thought of taking a bath and putting fresh clothes on; eating in a diner like civilised folk. But of course that wouldn't happen. They wouldn't be able to walk around like normal folk at all. There were law enforcement agencies out looking for them, their pictures wired from coast to coast.

Rooting around in the master cabin she found an expensive-looking top. Unable to resist, she slipped it on, the silky material cool against her skin. The fabric seemed to stretch and mould itself to the contours of her body like it had been made for her. By wearing it she was making a statement, a kind of defiance at the ghosts of the previous owners. They could complain all they liked but it wouldn't make any difference. She'd learned to ignore their voices. Shut the damn things out of her head.

Johnny raised an eyebrow as she came up on deck. She did a little pout for him, hand on hip like one of the girls on Sunset Boulevard.

'What do you think?' she said.

'Didn't you hear what I said? We got a storm coming in.'

'I'm just trying to have a little fun, Johnny.'

'You can have all the fun you want when we get to Mexico. Right now I need you up here with me.'

Crushed by his attitude, she let her shoulders sag. He watched her intently, shaking his head.

'And put that goddam top back where you found it. I don't want to see you wearing her clothes again, you hear?'

They could have been out on a day trip along the coast, enjoying a little respite before dinner, wondering what clothes to wear and which clubs to call in on later. Instead, they had this. The unspoken agreement between them not to talk about what had happened. The certainty that life would never be the same. And Johnny's insistence on spoiling what little enjoyment she might get from the situation by turning into a goddam square.

She opened a bottle of wine and took it up on deck. Johnny took a sip, and nodded with quiet satisfaction, announcing in one of his highfalutin voices, 'Well, Laura-Mae, I do declare – conditions are what you make 'em. Wouldn't you agree?'

The wine produced a dull sedative effect. Her mind strayed to territory she'd rather forget. Images and people from a far off place. Hollywood, where the rich and powerful held court and looked down on everybody else. Always so glamorous and seductive from the outside until you took a peek behind the curtain and saw how it really was. But she missed the uncertainty, the people. The not knowing where you were going to be from one day to the next.

'Will I have to get a job when we get to Mexico?' she said.

'Guess you'll have to wait on tables like you did before.' He grinned at her. 'Unless you can think of a better way to make a living.'

'Like what?'

'Well, maybe I could put you out on the street. I figure you got a few more years left in you.'

'Thanks.'

'Don't mention it, honey.'

She drank more wine, and listened to the creaking hull. The drop in wind created a more leisurely feel. Perhaps this too was an illusion. Somewhere out there was the unknown enemy, the authorities collating information and sending radio messages to pinpoint their position. It only felt like they were alone.

'What if we changed course and went to New York?' she said.

'Just like that?'

'Why not – we can do whatever we like, can't we?'

'New York's a long way, honey.'

'So's Mexico.'

'Let's just stick to the plan, huh?'

Barthez said the movie business started in New York, before the exodus to California. She got an ache in her heart thinking about it. What her life might have been like had she stayed there and tried to work it out. Johnny said they were all snakes, every one of them, just about the worst collection of undesirables you could have the misfortune to meet. But she didn't always see it that way. Some of the movie folk had tried to help her. People like Mrs Seberling and Van der Hass, who she'd taken up with for a while. But it was the industry itself that had really seduced her. Once you had a glimpse of that life it hurt to leave it behind.

'Know what I'd like right now?' she said.

'What's that?'

'A big ole ice cream sundae like we had in Mirabella's. Wouldn't that be something?'

'Sure would. But we got everything we need right here, honey.' The look in his eye made her weaken, drew her in to his world where he wanted her to be. At least he wasn't mad at her anymore. She'd changed the top, put her shirt back on. Did what he wanted her to do.

'Why don't you get some sleep?' she said.

He stood, stretched and yawned. 'You gonna be OK up here?'

'Sure, baby. I'll wake you when we get to Mexico.'

He smiled and brushed her hair with his fingertips, and in that moment she felt safe. Something was surely looking out for them, making sure they had safe passage. The God she sometimes prayed to, keeping all the darkness behind them.

*

A familiar drone came from far off. Looking up, she saw a plane in the distance, a vapour trail weaving behind in the clear blue sky.

'You think we should change course?' she said.

'What for?'

'They might have seen us.'

'You worry too much, honey. Probably just some rich kid trying out his new toy.'

The plane flew over, little more than a blip in the sky. She imagined the people on it, gazing down at *Indigo*, wondering who they were and where they were going.

'What if they're out looking for us?' she said.

'No one's looking for us, I told you that before. Far as anybody's concerned we're still in California.'

'But what if – '

'Stop the goddam worrying, OK? Go make us something to eat.'

Barthez had his own plane – a two-seater he kept on his estate. It was said that he used to take girls up in it and terrify them with all sorts of dazzling manoeuvres. She'd never been invited, and would have declined anyway, but the thought left an odd yearning; one more aspect of the life she'd given up, opportunities she'd never get to discover.

Then they were alone again. She gave up the position at the helm, glad for Johnny to take over. The concentration needed made her eyes ache – staring at the same point on the horizon for what seemed like hours, seeing the same vast ocean. They had chores to get on with, the maintenance of the yacht to keep them occupied. But the plane flying over left her feeling anxious. No matter how far they got from the mainland there would always be someone out there looking to hunt them down.

The cramped galley added to the lack of comfort, an interior designed for the rigors of sailing rather than a luxury voyage. She tried to adapt, tried to be philosophical about the whole thing. Johnny talked about hardship and the need to endure, but what was the point in unnecessary suffering? Better to find someone who could get you what you wanted – a guy like Barthez, who had an eye for talent and a phone book filled with useful connections. He might not have looked much but he had the two things everyone wanted – money and influence. The whole town knew who he was and what he could do.

She cooked rice and chicken on the tiny stove, trying not to think too much. The cabin fixtures groaned with every undulation. If the dead could speak they would surely find a voice through the timbers that once housed them. She heard their cries on the wind, their mournful accusations. Why did you do it? Why did you abandon us to this?

They'd been over every inch meticulously. Washed the walls with disinfectant. Scrubbed the upholstery, the wood. Johnny said they should leave no trace, nothing to incriminate them. But still she couldn't shut the whole thing out completely. The awful screams that rang out, the cries of an animal in pain and terror, that she thought would never stop. Then the silence when it was all over, and it was just her and Johnny to clear up.

She filled a bowl with water, and scrubbed hard. First, the abutment to the seat where the blood had congealed. Then the wooden panelling above, where there was still some residue. Here it was even more resistant, so she scrubbed harder, desperate for it to go away.

Johnny found her later, sitting there staring at the walls, spent.

'What you doing?' he said.

'Nothing.'

Sensing the cause of her unease, he looked around the interior and shook his head. 'What did I tell you when we left the mainland? You gotta forget about it. Put it outta your mind like it never happened.'

'I'm trying to, Johnny.'

'Well try harder.'

She nodded meekly, ashamed of being weak when he was so strong and in control. But still she needed reassurance, the promise he wouldn't abandon her this way.

He went to the chart table, and bent to study the map. She watched him until she couldn't bear the silence any longer.

'Do you love me, Johnny?'

'Course I do.'

'Be truthful now.'

'I am being truthful.'

'Sometimes it don't seem that way.'

He looked up, his concentration broken. 'You gotta stop worrying. Everything's gonna work out fine, just like I told you.'

Time lost all meaning. They could've been out here for months, away from any form of civilisation. This was all they had. Sunrise and dusk, the unending seas in-between. Nothing to do but sail the yacht and scan the horizon, waiting for the first glimpse of land.

Vanity cried out when she least expected it. The face in the mirror was of someone else, someone she didn't recognise. Her skin, usually pale and sensitive, had reddened at the neck and shoulders, scored by the sun and the wind. But the eyes were clear and bright. A keen observer might have looked into that face and seen the truth, but she'd learned to keep such frailties well hidden. In her fantasy world she was a famous actress with an entourage of willing helpers. Not just plain old Laura-Mae Ellis from Cooke County, who at 25 years of age had seen her career wiped out and her prospects fading.

Johnny said she looked good even without makeup, and a part of her wanted to believe him. All her life she'd been hearing the same thing. How important it was to look your best, even when the clothes you wore were patched-up, or handed down from some cousin or older sister. Poverty meant hardship, and there sure wasn't any fun in that. No fun at all. The life she aspired to was filled with glamour and riches and fascinating people. Once you had a taste of it you wanted more.

*

Late afternoon, a speck appeared on the western horizon. It grew steadily into a discernible shape: a passenger ship of some sort, perhaps.

'What do you think it is?' she said.

Johnny peered out over the guard wire. 'Looks like a cargo ship.'

'Is it heading our way?'

'Can't be sure. Go fetch the binoculars.'

The glasses were in a worn leather case in the hold. Slinging the strap around her neck, she headed back through the saloon, heart beating.

Johnny took the glasses and gazed out at the horizon.

'Can you see anything?' she said.

'It's a cargo ship of some kind. Looks like it's heading way off on the starboard side.' He let the binoculars fall at his chest, observing the ship in silence. It kept coming, bigger than a yacht, but still far enough away to be indistinct.

Taking the binoculars, she looked for herself. The lens brought the horizon into sharp relief, but at first she couldn't see anything. Then it appeared, its hulking grey sides high above the waterline, streaks of rust from its portholes, twin beads of phosphorous trailing in its wake. Deckhands were visible, too distant to make out, and too busy to break from their labours to notice a solitary yacht with a couple on-board.

'You think we should try to make contact?' she said.

'What the hell for?'

'Find out how close we are to Mission Bay.'

He shook his head, perplexed by her lack of understanding.

Just as the plane had disappeared, so did the ship. Relief came, but disappointment also. The closest they'd been to human contact in days and it was gone, snatched away like an illusion. Not much in the way of entertainment on-board *Indigo*, except for the wine they drank and the mind games they played with each other. Being in such close proximity they couldn't help but get on each other's nerves from time to time. Johnny had become increasingly remote, focusing on the maintenance and setting a course for Mexico. She'd become a kind of galley slave, cooking meals and washing dishes. The thought of seeing someone else had become more and more appealing – just to have a normal conversation without some angle attached.

'How far now?' she said.

'Not far.'

'Will we make it there by nightfall?'

'I can't say, honey.'

'I thought you'd sailed these waters before?'

'You gonna get on my case again?' He dared her to respond. 'We'll get there when we get there, OK?'

'You don't have to yell at me.'

'I ain't yelling at you. Jesus Christ. You keep asking the same goddam questions over and over again!'

She found the sun-cream in the hold, along with the wet weather gear and the fishing equipment – a surprising lack of essentials necessary for long voyages. The previous owners had only ever sailed the coastline, preferring the luxury resorts to the dangers

of open sea. Their friends were all wealthy types from Beverley Hills and Laurel Canyon, real estate developers and movie people. Most of them had come from somewhere else, taking advantage of the great migration, like predatory birds in search of a rich harvest. They brought out the worst in her, made her feel envious and resentful, conscious of the place she came from.

The sun climbed to its noonday position high above, the elements conspiring against them. She longed for the cool of hotel air conditioning, the luxury of a swimming pool to dive into. The ocean was different. The depths frightened her. Unfathomable, like the mysteries of life itself.

They swam across an inlet once, from one side of the rocks to the other. Johnny went first, holding their clothes aloft with one hand. Standing on the rocks on the other side, he beckoned for her to follow, but she couldn't move, transfixed by the deep blue water. Finally, she jumped in and thrashed her way across in the comic parody of an Olympic swimmer. Johnny helped her up out of the water, laughing, telling her to calm down before she cut herself to pieces on the jagged rocks.

Watching his manoeuvres up at the bow, she had to admire his athleticism. His muscles glistened with sweat. The frown lines in his forehead gave him a look of noble concentration. Surely, he would have been just as comfortable on his own, steering the yacht and plotting the coordinates, sleeping in snatches. Having her on-board only added to his burden, his sense of responsibility.

'Need a hand?' she said.

'I'm fine, honey.'

'You said you'd teach me how to tie a bowline – remember?'

'And I will, too. Johnny Boy gonna teach you everything he knows, and some.'

The hours went by in ponderous slow-motion. She felt the effects keenly – the bags under her eyes from lack of sleep, the drain from having to remain vigilant at all times. A permanent state of discomfort spent in either of two extremes: soaked through for hours on end, or burning under the sun. The further out they headed the rougher the passage became. Just when she thought they were making headway, the elements seemed to turn against them – or at least that was how it seemed. Strong currents buffeted the yacht, whipped up by the wind. Small waves broke over the bow. Ever-changing conditions that reinforced a sense of powerlessness. They were at the mercy of something mysterious and all powerful that could destroy them in an instant.

According to Johnny, they were roughly 20-miles from Mission Bay – allowing for drift that meant they were at least heading in the right direction. The plan was to stop there briefly to refuel and pick up supplies en-route to Mexico. Her spirits lifted at the prospect of land, sanctuary. *Indigo* barely stirred, the point of the mast high above them. Easy to understand the affection people felt for the vessels that carried them; the sleek lines and the craftsmanship; the feeling of oneness developed through adversity. The sea was the antagonist, its moods often set against them, but the yacht was their ally, built to withstand tremendous upheaval. She prayed that nothing would happen to them, that *Indigo* would carry them to safety.

'Will the Colonel help us find somewhere to live?' she said.

'Sure, he will. But first we gotta lie low for a while, make sure we don't attract attention to ourselves.'

Johnny said they couldn't take any chances. All the jewellery and the heels, the expensive eveningwear the previous owners liked to travel with would have to go. Their clothes and valuables would have to be bagged, along with all the other incriminating paraphernalia, and gotten rid of at the first opportunity.

She understood the logic, the cold practicalities of what they had to do – even the unspoken decision not to mention the previous owners by name. Referring to what happened in the abstract created a suitable distance between them and what they'd done. Like a rewritten movie script – if you didn't like certain parts you could change it and put something else in. And with Johnny directing the scenes all she had to do was play along. The payoff would come at the end when the shoot was finished and the picture was up there on the screen.

Sometimes it felt just like that. The two of them making a

movie, each one competing for the lead role. But she longed for a time they wouldn't have to pretend anymore. The people they couldn't talk about would no longer take up space in her head.

*

Johnny picked at the meal she cooked, a sign his health wasn't too good – not that he'd ever let her know how he was feeling. Worrying about him made her lose her appetite too. A special kind of loneliness set in, inspired by the sea.

'You ever think about home?' she said.

'Which one?'

'I meant where you come from, the folks you left behind.'

'What's to miss?' He stabbed a small potato, and popped it in his mouth. 'I could go back tomorrow and it'd all be the same. Same people doing the same jobs. I came out here to get away from all that.'

Home meant less and less the further she travelled. Just a bunch of dirt track roads and endless fields, where the sharecroppers spent their whole lives never knowing any different. The thought of going back made her feel bad. Another part of her she'd like to erase from her mind completely.

'I wouldn't care if I never saw that place again,' she said.

'Well that makes two of us, honey.' He reached out and squeezed her hand. 'I just wanna be out here with you. That's all I ever wanted.'

All of life was this way, it seemed. You got blown along with the wind and had to adapt, wasn't much you could do to change it. Soon they'd be in Mexico with a different set of people. But a small seed from the past always remained, a part of you that you couldn't get rid of.

She saw herself as a little girl, enduring the summer heat and the winter cold, the changing seasons. The men coming in from the fields, the sweat and the toil wearing new lines in their faces. The women putting whatever food they had on the table, taking it upon themselves to hold it all together.

'Sufficient unto the day are the evils thereof.'

Johnny looked up. 'What was that?'

'It's from the Bible. My mammy used to say it.'

'Well quit saying it round here, I got enough problems.'

She sipped the wine, her thoughts moving on to different people and places.

'You think you should wire the Colonel when we get to Mission Bay?' she said.

'What for?'

'Just to let him know where we are.'

'He's a busy man, he don't need to know where we are. He'll help us out when the time's right.' He licked his fingers, quiet, withdrawn to a place she couldn't reach. She felt chastised, dismissed, like a child denied the right to her own opinion.

'You still angry with me, Johnny?'

He gazed out at the ocean, distant as the wave tips. 'Guess I don't feel the same way you do.'

'What's that supposed to mean?'

He looked at her lazily. 'Let's just get to Mexico. And quit telling me what your goddam mammy said.'

She took his plate and walked away, cheeks burning.

'What's up?' he called after her. 'You ain't talking to me no more?'

'I'm going below.'

'Well you do that, honey. And don't you go getting sore at me, you hear?'

As a protest against him and his mood swings, she stayed in the master cabin and read the journal. All those precise lines and fancy letters, stories about people she'd never met before. The previous owners were always going somewhere – setting sail for San Francisco, or visiting friends in Pasadena. A life of idle pleasure, where the money stopped boredom from setting in.

Turning the page, she read the entry for June 17: "We stopped at the house once owned by Lois B. Mayer. Now that was a man who knew how to get things done. After all, he was the one who discovered Joan Crawford and Greta Garbo!"

Gripped by a sudden envy, she put the journal back, and sat for a while, rocked by the motion of the yacht. It didn't seem right, soaking up the thoughts of someone no longer around. The words in the journal were personal and ought to stay that way. But somehow they drew her back, aroused in her an undeniable curiosity.

The set of photographs she found in the hold inspired a different kind of thrill. The subjects were female, partially-naked, captured in erotic poses. Actresses, maybe, or models, like the ones on Sunset Strip. Part of a secret collection, hidden away where no one would find them.

Johnny glanced over them without interest, and handed them back. 'Maybe you oughta stop poking around down there.'

'I thought you'd want to see 'em, that's all.'

'Well, I don't, OK? I got enough to think about trying to keep us on course without you breaking my concentration every time you feel like it.'

Later, he tried to get a weather forecast. The reception wasn't good, the broadcaster's voice lost in static. The scene reminded her of home when she was a child. The nightly ritual around the radio, listening to dispatches from the war. Two uncles and a cousin lost, but nobody said a thing because it wasn't good for a child to hear such things.

'Sonofabitch,' Johnny said. 'We'll have to try again later.'

'Does it matter that much – I thought we were getting closer to land anyhow?'

'Weather's changeable. We need to know what we're heading into.'

She didn't question his authority. Out here, hundreds of miles from anywhere, the world took on a different shape. All the things she associated with her former life no longer applied. The sense of time got distorted; the ceaseless lapping of the sea against the hull had an eternal quality that dulled the mind. She wore a watch, but barely glanced at it – a pointless decoration like the jewellery and expensive clothes packed away in the hold. Beyond the wind and the waves, nothing else mattered.

*

'Shit!'

Looking up, she saw Johnny bent over the stern.

'What's the matter?' she said.

'We got a problem.'

She joined him, and looked down at the swirling water.

'What is it?'

'Something's fouled the prop. I'm gonna have to take a look.' He slipped off his shirt, and kicked off his deck shoes.

She grasped the implications. 'You're going in?'

'Well, yeah. Unless you got a better idea?'

Watching him strip and prepare to dive in, she felt unusually fearful.

'Please be careful, Johnny.'

'Nothing's gonna happen. Stay here and keep watch.'

Clutching a knife, he slipped from the stern and into the deep. The impact caused a mini whirlpool of bubbles to rise to the surface. Then he was gone, his dark outline slipping from sight beneath the hull.

Bad thoughts set in. What if he got caught up underneath and drowned? What if a shark came along before she could yell a warning? How would she cope without him, stranded out here on the ocean without a prayer?

He surfaced, gasping mouthfuls of air.

'What is it?' she said.

'Something's caught up real good. I need to go down again and cut it loose.'

Drawing a lungful of air, he went under again. Sunlight played on the surface of the water, obscuring his outline. He stayed down for so long it didn't seem possible. Then, at last, he came up, gasping, holding something in his left hand.

'What is it?' she said.

Hauling himself on deck, he sat there dripping wet and breathing hard, staring out at the water.

'You OK, baby?' she said.

He tossed the sodden object on the deck a few feet away.

'That's what was holding us up.'

Just an old rag, she thought. One of the many pieces of debris that washed up on the ocean.

She looked closer. The buff material had a familiar chequered pattern . A warning of some kind.

'Oh, my God!'

'It don't mean nothing,' Johnny said.

'How did it get there?'

'Probably got caught up in the tide, like driftwood.'

His answer didn't make sense. Now she had another voice in her head to fuel the accusations. A sign from the grave that couldn't be ignored. The unmistakeable arm of a man's shirt tangled around the prop. A shirt that once belonged to Donald Simpson.

*

Indigo's bow cut through the waves and kicked up spray. Johnny unfurled the mainsail, a moment of anticipation for them both as the wind caught the canvas and stretched it tight against the mast. The mood of the ocean changed, from glassy indifference to a choppy waltz. She felt gladness and relief. Soon they would reach Mission Bay, on track for their next destination.

Signs of wear and tear had started to show. The mainsail had torn, a section flapping in the wind. Johnny was supposed to know how to fix these things, but judging by the amount of curse words he used she wasn't convinced. Such complexities left her feeling useless and unable to contribute. She'd picked up the rudiments – the basics of sailing a yacht in turbulent seas – but the business with the tangled prop brought the situation home clearly. If something happened to Johnny, she'd be forced to take over alone.

Sunset, a vivid painting on the horizon that did little to change her mood. Instead, a vague feeling of premonition. All that lay before them couldn't be avoided, a direct result of decisions they'd made and actions they'd taken. Something haunting about the evening when the sun went down, the shadows filled with sadness and regret. The ebbing of life itself, and all its vain struggles drawing to a close.

'Looks like the skies are on fire,' she said.

'Sure does, honey.'

Evening light cast shadows on the water, an illusion of calm. No longer were they sailing on such a vast, open tract, but on a smaller more intimate space. Most of the surface lay in darkness. The lapping water against the sides made a distant, plaintive sound that increased the feeling of isolation and loneliness. Overhead, the spectrum of the night sky, the stars like jewels. Such beauty in the world, but always beyond reach.

'I can't stop thinking about that shirt,' she said.

'I told you, it don't mean a thing.'

'But what happens if they find him? … And her? … The two of them just wash up on the beach somewhere?'

'Who cares anyhow? We'll be in Mexico by then.'

They drank to the unknown future, and Johnny's refusal to let doubt set in. But his long silences worried her, the periods of brooding he fell into that kept her out.

'We shoulda stayed in California,' she said.

'What for – so you could be Barthez's cute little run-around?'

I had a career ahead of me, she thought. Barthez told me so.

Johnny flashed her a curious, disapproving look, like he knew what she was thinking.

'You happy out here with me?'

'Sure, I am'

'Because you wanna be, or because that's the way it worked out?'

'I'm here, ain't I?'

'That ain't the answer I was looking for, honey.'

She fell silent. Her whole life consumed by roles and responsibility not of her own choosing. Her personality buried beneath layers of stage paint and acting up. In California she found freedom for the first time, and so many likeminded people to help indulge her fantasies. Now that had all been taken away and she couldn't help blaming Johnny.

'Do you believe in fate?' she said.

'What – the kind that puts a nickel in the church collection like your mammy used to?'

'I mean that everything's meant to be. We can't change any of it.'

'Only thing I can't change is the goddam weather.'

All the folk they met were either in the movie business, or hoping to break into it someday. Even the fortune teller she went to in Los Angeles had connections to the stars and the studios, with signed photographs on the walls and endless stories about the early days. The area had once been an empty tract of farmland and citrus groves before the movie folk descended – Sunset Boulevard little more than a dirt track road where horse-drawn carriages rode. The place just opened up doorways in her mind, welcomed her with the sunshine and the ethereal light.

The night swell closed in; the sound of the yacht's passage soothed her unease. Bad memories lost their hold, fading into the darkness beyond. What remained, troubled her only vaguely, the strains of a familiar tune playing on the wind. Sometimes it felt like someone was watching over her, adding up all the little things she'd done. The God she prayed to keeping tally. Things happened that couldn't be accounted for, like the day her daddy upped and left and didn't come home, and her mammy took up with men who didn't treat her right. Wickedness and sin, as a consequence of things people did here on this earth – lessons the Reverend Calhoun talked about on a Sunday morning to a rapt congregation. Nothing she did would bring her daddy back, and nothing could ease the sense of loss she felt at his leaving. So she pushed it deep down inside her and never spoke about it, just like her mammy did. But the hurt remained and wouldn't go away.

Johnny's berth was empty when she looked in. He never seemed to sleep. Even in the house in Laurel Canyon she'd wake to find him gone. Sometimes she longed for his embrace, his warm body beside her, if only for the comfort and security it might bring.

Other times she was glad to be alone, away from his moods, the disturbance he caused just by being in the same room.

Sometime before dawn, she heard his footsteps in the galley, and pretended to be asleep – another habit from childhood she'd yet to overcome.

He stood in the cabin doorway looking in.

'Time to get up,' he said.

She yawned and stretched, turned to face him.

'Huh?'

'I said, time to move, honey. We gotta storm coming in.'

*

Wind howled through the cleats and rattled the sails. Whenever the bow dipped into a trough, spray flew back like a whiplash. She'd forgotten the exhilaration of being out in rough weather. What they'd been through before was nothing, a minor blip on the spectrum compared to this.

Johnny pointed out the grey horizon, the formation of dark clouds up ahead. 'Looks like we're in for one big one. I'm gonna trim the sails.'

She caught the excitement in his voice, and looked beyond the bow, to the rising swells, high as a house. 'What we gonna do?'

'Go below and close all the hatches. Make sure everything's stowed away tight.'

Stirred by the wind, the ocean became a destructive force. The oncoming mist gave everything an ominous reality, each successive wave coming on in sickening slow motion. Johnny struggled to change down to the storm jib, and slipped on the decking. She yelled out for him to be careful, regretting the note of panic in her voice. Lashed by the waves, spray glistening in his hair, he made his way along the starboard side to grab at the halyard. She couldn't help thinking how heroic he looked – like the pirate played by Randolph Carlson in *Blackwater Moon*.

Inside the cabin she breathed easier, an illusion of safety. *Indigo* rolled with each swell, the timbers groaning as if they might come apart at any moment. Angry spray beat against the porthole glass as a reminder.

A sickening fear caught in her throat. This was surely the end. *Indigo* was shipping water and couldn't possibly sustain the same punishment much longer.

'We're sinking!' she yelled through the hatch.

Johnny looked back. 'What?'

'Below – there's water everywhere!'

'Start bailing out!'

'How?'

'Grab the bucket and start pitching over the side!'

Bailing out seemed futile. For every bucket she heaved out, another cascade found its way in. Her fingers ached and her clothes were soaked through. And with each frantic effort came the shrieks and wails of angry spirits unleashed by the wind. She prayed constantly, a jumble of meaningless words while the seas grew higher. It seemed impossible they might survive without being dragged under. Each successive wave swamped the deck, flooding the cockpit. Johnny's efforts to change sails and make good on deck might have been comical had she not been so concerned for his safety. Body angled against the pitch of the yacht, his feet slipped on the wet boards. At one point she thought she'd lost him, until he reappeared up at the bow, soaked through but strangely victorious.

'What you want me to do now?' she yelled.

'Just hold her steady. Stop her pulling into the wind!'

Salt spray lashed her mouth and stung her face, as *Indigo*'s bow smashed into the next wave. The darkening sky came down to meet them, trapping them in a vacuum, no end in sight. Surely, they would die out here, and no trace of them would remain. No graveside for mourners to stand around and offer their platitudes. Nothing but the ocean to swallow them up. Just like it had the bodies of Donald and Sheri Simpson.

*

Night became day. After what seemed like countless hours, the horizon line cleared, leaving a perfect view of the ocean. Far off on the edge of the world the first rays of the sun were coming up. They'd survived the night and this was their reward. One step closer to their destination, to dry clothes and a proper meal. The luxuries she'd been dreaming about since they'd left California.

The storm had caused chaos below, a malign force that swept through the yacht's interior, wrenching open doors and trashing the contents inside. Everything had to be shut tight and packed away again, like the contents of a house after a cyclone.

Another strange fear took hold. They hadn't seen land in three days. Johnny's claim that he knew where they were didn't ring true. By his reckoning they should have reached Mission Bay by now. But they were nowhere near the mainland.

'Where are we?' she said.

'Heading due east.'

'How come we ain't seen land yet?'

'We'll see it soon enough.'

'How come we ain't seen it already?'

'You wanna take over the goddam navigation?' He looked tired, his hair dishevelled, the trials of the last 48 hours beginning to show. His cough had worsened, too, a worrying aspect she didn't like to think about. Maybe he'd die on-board and she'd have to conduct a burial at sea. Say a few prayers over his corpse – a ritual he wouldn't have cared too much for had he been alive to hear them.

'You OK?' she said.

'I'm fine. It's the yacht I'm concerned about.'

She looked up at the mast, the battered sails. 'We gonna make it?'

'I sure hope so, honey. I got things to do.'

*

A thin grey outline appeared on the horizon. Could've been a mirage, something conjured up by her imagination. The more

she looked, the more it stood out.

Relief and joy welled up at such an unexpected sight.

'Land!' she yelled. 'Over there! … Can you see it?'

Johnny went below to fetch the binoculars. Her excitement settled into a mood of tense anticipation. Soon they'd drop anchor and reach the shore. Enjoy the experience of being on land again, without the constant motion of the yacht to upset the stomach and pummel the senses.

'What do you think?' she said.

He lowered the binoculars. 'Looks like some kinda island.'

'You think it's safe to go ashore?'

'Why not? … Let's motor in and take a look.'

She pictured an island paradise untouched by human hand, where rich fruit hung on trees and wild game foraged nearby. The fantasy didn't hold with reality – they were still only a spit from mainland California. She comforted herself with the fact that they must have been blown a few miles off course by the storm. Soon they would get the help they needed. Make contact with the Colonel in Mexico and be on their way. And yet such an unknown prospect brought its own anxieties.

'How deep are we?' Johnny called from the bow.

She looked at the gauge. 'About twelve fathoms.'

'Keep watching, and shout out the numbers. We can't afford to run aground now.'

Rounding the promontory, they sailed along the westward side of the island, steering clear of the shallows. The vegetation looked dense and uninhabitable, capped off a few feet from the shoreline.

Johnny pointed to an upcoming inlet a few-hundred metres to port. 'OK, bring her in here.'

Adjusting their position, she watched the water.

'Can't we drop anchor here?' she said.

'We're not close enough yet.'

Clearing the next outcrop of rocks, they caught sight of their destination. Set back from the rocky headland was a small bay, the still blue water protected from the currents that lay beyond the reef. White sands formed a small, deserted beach.

'What do you think?' he said.

'It's beautiful.'

He smiled, indulging her, as if the whole thing had been prearranged.

'What about people?' she said.

'Don't see too much of anything around here, do you?'

The water changed colour, from the deeper blue to a lighter shade, alluding to the shallows. But they'd cleared the reef, potentially the most dangerous manoeuvre of all. The bay offered shelter, relief from the unpredictability of the open sea.

Johnny put the engine into neutral, and stood. 'This is as good a place as any. Let's drop anchor.'

Unearthed from its coil, the chain rattled, and dived to the bottom. She listened out for the muted impact below, hoping the anchor would hold fast and prevent them from dragging.

He turned off the engine.

'Hear that?'

She listened to the eerie silence. 'I can't hear anything.'

'That's what I mean. It's just us, honey. Just you and me.'

The clear blue water looked inviting, nothing like the ominous depths beyond the reef. Rocks were visible on the sandy bottom; a shoal of minute fish swam in formation beneath the hull. Sheltered from the wind, the bay had a private, untouched feel, an aura of peace and tranquillity.

Johnny began an inventory of the damage to the yacht, reciting aloud all that he found. Ignoring him, she focused on the shoreline. The silence had an eerie, hostile quality, as if some human or animal presence must be hiding within.

'It sounds so quiet,' she said. 'I'm not so sure I like it.'

'Why don't you swim ashore and take a look?'

'I ain't going nowhere on my own.'

'Suit yourself, honey.'

The occasional rustle of branches signified a bird, or some other feature of wildlife. It looked like no other part of the coast that she was familiar with – a tropical island they'd happened upon by chance. Whatever it was she couldn't relax, couldn't get used to the feeling they were being watched.

Johnny came up, wiping his hands on a rag, his face coarse with sweat. She read his look of resignation and tried not to overreact.

'Have you fixed it?'

He shook his head. 'It's gonna need a complete overhaul.'

'So what do we do now?'

'Clean up and go ashore.'

'Is that a good idea?'

'You got a better one?'

ACT II

THE ISLAND

The sand felt firm but yielding beneath her feet. She slipped off her sandals and took a few paces, enjoying the simple luxury of being back on dry land. Ahead lay the dense foliage, tall palm-trees rising above, the leaves like giant fans. No pathways or tracks leading in.

Johnny looked over the green canopy, to the blue skies beyond. 'Let's head down to those rocks. Maybe we can climb to the top from there.'

'What about *Indigo*?'

'No one's gonna see her beyond the reef. Come on, let's go.'

The strip of beach led to a rocky impasse at the far end. Trudging through the sand, the dark foliage on one side, stunning blue sea on the other, she was struck by the contrast. Here they were, miles from the nearest form of civilisation, and yet so many questions remained. Did anyone live here? And if so, wouldn't they be suspicious of two strangers turning up looking for food and shelter?

Johnny said that if they kept heading inland they might come to a town or a settlement on the other side. But that only increased the worries eating away at her.

'What if somebody recognises us?' she said.

'Out here?'

'You said yourself you don't know where we are. We could be closer to the mainland than you think.'

'Just keep walking and leave the thinking to me, OK?'

Like explorers taking their first steps, they made their own imprint on the primitive terrain. She couldn't help but feel the lure of it, the challenge of the unknown. All the lavish production sets and parties in Hollywood might never have happened; her sunburned skin and calloused fingers told a different reality. And the clothes she wore, shrugged on for comfort and convenience rather than pleasure. All these elements took her one step further from the life she was used to. No longer Laura-Mae Ellis, the aspiring young actress, but a coarse, more cynical version turned that way by events beyond her control.

The ache in her thighs got worse. Finally, she gave in and called a halt.

'I need to rest.'

Johnny slipped off the backpack, and tossed her the water container. 'Don't drink too much, it's gotta last us.'

The water tasted warm and tainted, barely able to slake her thirst. She sealed the cap and threw it back.

'Ready?' he said.

'I think so.'

'Better shape up, honey. I might have to leave you here to get picked off by scavengers – how 'bout that?' He grinned at her, but she understood the challenge. Always the urge in him to dominate, to push her to new limits, even when his own health might be compromised.

They climbed to a vantage point that overlooked the bay. From here, the view was equally stunning. *Indigo* looked small and defenceless far below, waiting for their return like a faithful friend. She worried that someone might board her and sail off. Then they'd be truly stranded.

A lizard scurried off into the grass. Climbing further, they came across several more, their speckled bodies a perfect camouflage among the bracken. Still no signs of human habitation, only the wildlife to keep them company.

At the top of the next climb, they stopped and looked back. The bay was no longer visible, only the vast stretch of ocean they'd sailed in on. Now they were defenceless and vulnerable to the elements. Truly alone.

She took off a sandal and examined her foot.

'I got blisters already.'

'Never mind that, we need to keep moving.'

'Don't you care about me at all?'

'You'll thank me when we get to the other side. Now come on, let's go.'

The heat produced a trancelike state. Tramping behind Johnny, several voices fought for her attention. Barthez, reminding her of all the things he'd done for her; his fight to get her a job and have her included on the studio payroll. His promise that one day she would have her own stylist and clothes designer if she did what he said. To up and leave like she had must have left him confused and bewildered. Maybe she could find a way of contacting him and explain what had happened, why she'd taken off and abandoned her career without a word to anyone.

A gradual descent took them further inland. Gazing at the thick forest canopy below, she felt a part of something unexplainable. A primitive awareness, perhaps – an instinct for something that had been there all along. Being at sea had awakened it, made her appreciate the quiet, the solitude.

Johnny took off his hat and mopped his brow, the sweat giving his face a sickly-looking pallor. A bird squawked in the trees and took flight, soaring high above them.

'How much further?' she said.

'That's what we're gonna find out.'

'What happens if we get all the way over to the other side and there's nothing there?'

'Then we'll just have to come right on back and think of some other way.' He shrugged on the backpack, and moved off. She followed, reluctantly, loosening the buttons of her tunic, and fanning the air with her hat. Once again, she wished she'd never met him. If it wasn't for Johnny she'd still be in LA, eating breakfast in the diner on Vine Street, or getting ready to meet Mrs Seberling, for the voice strengthening exercises that had become a regular part of her routine. But these thoughts were fleeting, without substance. The truth was, she couldn't be without him. That was the way it was and always had been.

The midday temperature climbed higher, the harshness of the climate evident in the scorched bushes and dried-out grass. It seemed unlikely that anyone could live here. They'd come across the place through bad luck, and Johnny's insistence that he knew best. Now it looked like they might die out here, too, baked in the heat, their bodies left for the wolves, or whatever wild animals they had here on the island.

*

Atop the next rise they stopped. She drew in her breath at the sight before them. Just up ahead stood the most incongruous sight. A small chapel, domed and plaster-white, topped with a bell-tower. A wooden seat had been built around the foot of a nearby tree, the overhanging branches offering shade to the weary traveller.

'Oh, my God!' she said.

Johnny looked over, smugly. 'Didn't I say we'd find civilisation?'

A bell rang behind them. She spun round in alarm, to see the bony flanks of a goat, its hooves kicking up pebbles as it tore away across the bracken. Johnny laughed at her shocked reaction.

'It ain't funny,' she said. 'Scared the shit outa me!'

Dropping the backpack on the seat, he wandered over to the chapel.

'What you doing?' she said.

'Taking a look inside.'

'You think that's wise?'

'Who's to stop us out here?'

The arched door creaked on its hinges, the old wood cracked and faded with age. Johnny pushed it open to reveal a cool interior; the light from a small side window lifted the shadows. At the end stood a small altar covered in a white cloth. Hanging on the wall above was a wooden crucifix and various religious paintings.

'I don't think we should be in here,' she said.

'Relax, what's the matter with you?'

Stepping inside, she half expected a solemn voice to order them out. Clearly, the place was some kind of sanctuary, removed from the heat and the dust; the thick plaster left an imprint of fine white powder on her fingertip when she touched the wall. But why build it out here in the wilderness? It didn't make sense.

'Let's go,' she said. 'I've seen enough.'

Johnny put an arm around her waist and squeezed. 'What's up, honey? You got the heebie-jeebies over some old chapel?'

She shrugged him off and headed for the door.

'I'll wait outside.'

'Chickenshit!'

'Yeah – that's what I am!'

She sat on the seat beneath the overhanging branches. Barren earth and sparse vegetation all around; a place where only stray goats and lizards could survive. It seemed unnaturally still, the air thick and heavy. The kind of place Barthez would have liked for one of his cowboy pictures.

The chapel door groaned. Johnny came out, and shrugged on the backpack.

'OK, let's make a move.'

'You say a prayer while you were in there?'

'Oh, sure. I said the only one I know. Goes something like, Lord, show me the way and the road up ahead, that I might see mine enemies before they see me.'

'That ain't a prayer.'

'Well that's the best I could do, honey. Now come on, let's go, before the vultures start fixing to pick the meat from the bones.'

The scenery changed the further they headed south. As the track opened out, evidence of human habitation became more apparent. The thick brush had been cut back to form a path, wide enough for two people to walk side by side. More goats appeared like messengers, the tinkling bells around their necks giving them away – on occasion they even stopped to stare, mystified by the two strangers invading their territory.

Then, visible below like a mirage in the heat, tiled rooftops came into view. The stony path they were on joined a dirt road at an intersection, tyre tracks embedded in the surface. Further on, an enclosure bordered by a low stone wall. Single-storey wooden buildings with small verandas overlooked a narrow street, the rooftops descending into a valley. Beyond this the bright blue sea.

'We've made it!' she said, flooded with relief.

Johnny aimed the binoculars at the rooftops.

'What can you see?' she said.

'Just a bunch of dwellings and smokestacks.' He lowered the binoculars and looked at her solemnly. 'Just remember the story. We're on our way to Mexico, taking an extended vacation. We hit a storm and got washed up here.'

'You ain't gotta tell me that again, I know already.'

He grabbed her arm. 'This ain't a game we're playing here. So take that wiseass look off your face and start listening!' Relaxing his grip, he softened his tone. 'Just focus on the facts like I told you. We just need to find someone who can help us fix the yacht and get refuelled. Then we can head on to Mexico.'

*

The dirt road led down between rustic dwellings. Clothes hung from verandas. Smoke rose from stovepipes in lazy wisps. An old man sat outside a ramshackle house, smoking a cigarette. He watched their approach from his chair, detached, remotely hostile. She tried a smile, hoping for a reaction, but got the same blank stare.

'I don't think he likes us,' she said.

'Never mind that. Just keep walking.'

A narrow street offered shade from the sun. Like players on a stage, the inhabitants came out to observe them – or rather to stare at them – babbling in a foreign tongue that sounded like Spanish with some other influence thrown in. A dust-streaked motorcycle shot past, ridden by a young male; his female passenger turned her head to gawp at them in surprise. The whole thing felt surreal. A few hours ago they'd been alone, nothing but the cry of gulls and the choppy seas for company. Now they were here in this strange place, wary of the threat from an unknown source. No one smiled or called out a greeting. They were clearly 'foreigners' and should be treated that way.

They came to a set of stone steps worn smooth by generations of footfall. On their way down they passed several women making the journey up. The women carried bags filled with produce, a stoic acceptance on their wrinkled faces; if they were surprised to see two strangers in their midst they didn't show it.

At the bottom was a small square, wide awnings providing shade. The few tables and chairs outside suggested a diner or café, but there weren't many customers. She looked for any Europeans among the largely dark faces, overcome by a deepening sense of unease.

'They don't look too friendly,' she said

'It'll be fine. Just let me handle the negotiations.'

Turning a corner, they were greeted by a wide bay and the shimmering ocean beyond. A group of men worked at nets and lobster cages, shirt sleeves rolled up over dark, muscular arms; the pungent smell of fish drifted back on the sea breeze. Laid out beneath colourful awnings were more tables and chairs, in expectation of custom.

'Let's try here,' Johnny said. 'Maybe we can find someone who speaks English.'

They sat at a table facing the jetty. Almost at once, a rangy-looking cat appeared, followed by another. She tried shooing them away, fearful of any diseases they might be carrying, but like forlorn refugees they regrouped beneath the table, feral eyes imploring her for pity.

'Goddam things,' she said. 'Why won't they go away?'

Johnny seemed to find it funny. 'Looks like they see something in you they like. Must be the perfume you got on.'

An elderly man wandered over, and stopped at the table. From his stained apron and wary demeanour, she assumed he was the proprietor.

Johnny flashed an easy smile. *'Buenos tardes.* We just hiked over from the other side of the bay. Can we get coffee round here?'

The old guy frowned, black eyes inset beneath a stern brow.

Johnny made a drinking motion. *'Dos cafes, por favor?'* He pulled a dollar bill from his wallet and slapped it down on the table. 'There you go, *hombre.* Prime US currency, straight from the Federal Bank.'

With a curt nod, the old guy took the bill and made his way back to the café's interior.

'Did you see the look he gave us?' she said.

'What look? All that old fucker's interested in is the colour of the money.' Seeing her unease, he shook his head. 'Relax, honey. No one knows who we are. We'll find a place to clean up, grab something to eat, and be outta here.'

The place had a lazy, timeless feel – a small corner of paradise they'd come across by accident. Looking round at the vibrant harbour scene, and the men working on the lobster crates, it was hard not to be charmed by it all. Perhaps under different circumstances she might have been. But there was always the chance they'd be recognised and questions asked. The story they'd invented wouldn't hold up under scrutiny.

A stray cat rubbed against her leg, its mouth open in a silent meow. She clapped her hands, and shooed it away.

'Gotta give 'em credit for persistence,' Johnny said.

'It ain't funny – I don't want 'em near me!' The cats stirred a fear in her she couldn't articulate. They seemed to congregate beneath the table deliberately, their rheumy eyes searching her out in a sinister appeal.

The old guy brought the coffee, and set the cups down without a word. As he made to leave, Johnny stopped him. 'Hey, buddy – how can we pick up supplies around here?'

The old man curled his lip and shook his head, a garbled response neither of them could understand.

'Anyone speak English around here?'

The same black eyes stared obstinately back. Johnny put up his hands in defeat.

'OK, buddy, we'll go find someone else to help us out. Thanks for your time.' As the old guy strode away, Johnny called after him.

'*Gracias, amigo!* You sure gotta way with people!'

'Please don't make a scene,' she said.

He stared at her. 'What you think I am – stupid? I got us this far, didn't I?'

Now they were settled, no one seemed to pay them any attention, the men engrossed in their work. They might have arrived in some other dimension, one so far removed from their previous life as to be unrecognisable. And yet there was something else here that was harder to define. With the sun on the water and the fishing boats moored in the harbour, it felt strange, almost disconnected from reality.

Johnny drained his coffee. 'Right, let's go.'

'Where?'

'Find someone who can fix the yacht so we can get outta here.'

Strolling along the jetty, they passed the men with the fishing nets. One of them stopped working and gazed across at her. She sensed his interest, conscious of her pale, sun-reddened skin and western style dress. This briefest connection reassured her in an odd way. Even out here, ravaged by the storm and the harsh conditions on-board *Indigo*, she still had something of value.

A few locals sat outside a bar, drinking and reading newspapers. Cigarette smoke hung in the air, along with the distinct smell of alcohol.

Johnny sidled up to them, nonchalant as ever.

'Hi there, y'all. Anyone speak English?'

They stopped talking and stared at him.

'We're moored on the other side of the island, see? Hit a storm and got blown off course. Could sure do with some help getting fixed up again.'

A man with a fat, drooping moustache looked Johnny up and down.

'Where are you from?'

'California,' Johnny said, with the same easy smile. 'What's the name of this place?'

'El Joya, but you won't find it on any map.'

'How far are we from the mainland?'

The man conferred with his elderly companion in dialect. They seemed to be arguing over some obscure point.

'Sixty miles, maybe less,' the man said.

'Sixty?' Johnny scratched his head. 'Jesus. I guess the storm took us further than we thought.'

Peering into the gloom of the bar, she could make out more men inside, the murmur of low conversation and music. Their eyes lingered on her, assessing her face, her body, openly and without shame. She tried to look away, made to feel like a piece of merchandise, the way she was sometimes made to feel back home.

'Anywhere round here we can stay?' Johnny said.

The man with the moustache gestured along the front. There was one such place, he said. A Madame Diaz let rooms at a reasonable price. They could try there.

'Anyone around here help us fix the yacht?'

The man conferred with his friend. She thought she heard a derogatory word in Spanish but couldn't be sure.

'Ask for Henry up at the monastery,' the man said. 'He knows everyone.'

Johnny nodded, and gazed out at the sea wall, the fishermen working the nets. For a moment his confidence seemed to slip. Perhaps, like her, he found something unsettling in the atmosphere.

*

The room had clean sheets and air conditioning, luxury after the cramped space on the yacht. Lying back on the bed, she looked at the cracked plaster ceiling and reflected on their good fortune. A warm breeze blew in from the small balcony. Voices drifted in from the harbour. The owner, Madame Diaz, had even gone to the trouble of putting flowers in the room, and a sweet fragrance hung upon the dry air.

Johnny came out from the bathroom, drying his hair with a towel. He looked rested and well, as if the blight of illness had never touched him.

'Not quite the Fairmont,' he said. 'But it'll do for now.'

'How long we gonna stay?'

'Couple days, maybe. Until we get the yacht fixed.'

As homes went, she'd had a lot worse. Hollywood had spoiled her, given her a glimpse of the previously unattainable. Barthez's mansion in Beverley Hills, designed like a Spanish villa, with subtle lighting under the arched porticos and a beautiful waterfall on the forecourt. The night Randolph Carlson made his entrance down the grand staircase, a drink in one hand, cigarette in the other. One of the girls had pointed him out, warning her to stay away. By then his reputation had been mauled by the press, who took great delight in telling everyone his career was over. But no one else seemed to have his looks or his style, and she fell for him right there, without a word spoken between them.

Johnny's hold was of a different kind, like a shadow that crept over her by stealth. By the time she realised what was happening it was too late. She'd succumbed to his charms, given herself to him without reservation.

'I'm gonna talk to Madame Diaz,' he said. 'Find out what the deal is around here.'

'What am I supposed to do?'

'Just relax, honey. Look on this as an unexpected vacation.'

She took a shower in the small ceramic cubicle, the jets cleansing and invigorating after so long cooped-up on the yacht. Voices drifted in from beyond the balcony, merging with her thoughts. The prospect of a long voyage ahead didn't fill her with much enthusiasm. They had all the amenities they needed here on the island – access to food and shelter, a place of safety from the mainland. But sooner or later the money would run out and they'd have to find another source.

Lying on the bed, she drifted off – a kind of half-conscious dream where she was being driven down Hollywood Boulevard in an open top car. But when she looked over she saw it was Barthez driving and not Johnny. Barthez smiled with such tenderness and conviction that even in the dream it caused her to weep with a longing for those days to return, and for the company of those she'd left behind. The beach house at Santa Monica, where the servants always greeted them with a deferential bow and the offer of a cocktail as they were ushered out into the garden. Margot's serene face as she came out to meet them, and the smell of her perfume as she wrapped them in her warm embrace. Van der Hass, who seemed a little unstable to her at first, chain-smoking Gauloises and whining constantly about his latest novel. These people all lived on in the projection room of her mind, a place she could revisit whenever she felt lonesome.

Opening her eyes, she took in the room. The flowers on the table. The backpack, still on the chair where Johnny had left it.

Rousing herself, she went out to the balcony, and looked down at the street. The same foreign voices drifted up; the cry of gulls from the harbour. An unnatural still in the air she couldn't figure out.

Johnny had been gone too long. Something wasn't right.

Snatching up her hat, she hurried outside.

*

Wandering along the front, she sought the shade beneath the awnings. The local women eyed her with open suspicion, as if she was a threat to them in some way. Back in California such looks wouldn't have bothered her at all. Here, they inspired a mild claustrophobia made worse by the heat. Conspicuous and vulnerable, she moved among them, searching for Johnny, expecting at every turn to see his face, his curious half-smile, like it was a game they were playing that he'd devised.

Labourers toiled on a piece of land up ahead, their picks and shovels ringing out on the hard ground. The sounds reminded her of Sunset Strip when she'd first arrived: an olive grove with cypress trees and a small stream. Studio bosses had it levelled, and a huge warehouse put up with a tin roof that reflected the sun. People said how ugly it looked, but that didn't bother the studio bosses none. Just to show their indifference to public opinion they went right ahead and built another one on the same piece of ground.

The labourers' exertions caused her a jolt of unease, hard physical labour always associated with the poverty of her childhood, the dirt-ingrained fingers and exhausted faces of the menfolk coming in from the fields. She checked her breathing, and remembered how important it was not to show fear, one of Johnny's favourite admonitions.

Pausing at a stone monument, she looked out over the front. The café with the feral cats was open, check tablecloths flapping in the breeze. Sunlight glanced on chair backs and awnings, the fishing boats moored in the harbour.

Two men were sat at a table, one wearing a distinctive white jacket, a coffee cup poised at his mouth. She couldn't see his face clearly, but guessed he wasn't a local – probably a European from the mainland.

The men stood and shook hands, as if concluding a deal. The one in the white jacket wiped his forehead with a hankie and put on a hat. His companion stepped away from the table and into view. She saw then that it was Johnny.

*

Water ran in the sink; she heard him splash his face and sigh with relief. On the table was the bag of provisions he'd dumped on his way to the bathroom. No greeting. No hint of an explanation as to where he'd been.

He came out, drying his face with a towel. 'What's up, honey?'

'Where the hell have you been?'

'I went out to buy a few things – what's the problem?'

'Why didn't you tell me? I was worried sick wondering where you were.'

He stopped drying and looked her over. 'I'm the one trying to get us outta here. You ever think about that?'

She didn't have an answer, the scene at the café still fresh in her mind.

'Where did you go?' she said.

'Along the harbour front.'

'Did you talk to anyone?'

'Couple of locals.'

'Anyone else?'

'Jesus Christ – what is this?'

'Who was the guy you were talking to outside the café?'

Johnny's whole demeanour changed. He narrowed his eyes like he'd been caught out.

'You follow me down there?'

'I came looking for you because you just upped and left me all on my own. What was I supposed to do?'

He tossed the towel over the chair, and fussed his hair in the mirror.

'The locals call it El Joya. When you look down from the highest point it sparkles in the sun.'

'Johnny – who did you meet at the café?'

He opened the backpack and took out a crumpled shirt. 'Gonna buy me a whole new wardrobe soon. Walking round looking like a goddam hillbilly.'

'I said, who did you meet!'

Dropping the shirt, he stood gazing out at the balcony, presenting her with the scarred and muscular contours of his back.

'His name is Henry Linklater. He's staying up at the old monastery on the hill, doing some kinda conservation work. One of the locals pointed him out, thought I'd go over and introduce myself.'

'Just like that.'

'Sure, honey. Just like that.' He turned to face her, defying her to challenge him.

Still it didn't seem right. The image of the two of them, sat there at the table deep in conversation. Shaking hands before they parted, as if some kind of deal had been struck.

'What you tell him about us?' she said.

'Same thing I been telling everyone else around here. We hit a storm and got blown off course.' He ran his fingers through his hair, a faint smile lingering. 'Know what I think?'

'What?'

'This here's an opportunity. Your boy Henry turned up just when we needed him.'

'He ain't my boy. I don't even know him.'

Johnny's smile hardened. 'Let's not upset the balance of things when we just got here, huh? We gotta make the most of it. Take what we can get.'

*

One day became two. She got used to the small but comfortable room, with its balcony that offered relief from the heat, and the sounds of life that drifted up from the harbour. Madame Diaz replaced the linen and clipped dead petals from the flowers by the window, always quietly respectful and wishing not to intrude. But the look she gave them implied a certain distrust. The same look they got from all the locals.

Johnny went out to get help to fix the yacht. The Englishman, Henry, had given him details of a local boat builder who worked on the front. From him they might also be able to procure supplies and other necessities for the trip to Mexico. In the meantime she was to stay in the room and not talk to anyone – an instruction she thought was unfair given the circumstances. But Johnny's word was final. He knew best and she ought to listen to him.

'What am I supposed to do while you're gone?' she said.

'Tidy the place up. Rearrange the flowers.'

'That ain't even funny.'

With a quick kiss on her cheek, he was gone.

From the balcony she watched him make his way towards the harbour, past the café where she'd first glimpsed the Englishman in the white jacket – an innocent enough scene, and yet one that tormented with its ambiguity. How had Johnny come across this man, who presumably he'd never met before? And why the apparent secrecy?

Pungent smells from the fish market carried along on the warm breeze; the voices of the locals calling out to each other in their strange dialect. She grew restless. The room itself became a prison cell, like the confines of *Indigo*, that no amount of luxury could relieve.

A lone figure wandered down towards the harbour, her head covered by a black scarf. It was only after she turned a corner that Laura-Mae realised it was Madame Diaz. Something about her appearance that contrasted with the picture-book harbour and the blue sky. Solitary and self-contained. Comfortable in this her natural environment, needing no one else.

On impulse, she decided to follow her.

*

The set of steps led to the flagstones below. Descending quietly, in her wide-brimmed hat and loose-fitting shirt, she hoped to blend in. No one seemed to pay her any attention as she strolled among them, beneath the wide canvas awnings along the front. Perhaps she'd imagined it before, over-dramatizing the looks they seemed to give her, and the heavy, oppressive atmosphere. Just a simple town like any other, with the ordinary folk getting on with their lives.

Madame Diaz turned a corner up ahead. Following at a discreet distance behind, she wondered at the wisdom of such a decision. Johnny had told her to stay in the room. What if she got involved in a situation she couldn't handle and put their liberty at risk? Maybe she ought to go back. But something drew her on. That same uncanny feeling she was being lied to.

A dusty track rose in a slow incline, crumbling stone walls on either side. Away from the shade of the awnings, the heat intensified; even the trees had a parched, dried-out look, everything deprived of water.

Pausing at the top, she caught her breath. A high stone wall formed a boundary; a set of wrought-iron gates to discourage visitors. Beyond this, a long driveway and neatly-cut lawn led to a four-storey building that rose impressively from the heat and dust. Small balconies jutted out in front of high, stone mullion windows. A sense of faded grandeur that had long since passed.

Madame Diaz was nowhere to be seen.

A dust blown car approached along the track. At a signal, the gates swung open, and the car cruised in. The gates stayed open. It seemed the most natural thing in the world for Laura-Mae to stray over the threshold into this strange new territory. Several men sat around on the lawn, reading newspapers and sipping drinks beneath high umbrellas that shielded them from the sun. They didn't look like locals, more like a bunch of middle-aged academics on vacation.

Johnny's warning came back to her. How important it was to appear natural and spontaneous among strangers, never giving too much away; a lie was only as good as the truth you weaved into it. They'd been over the story so many times she could recite it backwards, even adding bits herself to make it sound more convincing. But still she had no right to be here. The only solution was to hide among the trees at the back, and observe the goings-on from there.

A man came out, the brim of his hat casting his face in shadow. He strolled across the lawn, and took a seat at an ornate white table. Even without the distinctive white jacket, she identified him as the Englishman, Henry.

Then, from the same entrance, running his fingers through his hair and smiling at some private joke, came Johnny.

She watched, fascinated, as he joined the Englishman at the table, the two of them relaxed, enjoying a leisurely conversation, as if they'd known each other a long time. They could have been the guests in a secluded hotel enjoying a siesta. But there was something badly wrong with the picture. Something she just couldn't figure out.

*

Johnny came back, tired and irritable from his attempts to get help from the locals. Wary of his mood, she tried to distance herself from him, still reeling from what she'd seen.

'What did you do while I was gone?' he said.

'I went for a walk along the harbour.'

'I told you not to go out – didn't you hear me?'

'Yeah, well I got bored waiting for you. How'd you think I felt, stuck in here on my own in all this heat?'

He stopped pacing and stared through the open window. 'It's gonna take a few more days to fix the yacht.'

'I thought you said – '

'Don't matter what I said. They do things different round here. We'll just have to wait.'

She chose her moment, waited for him to calm down. 'What about this Henry – can he help us?'

'How should I know?'

'I thought you'd been talking to him?'

He grabbed an orange from the bowl, and tossed it in the air a couple of times.

'You buy these?'

'They were here when I got back. Madame Diaz must've left them.'

He dropped the orange in the bowl, and sat on the bed, taking off his shoes.

'Henry knows a lotta people. He's got influence here.'

'So you did see him?'

'Yeah, I did – what's wrong with that?'

'Where – up at the monastery?'

He looked up, slowly. 'You been spying on me again, Laura-Mae?'

'I just don't like the idea of you doing things behind my back.'

'Oh, yeah? And how does that work out?' Her silence goaded him. 'You gotta better way of doing things, you come right out and say it.'

'I just wanna leave. Get off this island.'

'And that's what I've been trying to fix up all along. You gotta trust me on this one, honey.'

Later, he was rough with her, pulling off her top and mauling her with an intensity she both feared and understood. She yielded, no longer a person, but an object to be used and brutalised. He cursed her in low whispers, her cries and moans only inflaming his passion. Then, when it was over, he lay quiet beside her, his chest rising and falling. She lay still, counting the cost of being with him and his demons.

The sounds of the men working on the harbour drifted over the balcony. At some point they'd be underway. The little apartment with all its colourful flowers and rich fruit would be a memory. They'd be alone again, sailing into unknown territory.

'Tell me about Henry?' she said. 'What's he like?'

'Why?'

'I gotta right to know, haven't I? You don't tell me nothing. Expect me to figure it all out for myself.'

'You'll meet him soon enough.'

'When?'

'When I say.' He got up, and shrugged on his pants. 'The less questions you ask, the better it'll be for the both of us.'

Perhaps it was the dry heat making him ornery, the frustration at being stranded on the island. Or the fact the Colonel hadn't replied to the telegram he'd sent when they were still on the mainland. He didn't think about all the things she'd given up, all the sacrifices she'd made and the people she'd left behind. Innocence and naivety couldn't help her none here, except perhaps as an act put on for strangers. Men were stupid, by and large. Revealed their hand too quick, as Johnny would have said. Made their intentions known by the looks on their faces.

She'd learnt a lot in such a short time. Having to figure out ways and means of survival at such a young age. Leaving her family behind to seek a new life in the city, only to find remnants of the old still remained and were harder to get rid of than she'd imagined. So she used the only thing she knew she could count on that had always worked before. The thing that men wanted more than anything else in the world, that often made them reckless and irresponsible in their efforts to take possession of it.

Margot had it too. The great actress knew how to inflame men's desire by keeping it withheld for as long as needs be. Like the light flickering on the screen that created the perfect illusion. No one knew who she really was, or the lengths she was willing to go to get her own way. That's what separated her from all the other hopefuls who set foot in Hollywood looking for fame and adulation. Margot knew the secret. To get to that venerated place, you simply had to want it more than anybody else. It had to be your entire life's purpose.

*

Johnny went out the next morning, to chase up the local who was supposed to fix the yacht. For three days, *Indigo* had floundered out in the bay on the other side of the island, her sails torn and her engine in need of an overhaul. It only seemed right that they get across to her and carry out the repairs. Soon as that was done, they could load up with provisions and head for Mexico.

Watching the harbour life unfold from the balcony helped pass the time while she waited for Johnny. The men worked on the lobster crates, unloading them from the fishing boats to the jetty. Local women milled by the cafes, distinctive in their headscarves and long skirts, the coils of homemade jewellery they wore that gleamed in the sun. They seemed insular, linked by an invisible thread. A little like the extras she'd worked with in Hollywood, who formed small cliques, aware of their inferior status among the townsfolk, who despised actors and actresses. The indigenous people on the island formed the majority, and didn't particularly care for outsiders

Alerted by a noise in the room, she turned with a start. Standing by the door, dressed in black, was Madame Diaz.

'Sorry,' Laura-Mae said. 'I was just sitting out on the balcony. I didn't hear you come in.'

Madame Diaz gave a little bow, which might have signified courtesy had her expression not stayed the same. She seemed content to stand and stare, her eyes dark, almost luminous in their intensity.

'Thanks for the fruit.' The words sounded forced and unnatural; an absurd thought that her shirt was unbuttoned and might be considered unseemly.

'I brought you fresh towels for the bathroom.' Madame Diaz's English was slow, but spoken clearly and without hesitation. 'Is there anything else you need?'

'No, I don't think so. Johnny's out getting help to fix the yacht. He'll probably bring a few things back with him.' She had the distinct feeling she was being assessed, looked over for flaws and conceits, traits that would have set her apart from the other women on the island. The silver cross Madame Diaz wore around her neck signified her religion, reminding Laura-Mae of the hellfire preachers back home, who used such symbols to whip up a frenzy among the congregation and ward off evil.

Madame Diaz turned to go. Laura-Mae felt abandoned, that childlike voice that said she hadn't been listened to and understood.

'Thanks for the flowers,' she said. 'They're very nice.'

With a single nod of recognition, Madame Diaz was gone. Almost without a word, she'd made her disapproval known. Perhaps it was the western style dress, the fact that in her eyes a woman's arms and legs should always be covered. Or the fact that Laura-Mae and Johnny were from the mainland and not to be trusted. Whatever it was, the older woman made her feel uneasy. One more reason to get fixed up and off the island.

Quickly and self-consciously she buttoned her shirt, even though she was alone in the room. Such impropriety must have been frowned upon, the tight-knit community on the island having its own morality, its own laws. All the more reason to make the repairs to *Indigo* and leave. Escape the awful feeling of claustrophobia that was closing in.

*

Johnny came back with good news. He's managed to find the local, who'd agreed to go with him the following day.

'How long will you be gone?' she said.

'Long as it takes. We get the engine fixed we can motor round. Tie-up in the harbour and get the rest of the work done here.'

Watching the locals from the balcony, she couldn't help a certain envy: whole generations who'd never been anywhere else, or known anyone but their neighbours and immediate families. The strange atmosphere made it hard to adapt – that dreamlike quality she'd felt from their arrival at the bay on the other side, to the hike over the hills. The discovery of the chapel, and the goats staring at them along the hillside path. Madame Diaz's unspoken censure that left her feeling so uncomfortable, especially as she was a guest in the older woman's home.

Perhaps this was how prisoners felt, incarcerated in some lonely, forgotten outpost, with nothing but their thoughts and memories to draw upon. As time went on, they would lose all the things that made them what they were, until in the end all they had left were fantasies, the things people dreamed up to compensate for reality.

'Madame Diaz brought us some fresh towels,' she said.

'She ask where I was?'

'I told her you went out looking to fix the yacht. That OK?'

He turned his back on her, indifferent, the subject closed. Her fears didn't figure too highly on his list of priorities, and wouldn't have made much sense to him anyhow. It was his job to get them out of there and off the island, away from the threat of apprehension. She understood her role in it: not to make any fuss, to be as unobtrusive as possible. But Madame Diaz had left an impression, made her feel uncomfortable.

'I don't like the way she looks at me,' she said.

'What d'you mean?'

'It's just … I can't explain it. It's like she knows something.'

'Only thing she knows is what you tell her, and that's it. Now quit trying to work everything out.'

'I'm just saying how I feel, Johnny.'

'And I'm telling you how it is. Don't matter a fuck what she thinks anyhow. Couple more days and we're outta here.'

He fell asleep on the bed – one of his many talents, that he could close his eyes and drop off anywhere, even if it was never for long. Looking down at him, she tried to feel something other than regret. The love she usually had for him wasn't there. Instead, the kind of sad affection a mother might feel for a sick child. But even in sleep there was an air of danger about him, as if he was coiled and ready to strike at the first opportunity.

Maybe his orphan status had something to do with it. She couldn't imagine what it must be like not to have parents – the ones she'd been born with had let her down badly enough. One of the reasons she felt such an affinity towards Johnny when they first met. They were two of a kind. The world had been cruel to them in different ways, hadn't exactly given them a head start. All they were trying to do was even the score and make a little money.

He woke with a start, and rubbed his eyes. 'What time is it?'

'Just after four.'

'Why didn't you wake me earlier?'

'I thought you needed the rest.'

'Rest when I'm dead. Come here and lie with me a while.'

She lay beside him, passive, arms at her sides. He ran a hand over her thighs, and onto her belly, all the while staring down at her like he was mesmerised. Something primal about him in that state that made him almost unrecognisable from the Johnny she knew. The beard he'd grown to avoid recognition made him look older, framing his dark, sunburned skin. He could almost have been mistaken for one of the locals, the fishermen toiling in the heat.

'You ever think about leaving me, Laura-Mae?'

'All the time.'

'Don't get clever now.' His fingers slipped beneath her top, light on her skin. 'What would you do without ole Johnny Boy?'

'I can think of a lotta things.'

'Well I can think of one thing you'd miss for sure, honey.'

Love was a strange thing, a gift and a burden at the same time. Sometimes it seemed the love she felt for Johnny was a game they played that could only end in tragedy. Leaving everything behind like they had made them fugitives, forced to rely solely on each other. Here in this tranquil place they had to renew their commitment on a daily basis, knowing there were forces in place that could tear them apart.

After they fooled around some, he lay back, breathing heavy, a sheen of sweat on his face.

'You OK?' she said.

'I'm fine.'

'You don't look too good, that's all.'

'I said I was fine, didn't I?' Seeing her wounded reaction, he took hold of her wrist and gazed up at her with tenderness. 'How 'bout you put some clothes on, and we go out and meet Henry?'

She sat up, startled.

'What?'

'He wants us to have dinner with him down on the front.'

'Why didn't you tell me earlier?'

'I'm telling you now. Don't make a big thing out of it, OK?'

She got up and made for the bathroom, unable to take him or his lying any longer.

'What's up, honey?' he called out.

'You do what you gotta do. Just don't expect me to play along with it.'

His laughter rang out behind her, mean and disrespectful, like he got a kick out of it somehow. One minute he was reminding her how careful they had to be around people, the next he was acting like it didn't matter who they met up with. The whole business made her tired and confused, unable to think straight.

Later, he was more serious, going over their roles and responsibilities, and how she was supposed to act.

'Whatever I say, you just smile and nod your head like you heard it all before.'

'What if he asks me questions I can't answer?'

'Then you just keep your pretty mouth shut and let me do all the talking.' He relaxed visibly, and put his hands behind his head. 'You ain't gotta worry about a thing, honey. Johnny Boy got it all worked out.'

*

Small children frolicked at the harbour's edge. A few old men played cards beneath the awning of a café. Breathing in the warm evening air, she relaxed a bit more, the tension slipping away.

Henry's voice made a pleasant accompaniment, pitched just right – not rude or insistent like Johnny's, but more refined and genteel in the way the English had of articulating every syllable. Entranced by the mood at the table and the evening heat, she felt herself warm to him. He seemed to take a special interest in them as guests, keen to tell them all about the island. But always at the back of her mind the need for vigilance, the constant reminder that they were in a strange place.

Intrigued by their intention to sail to Mexico, Henry asked questions. Emboldened by the wine, she took the initiative, telling him about their shared love of the sea. How they'd both become jaded with the city and decided to leave.

'We thought the climate would be good for Johnny's health. That's what the doctor's told us back in Chicago.'

'You lived in Chicago?'

'Only for a while, until we saved enough to come out to California.'

'That's right,' Johnny said. 'We robbed banks like Bonnie and Clyde.' He grinned and raised his glass. 'Here's to the island, and to your hospitality, Henry. I gotta admit, it's some place you got here.'

'Well, it isn't my place exactly, but I can at least vouch for some of the cuisine. Shall we eat?'

The waiter brought out an enormous seafood platter that they all shared. She filled her plate, aware of the journey ahead and the prospect of going hungry again. The spread was magnificent: shrimp and sea bass, fried vegetables and hunks of bread in a basket. The whole thing washed down by the sour-tasting wine.

'Bon appetit,' Henry said. 'It's a pleasure to be in such good company.'

Johnny nodded in agreement, as comfortable here as he was anywhere, and clearly enjoying the routine. But she wanted to know more about Henry, and how he'd ended up in such an isolated setting.

'What is it you do here?' she said.

'Well, that's a good question. I sometimes wonder myself.'

'Henry's been hiding out from the British government,' Johnny said. 'Gotta lie low till it all blows over.'

'Nothing quite as dramatic as that, I'm afraid.' Henry smiled, a little distant, perhaps. 'I'm actually a writer, of sorts. At least I was until I turned my hand to conservation.'

'You write books as well?' she said, intrigued.

'Well, I've written a book, which was published somewhat reluctantly by the National Geographic last year. Then my slender pool of resources dried up, so to speak, and I ended up here on the island, where I've been ever since.'

Henry's background inspired in her a real fascination. With a little prompting, he opened up about his interest in the indigenous people, and how he'd lived with a tribe of Mexican Indians for three years, observing their customs and rituals.

'Wow – that's amazing,' she said, unable to contain her admiration.

Henry gave a modest shrug, reluctant to go into details. Perhaps because he was embarrassed by the attention and wanted to disassociate himself from his obvious success. Maybe there were other reasons. Johnny always said that when you found something out about a person it gave you control over them, and you could use it to your advantage later. There were ways of drawing people in to your confidence and making the circumstances ripe for confession. Knowing this made her feel anxious again. Johnny had already seen this vulnerability in Henry and would use every opportunity to take from him what he could.

The conversation turned to the other 'foreigners' on the island, men who'd arrived for whatever reason and who, like Henry, had ended up staying.

'I'll have to introduce you to Dr Martinez,' Henry said. 'He's from Cuba. He's studying a species of rare bird they've discovered here.'

'Seriously?' Johnny said. 'He came all the way from Cuba for that?'

'Oh, you'd be amazed at his dedication. He really is quite a remarkable man, although a little on the eccentric side, perhaps.'

There was an endearing quality to Henry, a thoughtfulness in the way he spoke; the way he reserved his comments and gestures so as not to dominate the conversation. When he did catch her eye, his gaze was intense, even troubled, perhaps, although she couldn't think why.

'How long have you been here on the island?' she said.

'Too long, I'm sure. I think I may have outstayed my welcome.'

'He knocked up one of the local girls,' Johnny said. 'Now her daddy's come around looking for him, so it's time to say bye-bye.'

Henry smiled, indulging Johnny's coarseness, as if already he was used to it. 'As I said, I'm involved in the conservation of the monastery. It isn't a profitable cause, but it's taken up enough of my time, that's for sure … More wine anyone?'

She could see Johnny's mind working; his nose for opportunity. If they stayed long enough he'd find a way to manipulate the situation no matter the danger it might put them in. Tonight he was all bon homie and good humour, toasting Henry with the wine they enjoyed so freely, joking that there were no cops here to raid the place and throw them all in jail. The covert looks he gave her confirmed her suspicions – whatever he was cooking up she would be expected to go along with it. It wouldn't just be a case of repairing the yacht and leaving.

Henry's presence created new complications. His questions, seemingly innocent, were always probing, intending to draw them out. In spite of his hospitality, she began to feel uncomfortable and eager to move on.

But Johnny was having too much fun. He talked about *Indigo* and the battering she'd taken during the storm, bragging about his navigation skills, and how good he was with a sextant, like the mariners of old.

Henry listened with great interest, amazed that they'd pulled through. 'How fortunate you ended up here. It could've been a lot worse for you.'

'Ain't that the truth. We could be at the bottom of the ocean by now and no one would know any different.'

The late evening symphony of cicadas had started up. Lights from the bars and cafes spilled onto the flagstones, laughter and music coming from inside. Johnny became more reckless, indulging his love of playing games. Now she had to be his foil, the recipient of casual remarks he made to see how far he could go. He talked about people they knew in Chicago, weaving grand stories about them like a Hollywood impresario. But the drink made him careless. Once or twice she thought he'd said too much, but when she looked across the table, Henry's face reflected nothing but polite interest, the smile of someone used to indulging precocious children.

'What was it like in Hollywood?' Henry said.

'Oh, just about as crazy as it could get.' Johnny took a sip of his drink, thoughtful. 'You wouldn't believe how much some of them big stars get paid.'

'Perhaps I should pack up and try my hand over there.'

'Why not? They even had Scott Fitzgerald holed-up in a room at M.G.M., turning out scripts all day. Damn near finished him off.'

'Did you ever meet him?'

'Fitzgerald? Hell, yeah. We used to sit in a bar downtown of an evening, and he'd tell me all his troubles. How the studio bosses didn't appreciate his talent, and how he'd turned into this overworked hack with a drinking problem.' Johnny nodded to himself, as if recalling these poignant scenes. 'I did what I could to help him, but I guess some folk are just too far gone. Best you can do is keep out of their way.'

She was pretty sure Johnny had never met Scott Fitzgerald, but the story rang true in the way that he told it. Henry looked on with a kind of rapt fascination, willing to believe anything, it seemed.

Next, Johnny launched into an attack on the wealthy landowners in California, who kept their huge reserves to themselves while everyone else went without. As he talked, his expression changed, an anger in his voice he couldn't disguise. She'd heard it all so many times before that she withdrew quietly, trying to focus on the scenery instead. But Johnny's bitterness was inescapable, highlighting the divisions between rich and poor, the scandalous indifference of successive governments in righting the disparity. Henry seemed to agree, but only as a token of courtesy; as the host, he was obliged to put up with his guests' idiosyncrasies. She was reminded of a comment Barthez once made, about the English always playing their hand close to their chest.

'Do we have to talk about all that?' she said. 'It's so peaceful here, why spoil it?'

Johnny stopped short and stared at her. 'Well, sorry if it's spoiling the food for you, Laura-Mae. What would you like us to talk about?'

'I just thought we could – you know, lighten up a little bit. It's such a beautiful place.'

'It does have a certain charm, you're right.' Henry picked up on her cue and followed her gaze across the harbour. 'Something of a sanctuary from the rest of the world.'

'A sanctuary – yeah, I like that,' Johnny said. 'A secret hideout for people running away.'

'Well, yes, I suppose you could call it that. If you follow the assumption that we're all running from something.'

'What are you running from, Henry?' She couldn't resist the question, surprised by her own boldness.

Henry smiled, indulging her also. 'My past is rather boring, I'm afraid. I came out here to escape the routine of life back home. Family expectations, that sort of thing.'

'Were you married?'

Johnny made a tutting sound and shook his head. 'I don't think Henry should answer that kinda question without a lawyer present.'

'Oh, I've nothing to hide in that respect. I've always been too dedicated to my work to settle down.'

She hoped Johnny hadn't noticed the locks Henry gave her – too preoccupied by the food and drink, and his vitriolic assassination of the moneyed classes to bother with that. But she knew how jealous he could get; how easy it was for him to embarrass himself in public, drinking too much and saying the wrong things.

Henry described the island and its people, how their culture was founded on a mixture of folklore and superstition. The indigenous people had known much tragedy, having survived a massacre by European settlers that had almost wiped them out. But they managed to keep their customs going, much like the tribe he'd lived with in Mexico.

'Tomorrow is the Festival of All Souls,' he said. 'The entire island turns out in celebration.'

'Can we go?' she said.

'Of course. In the meantime, perhaps I could show you more of the island – if you've nothing else to do.'

'That would be real nice, thanks. What do you think, Johnny?'

'You go right ahead, honey. I'm sure Henry's just the boy to show you all you need to see around here.'

*

They climbed higher, to the chapel way above the town. The familiar tinkling of bells announced the appearance of stray goats who peered at them suspiciously before darting away. Henry told stories about the island, and some of the more colourful characters he'd met there. As they climbed further, she felt she knew him a little more, that in some way he was reaching out, doing his best to make her feel looked after and entertained. Without Johnny watching her every move she could relax, breathe a little easier.

At the top of the next rise they stopped and looked out over the bay, the highest point on the island that took in the sun-dappled ocean and clear blue sky.

'Here's where the tour ends,' Henry said. 'Unless you want to keep walking?'

'I'm just about ready to collapse.'

'Well, let's just sit for a while and recuperate.'

They sat in the shade and drank the bottled spring water

Henry had brought along. Out of courtesy, he positioned himself a discreet distance away, discussing the ongoing repairs to the yacht while she fanned herself with her hat. Now that Johnny had found a local who'd agreed to fix *Indigo*, they had no reason to stay any longer than necessary – the time it took to buy the provisions needed for the coming journey and organize the fuel. She should have been relieved, glad to be moving on. Instead, she felt saddened at the thought of leaving. Particularly, the thought of leaving Henry, who she'd only just got to know.

'Who built the chapel?' she said.

'The Spanish, when they first arrived. Their intention was to convert the entire island to Christianity, but the old habits and customs proved hard to break.'

'I couldn't help noticing the atmosphere. Bit like New Orleans when you first get there.'

'Well, I don't know about that. But some of these people still take their cue from soothsayers and witchdoctors. Everything's based on some ritual that's been handed down from previous generations.' He grew quiet, gazing out at the horizon. 'I sometimes wonder if we're doing the right thing.'

'How's that?'

'Well, we come along with all these ideas on how to change everything. Maybe Johnny's right. It's the monster of capitalism that's to blame.' His smile was intended to pacify her, but she wasn't taken in.

'I don't think they like foreigners here,' she said.

'What makes you think that?'

'Just the looks they give me. Makes me feel uncomfortable.'

'They're suspicious of anything they don't understand. I think I felt the same as you when I first arrived, but you get used to it.'

She pictured Madame Diaz, who'd appeared suddenly in the room that day with that look of quiet disapproval. But people were the same wherever you went. Some good, some bad. And sometimes, just to put a smile on your face was all it needed to break down their defences. Then they were more likely to do what you wanted.

Henry asked about their upcoming journey. Would the equipment and the supplies they'd asked for be enough, and would *Indigo* hold up this time. And then of course there was the issue of money.

'How much do you need?' Henry said.

'Hard to say.' She tried to appear vague, as if they hadn't given it much thought. 'Could be as little as a couple hundred to get us going. But then again it could be a whole lot more.'

'What will you do when you get to Mexico?'

'Probably find a buyer for the yacht. Then settle down somewhere. Johnny's got a contact there who can get him a good job.'

Her attention drifted in the heat. So many things she would have liked to say but couldn't. The longer she spent in Henry's company the more the differences between him and Johnny became apparent. Henry was educated and reserved, not given to anger and wild accusations. Comfortable in his surroundings, he didn't seek an audience for everything he said. And being more cultured, he was possessed of a knowledge and wisdom Johnny didn't have. In comparing the two men, she found herself straying from her chosen course – to support Johnny in every situation, to be his 'eyes and ears', as he often liked to say.

But Henry posed a threat to their security. Any intimacy that developed between them, however superficial, would have to end.

'Tell me more about the festival,' she said.

'It's the annual celebration of fertility. What you might call a pagan ritual. All the townsfolk get together and give thanks for the crops, the generosity of their ancestors for making it all possible.'

'What will they make of two strangers turning up?'

'Well, you're hardly a stranger, are you? … Not to me, anyway.'

The rise overlooked the town and the blue sea, the same viewpoint they'd seen on their first day on the island. It felt familiar, like the lemon grove in California they could see from their window. Wherever she ended up became home eventually, an adopted retreat that soon took on a significance of its own. The island had unique customs and a colourful history. You could feel the struggle for survival in the surrounding hills and wild terrain, the scorched landscape. The locals wanted only to preserve their way of life and ward off evil, holding on to superstitions that had no place in the real world but gave them an identity, a purpose.

'Johnny says you're an actress?' Henry gave her his cautious smile. 'Have you been in anything I might've seen?'

'Oh, I doubt that very much. I was just kinda starting out when we left California. But I might go back one day.'

Henry nodded, as if he understood. But he could never know the ache it caused her inside. The life and the people she'd left behind that was always on her mind, like the fragments of a dream upon awakening.

'I suppose we'd better head back,' she said.

'Yes, of course.' Henry helped her up, one hand lightly placed beneath her arm to steady her on the stony track. For a moment they were linked, his touch a mild act of impertinence that seemed to challenge her for a response.

'Thanks,' she said, relieved when he stepped away. Now they were heading back to town, and she could assume the role Johnny had assigned her, always careful not to say too much.

But sometimes, when Henry looked at her, she wondered what he was thinking. Could it be that that in that sad and mournful gaze he'd worked out something wasn't right?

*

The dirt road led into the old town on the eastern side. They walked along the verge in the fading light. A car went by, coated in the standard layer of dust, the passengers calling out to them from the open windows. The young couple they'd seen the first day zipped by on a motorcycle, the girl in a thin floral dress and jacket, her arms around the man's waist. The mood reminded her of wild nights in LA, drinking and dancing until the morning light. The locals were seized with the same festival spirit, an electricity in the air that was palpable.

Henry looked back at her. 'Can you hear it?'

She listened out, the motorcycle's engine fading up ahead.

'I can't hear anything.'

'Keep listening.'

A faint drumbeat carried along on the breeze, like the distant roll of thunder. More cars passed, and even the odd battered-looking truck, filled with excited locals on their way to the festival. The drumming increased in volume the closer they got, a magnetic pulse beat luring the inhabitants from all corners of the island.

Soon they were on the town's outskirts. A sprawl of wooden shacks with small verandas rose up either side of the dirt road. The locals were out in numbers, some in costumes and disguises, children wearing ghoulish masks and waving streamers. And in the background, the drumbeat coming from the beach where everyone seemed to be heading.

'We'd better be careful,' Johnny said. 'Might be a few crazies running round down here, all fired up on the local moonshine.'

Henry slapped him playfully on the back. 'You may not think it, Johnny, but you're very privileged to be here. This is something few outsiders ever get to see.'

The beach was filled with people, as if the whole island had descended on it in anticipation. Fires had been lit at intervals, tended by the young men, the whole area infected by a lively carnival atmosphere. She couldn't believe the change. The sleepy, soporific quiet of the daylight hours replaced by this wholesale celebration.

'Let's get a bite to eat,' Henry said. 'Then we can find somewhere to watch the dancing.'

They followed Henry down to the shoreline, assailed by the aroma of barbequed food and the pulse of tribal music. Finding a spot near the dunes, set back from the crowd, they ate the food served on paper plates. She savoured every mouthful, the skin of the chicken flavoured with local herbs and spices. The drink came in Dixie cups – a sweet-tasting mix that Henry said was extremely potent. He seemed to know everyone, and was treated with a respectful, almost reverential air. They called him 'Mr Henry' and bowed their heads as he passed by, as if to a visiting dignitary.

'You seem real popular round here,' Johnny said. 'You sure you ain't been holding something back from us?'

'Well, that would be telling now, wouldn't it?' Henry gave her a playful, sidelong look that excluded Johnny. She felt awkward, compromised in some way. But they were together, the three of them. All she had to do was keep her head and enjoy the evening.

The drums stopped. An officious-looking local stepped up to make a speech. He held a microphone with a long lead attached to a speaker pitched at an angle in the sand. Henry explained who he was and what he was doing. 'He's going to talk about how grateful they should all be that he's the mayor, and how much he's done for the town since he's been in office.'

'They have a mayor here?' she said.

'Oh, yes. It's quite the burgeoning democracy – courtesy of the British influence, of course.'

The official finished his speech and stepped down. The drums started up again, reigniting the festival spirit.

'Now the fun starts,' Henry said. 'This is the best part of the evening. You'll see the locals in a different light.'

A group of young girls in white raffia dresses filed into the enclosure and lined up with their backs to the sea. The musicians assembled to one side awaited a signal. Then a drum-roll and a high-pitched whistle. The girls stepped out onto the sand in unison, inching forward rocking their hips suggestively. They looked like the dancers in a burlesque on Sunset Strip, except this time it was for real.

How compelling it seemed to Laura-Mae, this primitive ritual acted out in such an exotic setting, the darkened sea and the rolling surf in the background. Henry kept up a commentary, filling in the missing details. How the locals had kept their past and its culture, not allowing it to be undermined by modernity and consumerism. There was no airstrip and no high-rise hotels on the island; no greedy developers looking to exploit the natives. And yet these people had their own belief system that influenced everything they did: soothsayers and astrologers, medicine men and witchdoctors who studied ancient texts and read palms, making sacrifices to placate the gods. The organized religion that found its way into the community several centuries ago had never quite managed to gain a foothold. The old idols continued to dominate.

'What do you think?' Henry said.

'They look incredible,' she said. 'There's so much energy and colour.'

'What happens next?' Johnny said. 'Does it all end up in one big orgy on the beach?'

'I'm afraid not, Johnny. Sorry to disappoint you.'

Johnny stood, brushing sand from his pants. 'Well, I don't know about you folks, but I'm gonna get me another drink. Any takers?'

Both Laura-Mae and Henry declined, and together they watched Johnny trudge through the sand towards the drink station.

Henry took the opportunity to move closer, his smile somewhat unnatural in the light of the fire.

'I hope you've enjoyed it tonight,' he said.

'Oh, I have. It's been a real education.'

'I'll be sorry to see you go.' He saw her reaction and hesitated. 'I've got used to your company. Both of you.'

'You've been a really good host, Henry. And we appreciate it.'

His face seemed to glow in the light from the fires, his eyes imploring her with a silent yearning. Then, without warning, he leaned in and kissed her on the mouth. Mesmerised by the music and the atmosphere, she allowed it to happen, yielding to the impetus, the tug of desire that made her heart leap.

Henry sat back stiffly. 'I'm sorry … I don't know what came over me.' He glanced in Johnny's direction and shook his head. 'I don't know what to say.'

'You don't have to say anything. It doesn't matter.'

'But it does …' He fought for the right words, barely able to look at her. 'My behaviour was inexcusable.'

Aware that a line had been crossed, she sat still and tried not to think. But the pleasant sensation lingered – the illicit thrill of his mouth on hers, the seclusion of the dunes and the light of

the fires in the background. For a moment it could have been the two of them, alone together at the start of some great romance. The music and the evening warmth washed over her, a feeling of almost unbearable rapture. Then she saw Johnny, making his way back across the sand, and the fantasy ended.

'Did I miss anything?' Johnny said, sinking down beside her.

'No, nothing at all.' Henry glanced at her, a look that silenced any doubts she might have had. And she played along, as she'd always done, knowing that fate had intervened and set up events that couldn't be reversed.

The dancing and celebration continued well into the night. The women gyrated on the sand to the tribal drums, and the men waved their arms in a frenzy, invoking their ancient gods. The fires crackled and spat, smoke rising in the night sky. Phosphorous from wave tips broke along the shoreline. A night she would surely remember, made all the more poignant by Henry's sudden kiss.

A cry went up along the beach – an urgency and desperation that caused a stir among the locals. Heads turned in the direction of the disturbance: a woman's voice calling out for assistance. The unmistakeable note of grief – hysteria even – at odds with the festival atmosphere.

'What's going on?' Johnny said.

Henry strained to see, his view blocked by so many dark figures. Most of the men carried on dancing and drinking, the woman's cries unable to disturb their fevered state.

Then she appeared on the beach, a local woman of ample proportions, a garland of flowers around her neck and a coil of bracelets on her arms; in the firelight, her dark skin looked slick and oily like the figure in a painting. She grabbed one of the men, insistent, wringing her hands and wailing, pleading with him to help her, pointing in the direction of the dunes where the outer darkness lay.

'Maybe she's lost her boyfriend,' Johnny said, but his quip fell flat.

Laura-Mae turned to Henry. 'Can you make out what she's saying?'

'I'm not sure … I think it's a child gone missing.'

They watched the scene play out, a grim pageant lit by the fires and the distorted faces of the locals. The woman hurried back along the beach towards the dunes, followed by a few of the men. And still her wailing could be heard above the drums and the music, alerting them all to the unfolding tragedy.

*

She woke early, fragments of a dream that made no sense: riding a black stallion along a desolate shoreline; the stallion turned into a winged beast with fiery red eyes that carried her high into the sky where she looked down onto a glittering kingdom. In the dream she could have anything she wanted, but there was a price to pay. Maybe she'd already paid that price by ending up out here with Johnny.

Leaving him to sleep, she went out onto the balcony. The sun had yet to come up, shadows on the pale water, a few solitary lights along the shore. The events of the previous night played over, almost surreal and hard to grasp. Henry's sudden move that caught her by surprise. The two of them alone and shielded by the sand dune where they couldn't be seen. His remorse and need for forgiveness that had so thrilled and appalled her at the same time. Then the woman's cries of distress, and the news that a child had gone missing. The whole evening bizarre and otherworldly, as if conjured from her imagination.

Johnny came out and dropped into the vacant chair, yawning.

'Sleep OK?' she said.

'Kinda.' He scratched his head. 'Don't remember much about last night at all. Anything interesting happen?'

'I think you drank too much of that local moonshine.'

'Is that what it was? I thought maybe you and Henry had drugged me and left me for dead.' He put his feet up on the railing, relaxed and easy-going.

'What're your plans for today?' she said.

'Go find the engineer and fix the yacht.'

'Then we can go?'

He frowned. 'What's the hurry? Don't you like it here?'

'Johnny, we – '

'Couple more days, OK? Then we load up with supplies and we're gone.' He yawned and scratched his beard. 'Anyways, won't hurt to stick around a bit longer. Might be a way we can make us some money.'

'How?'

'You let me take care of that.'

She ignored the look he gave her, the insinuation that she ought to just follow him blindly in whatever he did. And why the sudden reluctance to leave? The longer they stayed on the island the greater the risk of being discovered, or something else turning up they hadn't figured on.

'Can I ask you something?' she said.

'Sure, honey.'

'The day we got here and you went off and left me … Was that the first time you met Henry?'

He closed his eyes, relaxed in the early morning sun.

'I asked you a question, Johnny?'

'And I'm trying to relax. Can't you leave me be for one goddam minute?'

'I just wanna know, that's all.'

He opened one eye, a flash of indignation. 'You think I'd lie to you? After all we been through?'

'No, it's just – '

'Saving you from that snake Barthez? All them assholes in Hollywood, trying to get a piece of you? Seems to me I was the only one looking out for you back then, but I don't hear you giving me no thanks for it. All you do is get on my case and gimme a hard time.'

She couldn't answer. He knew exactly how to turn it around and make her feel bad. And yet, by avoiding the question he increased her suspicion. Easy to recall the two of them at the café table, fleshing out the details of some obscure deal, then shaking hands like gentlemen. Then the night she was first introduced to

Henry, where Johnny acted like the two of them had known each other a long time. The doubts stuck in her mind and she couldn't get rid of them.

Johnny stood. 'I gotta go. You gonna be alright here till I get back?'

'Guess I'll have to be.'

He kissed her quickly and was gone, leaving her alone with the blue sky and the colourful flowers, so lovingly tended by Madame Diaz.

*

She wandered along the harbour to the café, beneath the striped awning and the cool shade. A few locals lingered by the storefronts and strolled along the jetty. Sunlight reflected back from the chrome chairs and the hoods of parked cars. Time had withdrawn from the scene leaving a pleasant vacuum.

Taking a seat at a table, she looked for the proprietor. Apart from her, there were only two other customers, older men, smoking cigarettes and drinking coffee. Almost at once, one of the wild cats appeared beneath the table, pacing up and down and meowing incessantly. She clapped her hands and tried to shoo it away, but with all the stealth of a street beggar it kept coming back, fixing her with its plaintive eye.

A sudden fear took hold, that here in this sleepy, idyllic place she might be in great danger. Apart from Henry she didn't know anyone. She was a stranger, stuck here on the island with no means of escape. The stray cat was a harbinger of some future event, a sign she was meant to pay attention to.

The fear passed, nothing more than an irrational impulse in the heat. But once again, she had that sense of fate unfolding, an unstoppable force she had no control over.

'Laura-Mae – what a pleasant surprise.'

She looked up in alarm, to see the familiar white jacket and homburg tipped low over the eyes.

'Can I join you?'

'Of course.'

Henry eased himself into the chair, and took off his hat. 'I was hoping to speak to Johnny, is he around?'

'He left to meet the engineer. Anything I can help you with?'

'Oh, it can wait until later.'

The proprietor brought coffee, leaving them without a word. She relayed the story of the obstinate local who'd finally agreed to help Johnny to fix the yacht. Henry saw it as a minor problem that could be resolved. These people were extremely set in their ways, he said. To get them to do anything was a trial in itself.

He looked at her with regret. 'I suppose you'll want to leave as soon as possible?'

'I think that's the idea.'

'Well, as I said before, I'll miss you both, you've been such good company.' He sipped his coffee, pensive all of a sudden. 'I feel I should say something about last night. I really don't know what came over me.'

'You don't have to say anything, Henry.' She forced a smile. 'We all had too much to drink and got carried away. It really don't matter.'

'All the same, it was unforgivable of me to behave in such a manner. I didn't get much sleep at all last night thinking about it.'

Henry's abortive kiss – a test she'd come through without any unwanted consequences; Johnny had been completely unaware at the time – perhaps a little drunk and indifferent to his surroundings. But she was guilty too, and couldn't escape the finger pointing. The fleeting wish that she might somehow end up alone with Henry now seemed absurd, brought on by the music and the dancing, the festival atmosphere.

'Did they find the child that went missing?'

Henry shook his head. 'The search will go on today, but I'm not very hopeful.'

It seemed such an awful thing to contemplate, especially in a place so outwardly tranquil. The harbour front with the men toiling in the heat. The bars and the cafes where the locals gathered to smoke cigarettes and drink coffee. It should have been a safe place where children could play without fear of harm or molestation.

'It all looks so peaceful,' she said. 'Hard to believe anything bad could happen.'

'A lot of things went on here. People don't forget.'

'What things?'

'The traders who came here before the turn of the century wiped out whole families overnight. Those who survived had quite a legacy to contend with. The memories get passed on through the generations and leave a sort of taint.'

Maybe that explained the atmosphere. The fishermen and the plantation workers, the children with their facemasks and streamers, the dancers at the festival. Their single greatest achievement the ability to survive the past, the curse of poverty and disease, the murderous inclinations of white Europeans. The town was a jewel that sparkled in the sun. But underneath was a darker, less polished side kept hidden from visitors. Superstition and religion entwined. A child disappearing in suspicious circumstances. Henry had seen it, and now so had she. A price had to be paid for living out here in such isolation, where the real world couldn't get in.

Henry fanned himself with his hat. 'Funny, even after all this time, I still can't get used to the heat. Saps the energy, don't you think?'

'Better the heat than the cold. Live in Chicago you'd feel the same way.' She kept her smile in place through an act of will; the actress in her, able to perform under any and all situations. But the strain of keeping it up took its toll. The feeling that the conversation was a bit contrived somehow, and she would have to rise to meet it.

Henry put down his hat and fixed her with a look of consternation. 'I hope you don't mind me being forward, Laura-Mae, but there's something I've been meaning to ask you.'

She waited, alerted by his obvious discomfort.

'Well, it's just ...' He shifted in the chair, unable to look at her directly. 'Did something happen in California?'

'How do you mean?'

'I just got the sense that things weren't right.'

She pondered her answer, aware of Henry watching and waiting.

'Johnny got in a fight with someone over money. We couldn't afford to pay the rent on the place we were living in so we decided to leave.'

'And that's why you came here?'

'We got washed up here on the way to Mexico. Just the way it happened, I guess.'

Muted conversation drifted over from the other tables; locals jabbering away in their obscure dialect. Even the cats had wandered off to seek a richer harvest elsewhere.

'You can talk to me, you know,' Henry said.

She feigned ignorance. 'I can?'

'Look – I know what Johnny's like. I've seen him. He's loud and aggressive, wants everything done his way. I like him, don't get me wrong. It's just … I care about you, Laura-Mae. And I can't help thinking you're in some kind of danger.'

She wanted to say, but you hardly know me. Instead, she sat there in the sun, accepting his interest in her without a word, knowing that it wouldn't bode well for her and Johnny.

Henry took a deep breath and smiled. 'Would you like to see the monastery?'

The change in tone caught her out.

'What, now?'

'Why not? I could give you a guided tour.'

*

They were in a long rectangular room with a high domed ceiling. Paintings in gold frames hung on the walls, portraits of stern-faced men who gazed down with unnerving perspicacity. She had the feeling that if she spoke too loud someone would rush in and have her evicted for spoiling the atmosphere. Even their footsteps on the tiled floor seemed overly loud, causing a distinct echo.

Henry stopped and pointed out a painting. 'This is the cardinal who ordered the building of the monastery in the seventeenth century. It was originally named after him until quite recently.'

The man in the portrait had a saintly air, his pale blue eyes radiating wisdom. The faint curl of his lips implied a hidden vanity, cruelty even.

'He looks quite pleased with himself,' she said.

'Yes, he does – and probably with good reason. You have to remember how powerful these people were. When the Spanish came here, the locals were little more than savages. The warships terrified them when they first appeared in the bay.' He stepped back courteously. 'Shall we move on?'

The top floor was a series of rooms formerly used for study and meditation. Guests could come and sit quietly whenever they liked, and make use of the small library; the books gave the place an academic feel, their red leather spines lining an entire section. But it was the silence that permeated, giving the place a solemn, spiritual feel.

'Why don't we stop here for a while?' Henry said.

'Is it OK?'

He laughed. 'Yes, of course. 'Did you think I'd take you somewhere prohibited?'

The two-seater felt comfortable, the sprung cushion firm beneath her. Looking round at the paintings and the gold, she got a hint of the opulence the early settlers must have enjoyed. The mansions of Hollywood seemed fake by comparison.

Henry took the armchair opposite, a considerable gap between them. Beams of sunlight fell through the high windows, lighting sections of the room. She felt an odd peace descend, Henry's presence lifting her weary heart, if only for the moment.

'Do you like it?' he said.

'It's amazing. So peaceful.'

'Yes, it is.' He looked up at the high ceiling, a token gesture as he prepared himself inwardly. 'So what made you decide to move out to California?'

Again, a subtle change in direction. She had to think, react. 'I got bored at home and joined a theatre group. We travelled around, went to different cities. Someone said Hollywood was the place to be, so I headed out there.'

'Did you ever meet Charlie Chaplin?'

She laughed. 'No, but I did see Randolph Carlson at a party one night.'

'Really – what was he like?'

'Not very nice. I think he'd been drinking. But he did have a certain style, and of course, the camera loved him.'

'Did the camera love you?'

'I guess so.'

Encouraged by his interest, she described Barthez's house in Beverley Hills, with its electric gates and long, sweeping driveway. Seeing Carlson enter with a small entourage, and being vaguely disappointed that he wasn't as handsome as she'd expected. Remembering the house and the people made her feel sad. Brief, transitory moments in life that were gone so soon.

'Are you planning on going back?' Henry said.

'I don't think so. I'm not sure I'd wanna go back right now.'

'And how did you come by the yacht?'

'Oh, Johnny bought it from a guy he knew. They used to make trips up and down the coast, until the guy got too old and didn't think he could handle it no more.'

The first outright lie she'd told. Henry nodded like he was taking it all in, but the deceit left her feeling uncomfortable.

'How about you, Henry? You ever think about heading back home?'

'Perhaps one day. Who knows?'

She wondered how he got his kicks – a man so outwardly in control of his senses. Did he go dancing or carousing, and wake the next day without any recollection of the past twenty-four hours – things she'd done regularly back in California. Or, was he like this all the time, the serious academic type, who preferred to analyse everything rather than actually experience it for himself.

'You said you'd never been married. Ever been, you know, involved with someone else?'

He hesitated, frowning slightly. 'There was someone a long

time ago. We sort of drifted apart in the end.'

'Were you in love with her?'

He smiled awkwardly. 'Well that would be telling, wouldn't it?'

Something nagged at her. The sense of well-being she felt in the old monastery rooms – like being drugged by the heat, an overpowering of the senses by an unseen force. Henry's questions, quietly insistent. The first intimation that he might not be as easy going as she'd first imagined, that there was something else there underneath.

And yet she was drawn to him; something in his look, the directness of his gaze. A shared need between them that went beyond the niceties of ordinary conversation. It seemed to her, that in that moment, Henry would do anything she asked him to do. Anything at all.

*

Johnny came back with a wild and agitated look. The local had found the fault with the engine, but didn't have the part to fix it. They planned to go back the following morning and try again.

'Why do we have to keep waiting all the time?' she said.

'Because these people won't do what you want 'em to. It's always tomorrow, or the next day, or the day after that. Too much sitting round in the sun drinking that piss-weak beer.'

She stayed out on the balcony and listened to him storm about inside. She couldn't hold a thought without it returning to the same source. The world had started to come apart and all she could do was watch it unravel.

When he'd calmed down, she chose the moment to talk to him.

'Henry turned up on the waterfront while I was having coffee. He was hoping to talk to you but you'd already gone.'

'What did he want?'

'He didn't say.'

Johnny went to the balcony rail and stood looking out. She recalled the monastery room where she'd sat with Henry. The feeling of contentment she found there, and how that in itself was enough to set off a warning.

'I think we should be careful what we say to him from now on.'

'Why?'

'He was asking questions.'

'What kinda questions?'

'Just about you and me. What we were doing in California. Where we got the yacht. That kinda thing.'

Johnny nodded, still gazing out. 'We won't be here much longer. He can get us the supplies we need. Help us get off the island.'

'What if he finds out?'

He turned to look at her. 'Finds out what exactly?'

'I just think we oughta be careful, that's all.'

'Well I'm real glad you're so concerned for our safety. Right now I got other things on my mind.'

'Have you heard from the Colonel?'

'Not yet.'

'Don't you think it's a bit strange he ain't responded?'

'He will in his own time.' He gave her a hard critical look. 'Why don't you freshen up. Might be our last night on the island.'

How many other occasions had she felt the same? Simply there as a good-looking foil for one of his deals. Not required to speak, only to look the part and to back-up anything he said, no matter how outlandish it sounded.

Being on the island had changed him, made him reckless and even more insensitive to her needs; they hadn't spent so much time apart since they'd lived together in California. But still she wanted to please him, to do whatever she could to make everything work out.

'Do you still love me, Johnny?'

'Sure I do.'

'Say it, then.'

'I love you, honey.'

'Can't you say it with more feeling than that?'

He draped his arms around her shoulders and gazed at her. 'You hankering for a piece of Johnny right now? Is that what this is all about?'

'I just feel kinda lonesome, stuck here by myself with nothing to do all day.'

He slapped her ass playfully, and started to walk away. 'Oh, we'll find you something to do all right. I'll talk to Dr Martinez, see if you can help find some of them goddam birds he's always talking about.'

'You met Dr Martinez?'

'Henry introduced us once on the harbour front. Fella's crazy as a bullbat, you'll like him.'

Again, she had the sense that Johnny was keeping things from her. But she had to go along with it, keep up the pretence that everything was going according to plan. Tomorrow it might be different. They'd fix up *Indigo* and get away. Just the two of them on their own again, heading for the promised land.

But the deceit made it harder to sustain. Even when she smiled and made conversation with Henry, a man whose attentions she desired, a part of her remained hidden and shut off. And in that dark place where secrets were buried, she remembered all the things she'd done and the people she'd hurt along the way.

Hair swept back, and a touch of makeup on, she stepped out of the bathroom. Johnny stared in admiration.

'Wow – what can I say? You look great.'

'Like you said – we ain't gonna be here much longer, so I thought I'd make the effort.'

'For who, me or Henry?'

'I ain't even gonna answer that.'

He cosied up behind her and put his hands on her waist. 'We've don't have to be anywhere for an hour or so. Why don't we fool around a little?'

'I've just spent all this time getting ready.'

He kissed her neck, his hands under the hem of her shirt.

'Johnny, please – '

Ignoring her resistance, he carried on, his voice soft in her ear, his hands all over her. She closed her eyes and detached, took herself away someplace else. His attempts to seduce her were no longer as desirable; the words he used to incite her to forbidden places no longer had the same effect. Encouraged by the rhythm of his breathing, she simply prayed for it to be over quickly.

After, he dressed, observing himself in the mirror, oddly quiet. Hard to judge his mood when he was like that; easier when he was sounding off about something, or working himself up to one of his rages.

She slipped the spare shirt back on, and buttoned up to the neck, remembering her propriety. Madame Diaz might come knocking at any minute, with that look of disapproval on her face.

'You discuss our finances when you were with Henry?' she said.

'Why?'

'He asked me how much we needed. I just thought you might've — '

'Seems to me you've been getting a bit too cute with Henry. Maybe I should keep the two of you apart from now on – how 'bout that?' He flashed her a look of scorn.

'I'm just doing what you told me to do, Johnny.'

'Don't you go getting clever with me now. You wanna get off this island, you better use your head a bit more, and keep your goddam mouth shut like I told you to!'

*

Henry met them in the old town. A sombre mood attached itself to the proceedings, moments of regret Laura-Mae found hard to put into words. He did his best to entertain them, as always the perfect host, choosing the wine and recommending dishes from the menu. But the fact they'd be leaving soon made it harder for her to relax and enjoy the conversation. An air of sadness pervaded everything. Waiters came and went, bringing trays of food to the other tables. A fountain gurgled nearby, a stream of water flowing over tiered rocks; a feature that seemed out of place on the island, but was effective nonetheless. Somewhere in amongst all that, the faces of people she'd known, whose lives had affected her in ways she couldn't have imagined. The past, always there to influence the present moment, the unborn future.

Doctor Martinez waved at them from a nearby table. Henry waved back, describing him as a fellow conservationist with a taste for the good life. He really wanted to be like them, Henry said – true radicals, who'd rejected the old, traditional ways for something more rewarding.

'He'd sure like San Francisco,' she said. 'Plenty of radicals there.'

'That's right,' Johnny said. 'And most of 'em are in Alcatraz. You been there, Henry?'

'Alcatraz? No, thankfully not.'

'But you've been to Frisco, right?'

Henry frowned, seemed unable to answer for a moment. 'Yes, I have … Once, many years ago.'

A strange understanding passed between Henry and Johnny. That mean look on Johnny's face, she'd seen so many times before.

'Are we getting more wine?' she said, hoping to change the mood.

Johnny slapped the table top. 'Now you're talking, Laura-Mae. I was always told to keep the wine flowing and the conversation takes care of itself!'

Henry ordered more drinks, and the tension eased a little. They talked about the coming journey when *Indigo* was fixed, and they were loaded with provisions and fuel. Henry seemed enthusiastic, almost disappointed he wasn't coming along.

'I must say, you make it sound so exciting. It makes my work at the monastery quite boring by comparison.'

'You want action, throw it all in and come with us,' Johnny said. 'Hightail it down to Mexico and make some real money.'

Henry smiled vaguely. 'I'm not sure I'd be much use to you. My seagoing skills aren't up to much.'

'Come along for the hell of it. Get off the island for a few days. You can always get a boat back, you get tired of the company.'

'I don't think Henry would like the conditions,' she said. 'There's barely room for two people on-board .'

'I'm sure Henry can answer for his-self. Ain't that right, Henry?'

'Well, it's an idea, certainly. I'll have to think about it.'

She smiled along with them, privately incensed at Johnny's recklessness. All the hours he'd spent hunched over the charts, plotting their position, yelling at her for questioning his ability to get them to safety. How he'd stressed over and over how important it was for them to be wary of strangers and not give anything away. Now, in one rash moment, he was offering Henry the chance to come with them. What would happen when they got to Mexico? Sooner or later they would have to cut their ties and get rid of the yacht. Make contact with the Colonel, and head inland. All of this done with the utmost secrecy. How could they possibly do it with someone else alongside?

The waiter brought out the brandy, and the conversation turned to the unpredictable nature of the sea. Henry told a story about a shipwrecked yacht the locals had come across. He'd gone out with a few of them in a skiff to investigate. When they got there they found the yacht caught on the reef, it's mast snapped and the sails torn. One of the locals tied a line to the guard wire and stepped on board. Henry joined him, and together they looked down into the cockpit where an eerie silence prevailed.

'There was no one there?' Johnny said.

'No one?'

'Just like the *Marie Celeste*.'

'Exactly.'

'What happened to the people on board?' she said.

Henry shrugged. 'They drowned, I suppose. Washed overboard.' He looked at her, deliberately, she felt; a moment of candidness shared between them. She tried not to react, to remind herself that he couldn't possibly know. *Indigo* was moored on the other side of the island, her previous owners' possessions all stowed away where they couldn't be found, the walls scrubbed clean, leaving no trace of what had happened there. But the reference put doubt in her mind. One more reason to be off the island for good.

Johnny played host, raising his glass to the three of them and their future good fortune. Rather than play along, she focused instead on the restful backdrop of palm trees and lights around the bay. They'd been on the island for three days, but already the atmosphere had seeped into her consciousness like the waves along the shore. If they stayed much longer she might never want to leave, lost to the warm breeze and the cicadas forever.

Henry gazed across at her with a fond smile.

'Is everything alright, Laura-Mae? You look troubled.'

'Oh, I was just thinking.'

'Now you see what I have to put up with,' Johnny said. 'Might as well be talking to myself sometimes.'

Henry's gaze remained on her, thoughtful and compassionate, but she looked away, unwilling to participate. All she could think about was the voyage ahead. How hard it would be to cope with Johnny in one of his dark moods; the extreme weather conditions and lack of sleep that would leave her exhausted and unable to perform. The prospect of having Henry on-board made it worse.

Dr Martinez joined them. Portly and slightly-dishevelled, he didn't look like a scientist – at least not how she imagined one would look. Taking a seat with them, he accepted a cigar from Henry's tin, making all kinds of complimentary gestures about the food, the island and the present company.

'These are my good friends from California,' Henry said. 'They're travelling to Mexico on a yacht.'

Dr Martinez fixed his good eye on them – the other being an opaque and slightly-sinister blue. 'Mexico, eh? Are you Catholic?'

'Not yet,' she said.

He smiled indulgently, and turned to Henry. 'She has a wonderful face, don't you think?'

'Well, now you come to mention it – yes, she does.'

Johnny couldn't resist joining in. 'Perhaps you'd like to make me an offer, Doc. I'm sure we could come to some arrangement.'

Dr Martinez puffed on his cigar, observing Johnny above the wavering candlelight. His scrutiny seemed to linger, as if there was something he couldn't work out.

'Have I seen you before?' he said.

'Sure you did. Couple of days ago, down on the harbour front.'

'No, I meant before that – here on the island?'

Johnny shrugged, bemused. 'Not me, fella. You must've mixed me up with somebody else.'

Dr Martinez nodded, accepting his mistake. To steer him away from more awkward subjects, Laura-Mae asked him about his work. The birds on the island were endowed with mystical qualities, he told her, a far more worthy subject for research than their human counterparts. It was his duty to record his findings and make them known to a wider audience. 'As a scientist, I spend my whole life in anticipation of one such moment. Then, when a discovery is made, I can rejoice.'

'You come all this way to study birds?' she said.

'Oh, yes. I dedicate my life to this work, it is my passion.'

Johnny flashed a lurid grin. 'I can think of better things deserving of my passion, that's for sure.'

'Can you really?' Dr Martinez fixed Johnny with his good eye. 'Perhaps you'd like to tell us what they are.'

Eager to oblige, Johnny told a tale about the people they knew who'd made the trek to California. The whole system of making pictures that consumed the entire lives of the folk who made them. The subject seemed of genuine interest to the doctor, so far removed from his own area of expertise. Even Johnny's habit of embellishing the details and sounding his own horn didn't appear to faze him too much.

The talk turned to the yacht, *Indigo*'s current predicament on the other side of the island. Dr Martinez smoothed his chin and looked intently at Johnny.

'And you sailed here, you say?'

'That's right. All the way from California.'

'You must be quite an accomplished sailor?'

'You could say that, Doc. In fact, I'd go as far as to say there ain't no one more qualified than ole Johnny. It's a talent I have, see? Right from a kid, I could turn my hand to most anything.'

'Yes, I'm sure. And you ran into a storm, you say?'

'That's right. Skies black as hell, waves bigger'n a house. It's a wonder we made it outta there at all.'

'But your expertise pulled you through, huh?' Dr Martinez turned to Laura-Mae with a smile. 'Lucky you were in such safe hands, my dear.'

'Luck's something you need on the card table,' Johnny said. 'We're talking life and death here, no mistaking.'

'Did you mark your position on the chart, and note the time you ran into trouble?'

Johnny frowned, weighing up this unexpected angle.

'Well, no, I didn't do that, Doc. I guess by then I had my hands full taking in the sails and keeping us on course.'

Dr Martinez nodded intently, the glint of amusement in his eyes. 'We had a similar experience in Bermuda a few years ago,' he said. 'Huge waves, 50-knot winds. You have to know what you're doing. Sometimes even expertise isn't enough.'

'But you survived to tell the tale, huh, Doc?'

'That's right. And so, it would appear, did you.'

Johnny stared back, a mean and obstinate set to his jaw. For a moment, the congenial atmosphere threatened to dissolve, until Henry stepped in to smooth things over.

'Well, I think more wine is required, don't you? Dr Martinez, will you stay with us a while?'

'Thank you, but I must get back.' The doctor stood, brushing cigar ash from his waistcoat, before bowing graciously. 'Henry, we'll talk tomorrow. Goodnight to you all.'

Johnny watched him go and shook his head. 'Jesus. Is he for real?'

'Don't be fooled by appearances,' Henry said. 'Dr Martinez is an extremely clever man. I can't vouch for his seafaring skills, but academically he's more than qualified ... Now, where were we? ... Ah, yes. The wine.'

The whitewashed walls of the fishermen's dwellings rose on one side, the sea on the other. Tiny pinpoints of light glinted from boats moored out in the bay; warm currents of sea-air drifted in from the swell. She couldn't relax. The doctor's claim that he'd recognised Johnny stuck in her head. Could it be that he was

right? Johnny had been here before?

As if to allay her fears, Johnny drew in a lungful of air and exhaled pleasurably. 'Ain't this grand? The three of us together out here, nothing but the wind and the stars for company.'

Henry seemed to appreciate the gesture of friendship, helped along by the wine and the atmosphere. She envied their closeness, however contrived it may have been. Johnny didn't have friends, only people he could use and manipulate. But seeing them together aroused a part of her she didn't care for too much. That feeling of being excluded and left out, made to feel she wasn't good enough to belong.

'Let's go for a stroll?' Henry said. 'Walk off all that rich food before we retire for the evening.'

'Yeah, let's do that, old chap!' Johnny said, mimicking Henry's accent. 'One always likes to take a stroll before retiring. What say you, Laura-Mae?'

'I think you're pushing your luck a bit too far, Johnny.'

'Really? And how's that exactly?' He put an arm around her shoulder, but she shrugged him off. 'Hey, come on now,' he said, laughing. 'I thought we were all friends here. You gonna give Johnny a hard time?'

They stopped at a bar on the harbour front, the table area outside filled with locals who watched them with detached interest. She felt the heat of their observation, an audience of the harshest critics around her, disapproving and cynical like some of the menfolk back home.

An odd defiance took hold, an impulse to sudden recklessness that would make them sit up and take notice. Henry had described the islanders as a patriarchal society, where the women had no voice at all. This was a chance to show them what it was like on the mainland where there were less restrictions. She could make herself loud and opinionated like the menfolk, and revel in their discomfort. Instead, she kept it all inside, absorbing the sights and sounds, just a she'd always done.

Henry insisted on paying the check. While he was gone, Laura-Mae turned to Johnny.

'Why did Dr Martinez say he'd seen you before?'

'How should I know? Maybe I gotta double. Either that or the old coot took a shine to me. How 'bout that?'

Henry came back, and she tried to put the idea out of her head. Soon they would be gone and it wouldn't matter. But the thought that Johnny might have lied to her on more than one occasion persisted.

'Well – I've got some good news for you,' Henry said.

'You couldn't cover the check,' Johnny said with a grin, 'and now you want us to skedaddle.'

'Actually, it's about the yacht. I've just spoken to the engineer. He's found the part you've been looking for.'

*

They sailed *Indigo* round the next day – Johnny and the little engineer, who took the helm as they chugged into the harbour. Already the heat had risen a few degrees, warming the flagstones. The locals were out fixing the fishing nets in readiness for the day's haul.

Watching from the balcony, she felt conflicting emotions. *Indigo* looked different in some way, as if the brief passage moored on the other side of the island had made her more resilient and ready for whatever lay ahead. Her bow cleaved the waves, her sides a glossy white. And yet there was something else that Laura-Mae couldn't work out. A foreboding of some sort, that eroded any sense of relief she might've had.

Johnny waved to her from the portside, ready with the mooring line. She waved back, affecting an enthusiasm she didn't feel. Always twin realities that ran in parallel; at times it was more desirable to live in one than the other. When the two worlds converged there was no escape from either; you were simply stuck fast in a place you didn't want to be.

She went down to meet them, aware of the few locals watching from the jetty. Johnny secured *Indigo*, and stepped back to wipe the sweat from his face. He looked pale and unwell, maybe suffering the overindulgence from the previous night.

Stepping on-board for the first time since their arrival felt strange. She had to reacquaint herself with the fixtures, the narrow space. And always the reminders of the previous owners whose spirits seemed to linger.

Below deck offered no surprises. The slight rocking of the hull warned of the trials ahead, the loss of comfort and security. Stowing her things in the forward cabin, she glanced over the cramped interior. Until the harbourmaster turned up there was nothing they could do but pack and repack, preparing for the coming journey as best they could. Once they were underway there would be no relief from the constant movement, the lack of space.

She found Johnny in the saloon, going through the storage compartments.

'When can we leave?' she said.

'Soon as we get refuelled.'

'And how long's that gonna take?'

'The way these fuckers operate? Could be another three days.' He whipped a cloth from his pants pocket and wiped his brow.

'You feeling alright?' she said.

'I'm fine.'

'You don't look too good.'

'Well that's real nice of you to say so, honey. Now make yourself useful before we get underway.'

Two hours went by and still no fuel. Johnny became more and more agitated, his contempt for local inefficiency increasing. 'I'll have to find the guy – drag him out of whatever bar he happens to be in!' He shot her a look of irritation. 'Go find Henry? Ask him what the hell's happening.'

'Now?'

'What else we gonna do? Sitting here hog-tied, like a couple of godamn fools.'

*

'I'm sure the chap with the fuel will turn up,' Henry said. 'It's just the rather ponderous way they do things round here, I'm afraid.'

'I don't wanna leave. Not with Johnny like he is.'

Henry laid a hand on her arm. 'I haven't seen you looking so distraught before. Is there anything I can do to help?'

'It don't matter.'

'Of course it matters. Let me order drinks and you can tell me all about it.'

The assistant brought coffee. Watching him stroll across the monastery lawn in a waistcoat and open-necked shirt, her heart sank at the thought of leaving. But she couldn't reveal the truth to Henry, couldn't even hint at it. The dark passion that had consumed her life with Johnny had drawn her into things she never thought she'd do. She'd always been loyal to him – the two of them together against the world, like he'd always said. Now she'd had a glimpse of what it might be like to live without him.

'At least the yacht's fixed,' Henry said. 'Now it's just a matter of loading up with supplies and you can go.'

'That's what I'm worried about.'

'Why?'

But the truth was, she didn't know why. The few days on the island had turned into an extended hiatus, giving her time to think. Johnny's behaviour had changed. He'd become more secretive and often morose, blaming her for every little thing. And yet it was more than that. The lies he'd told her. The fact that his illness might be getting worse, making him even more unpredictable.

'I'm afraid of what I'll find in Mexico,' she said. 'What if I get there and wanna come home?'

'Perhaps you're looking too far ahead.'

Glancing up at the monastery, she caught a glimpse of the transience, the illusory nature of all things. Each moment that slipped by was irretrievable, a personal loss you only felt looking back. And yet the desire to hold onto things, to people, caused pain in itself.

Henry grew quiet, wrestling with some intractable problem. Sensing his withdrawal, she peered closer.

'Something wrong, Henry?'

He looked up slowly.

'They found the little girl who disappeared.'

'Where?'

'In the sand dunes. Apparently, she'd been raped and strangled.'

'My God, that's terrible!' She recalled their night on the beach; the music and the dancing. Henry's clumsy advance by the light of the fire. 'Do they know who did it?'

'One of the local plantation workers has been detained. Apparently, he had some of her clothing in his room.'

How pitiful that the child had been discovered in that state. Here one minute and then gone. Laura-Mae recalled a similar case back home, when a sharecropper's daughter went missing. The veil of sorrow that descended over the neighbourhood when the child's body was found behind trash cans in an alleyway.

'The mood on the island isn't good,' Henry said. 'I think I mentioned before that they're very superstitious. To them, it could mean all kinds of things.'

The monastery's peaceful setting seemed incongruous, an affront to cold hard reality. Henry seemed overly quiet, brooding on the consequences.

'It's probably a good thing you're leaving,' he said.

'Why?'

'Things could change without warning. It wouldn't take much for the locals to see you as a threat in some way.'

'How? What've we done?'

'Some of the elders have already associated the girl's death with your arrival. I know it isn't rational, but that's the way they think.'

Too shocked to comment, she tried to figure it out. The terrible act committed that night seemed distant already, overshadowed by the concerns she had for her own safety.

'It makes things a bit difficult for me, too, I'm afraid,' Henry said.

'How do you mean?'

'Well, I'm the one who's been showing you around, taking you out for meals and things. Guilty by association, I suppose.' Henry smiled sadly. 'Most of my work here is finished. I was thinking about leaving anyway.'

'Where would you go?'

'I'm not sure. How would you feel if I came with you?'

She stared at him in confusion.

'It's just a thought, of course – and Johnny did offer. Plus, Mexico does have its merits – certainly appeals to my sense of adventure.'

His reasoning seemed inadequate, a sudden whim that had occurred to him while they were out drinking. Johnny's thoughtless comment about him joining them when they got the yacht fixed. But the implications would mean so much more.

'I'm not sure that you coming along would be a good thing,' she said.

'Because of my lack of sailing skills?'

'I just don't think it would work. Johnny can be so … unpredictable.'

He took her hand, his gaze imploring her with some inexpressible desire. 'There is another reason I want to come. I can't stop thinking about you, Laura-Mae. Ever since that night on the beach you've been on my mind constantly.'

She withdrew her hand, afraid of the ramifications. Henry's passion for her was a weakness, an aberration, temporarily blinding him to the truth. She could never love him as he professed to love her, never give herself to him in the way that he wanted. And yet …

In the midst of her confusion she saw the seeds of chance; the opportunity that always presented itself if you looked hard enough.

'I don't know what to say, Henry.'

'You don't have to say anything. Just think about it. But please don't underestimate the mood here on the island. I've seen it before. How quickly things can change.'

'What about the fuel?'

'I'll take care of that. You go back and talk to Johnny.'

*

She packed her few things in a case, sad in a way to be leaving the quaint little room that had been their sanctuary. They'd arrived on the island with a backpack and the clothes they stood in. In three days she'd managed to accumulate token souvenirs to remind her of their stay: a booklet from the monastery, postcards from the harbour front, and a miniature hand-painted chapel she got from a store. Johnny would have sneered at her for taking them with her, but she didn't care. They were leaving. It was time to move on.

Snapping the case shut, she sat on the bed and looked around. Madame Diaz had put fresh flowers in the room – the bright yellow petals seemed to have absorbed the sunlight and radiated outward. But the atmosphere had changed; an argument somewhere in the building during the night; voices raised, and doors slamming shut. Henry's warning about the mood on the island seemed ever more prescient.

Johnny came in, his face red from exertion.

'Y'all ready?' he said.

'Nearly.'

'Good, 'cause we leave tonight.'

'I thought we were leaving in the morning?'

'You heard what Henry said. We stick around here much longer we're liable to get lynched.'

He went onto the balcony and looked out over the harbour; his relief that the refuelling had finally been done was short lived. Now seemed as good a time as any to tell him.

'Henry wants to come with us,' she said.

'Hallelujah. Praise be the saints.'

'I thought maybe we could drop him off at San Diego. Pick up fuel and supplies then head on to Mexico.'

Johnny nodded to himself, still looking out over the water.

'You don't mind?' she said.

He turned slowly, with a look on his face she'd never seen before.

'Why should I mind? Extra pair o' hands might be just what we're looking for.'

ACT III

THE SEA REVISITED

The houses built into the hills got smaller and smaller as they motored out, a visual impression unchanged for hundreds of years. *Indigo* rocked gently on the swell, diesel fumes from the engine rising from the saloon. Johnny seemed happy that at last they were underway, his mood lifted by the forward motion, and the full tank of fuel delivered at last from the recalcitrant local.

Henry gazed out over their wake, surveying his previous home. 'I feel guilty to be leaving. Like I've abandoned my post and left the islanders to fend for themselves.'

She watched the diminishing landscape with mixed feelings. 'D'you think you'll ever come back?'

'Perhaps one day.' He looked at her wistfully, an unspoken desire held in check.

The island became a pale grey outline in the distance. Now they were truly at sea, forced to adapt to the changing rhythms of the wind and waves, the constant disruption to their footing, the creaking of *Indigo*'s fittings, a pleasant and familiar sound she'd actually missed while they'd been on land. That feeling of escape and solitude from being out on the ocean, away from people, the distractions of ordinary living. *Indigo* seemed to rise and fall on a surge of boundless energy, joyfully carrying them off to some distant land. For a moment she could forget the past and imagine them all bound up in an incredible journey. Then she glimpsed Johnny up at the bow and the fantasy ended.

'I can't believe I'm actually out here,' Henry said, taking in his new surroundings. 'I must need my head examined.'

'Wait till we hit a rough patch. Then you'll really wish you'd stayed on land.'

'Thanks.'

The sense of time no longer existed; only the occasional wind change and the ebb and flow of the eternal sea. These things would have a profound effect on Henry, who'd never sailed further than the island before – and never on a yacht. Being on firm ground for so long had left him unprepared for the voyage ahead.

'Would you mind taking the helm?' she said. 'I'd like to go below.'

Henry looked puzzled.

'Me?'

'Ship's rules. We'll all be sharing a watch soon, so you might as well get used to it.'

She left him with basic instructions to steer into the waves, enjoying the strained look on his face – the nervous apprentice taking his first lesson.

Johnny glanced up from the chart table. She thought she detected a strained and disapproving look from him but it was hard to tell.

'Everything OK?' she said.

'Good as can be expected. How's Henry?'

'He's taken the helm for a while.'

'Is that a good thing?'

'He's gotta get used to it sometime. And since he's part of the crew now, I thought it might be better sooner rather than later.'

Johnny leaned back and massaged his chin, his thoughts away someplace else.

'What's the matter?' she said.

He took his time, the vaguest hint of manipulation. 'I've been thinking,' he said. 'When we get to Mexico we'll need to make our own arrangements. We go one way, Henry goes the other.'

'I thought we were dropping him at San Diego?'

'Well sure, that's the idea, but things can change.'

'What things?'

'Hey, I'm just trying to cover all the possibilities here.' He gazed at her, solemnly, as if he'd imparted a great truth. But something about his manner she found contrived, an act he might put on for strangers. More than that, his probing was intended to unsettle her in some way. Keep her off balance.

'I'd better go back up,' she said.'

'Yeah, you do that, honey. Make sure ole Henry boy don't run us aground on the rocks.'

*

The sun went down; before them a rim of golden red, the dying of a great furnace on the eastern horizon. The island was far behind them and yet a strong sense of it still remained. A small part of her wished she was back there, climbing the hills to the little chapel, or sitting in a harbour side café. Mostly, she was glad to be underway, heading for Mexico. The unknown.

Henry came up and sat beside her. 'That really is an incredible sight. What happens next – do we navigate by the stars?''

'With a bit of help from the charts, of course.'

'Johnny showed me how to use the sextant, a most intriguing device.'

'Well you be careful now, or Johnny'll have you scrubbing the decking and changing the sails.'

Now they were companions, their bond strengthened by thoughts of the arduous journey ahead. But the strain of trying to balance this extra dimension made her weary. The effort it took to please Henry and answer his questions sometimes seemed too much.

'How many miles are we from San Diego?' he said.

'About sixty, I believe.'

'Did Johnny tell you about our arrangement? That you would

drop me there when you refuel?'

'Yeah, he did.'

'Are you all right with that?'

'Sure. Why wouldn't I be?'

He shuffled closer to her along the seating. She looked round for Johnny, and saw only the darkened bow, the light from the cockpit.

'The seas can be a dangerous place,' Henry said. 'People go missing all the time. But I'm sure you know that.'

A tiny pulse of alarm swept through her. Unsure of his meaning, she kept her eyes on the swell, the phantom white tips in the distance.

'That was always a fear of mine, you know.' He smiled reassuringly. 'To fall overboard without anyone knowing. Looking up to see the boat sailing off in the distance.'

'I'm sure that won't happen here.'

'I sincerely hope not. But then, I'm in safe hands, aren't I?'

She focused on the waves, the hypnotic rising and falling of the bow. Henry breathed in the sea air, a moment of pleasure they could both enjoy without fear. They could have been alone together, beneath the twinkling stars and crescent moon, sharing a moment like they had that night on the beach at the festival. In love, perhaps, but only in its most rudimentary form – the kind that meant very little and promised nothing in return.

'What will you do when you get to Mexico?' he said.

'Johnny knows someone there who can help us.'

'Who's that – the Colonel?'

'You know him?'

'I've heard Johnny mention him before. Isn't he the local bigshot or something?'

'I've never met him myself. All I know is, he can get us the papers we need, and a place to live. That kinda thing.'

Henry stared out to sea, the wind lifting his hair. He looked youthful, his skin soft and unblemished by the elements.

'Are you happy, Laura-Mae?'

She looked up, surprised by the question.

'Why?'

'I just wondered. I watched you on the island. You seemed ...'

'Seemed what?'

He smiled, his manner pleasant, his tone conversational. Maybe this was his idea of a pass at her, with Johnny lurking somewhere in the background. She felt again the exquisite tug of desire, the hint of danger that always added to it. Hard not to imagine Henry's mouth on hers, his arms sweeping her up and carrying her off someplace else.

'Perhaps I shouldn't have mentioned it,' he said. 'I should learn to mind my own business.'

Such power, to know she only had to say the word and he would draw closer, perhaps even risk his life to free her from her attachment to Johnny. And yet, there was a part of him that had not been revealed to her; a cautiousness and a secrecy hidden behind his courteous front.

She made a discreet move away from him, shifting her position on the seating. He seemed not to notice, relaxed in the warm evening air.

'Johnny told me about a couple he met in Hollywood,' he said. 'They were supposed to be involved in some kind of scandal that made the papers. Did you know about that?'

She checked herself, aware of Henry close by.

'I'm not sure. There were a lot of scandals in Hollywood when we were there.'

'Something about a real estate deal that went wrong. People lost a lot of money.'

'I don't think I heard about that.'

He hesitated, unsure of himself. 'I know something happened back there in California.'

She sat mutely, gazing ahead.

'You can talk to me, Laura-Mae.'

'There's nothing to talk about.' She stood. 'I'm going below. Johnny will take over from you soon.'

'Have I upset you?'

'No, of course not.'

'Then please stay and talk to me for a while.'
'I've gotta go, Henry.'

*

Johnny looked up as she came through the companionway.

'I've found the best course,' he said. 'We head for the leeward side of the coast and miss the heavier currents.'

'Henry knows.'

'Knows what?'

'About the Simpsons.'

'How exactly?'

'He says you told him about some real estate deal that went wrong. Now he's put two and two together and worked out it was us.'

Johnny tapped a pencil on the table top, eyeing her with amusement. 'That's what I always admired in you, Laura-Mae. You always had the ability to think ahead. That's what made us such a good team, don't you think?'

'Johnny, please. What we gonna do?'

'Find us a nice little place in Mexico, like I said. Raise us a few pigs and sheep. How 'bout that?'

'Stop fooling round. What we gonna do about Henry?'

Johnny's smile slipped, a coldness in his tone. 'I guess he gets a free ride to San Diego. That's the deal, ain't it?'

'Why did you invite him along, knowing it was gonna cause trouble?'

'I didn't invite him anywhere. He was so desperate to get off that goddam island he was practically begging to come aboard.'

She turned away from him, too drained to think.

'I'm gonna get some sleep.'

'You do that, honey. And don't you worry about ole Henry boy, I got plans for him.'

She stopped, caught the slick grin on his face.

'What do you mean?'

'What I mean is, I'm gonna work his ass raw till we get to San

Diego. By then he'll wish he never sees another sailboat again.'

She took to her bunk in the cramped forepeak cabin. Light from the saloon lit the shadows; *Indigo*'s creaking timbers in the background. Somewhere up on deck, Henry framed against the night sky, an invisible portal linking their two worlds. And there she was, stuck in the middle, not knowing who to turn to. Johnny, as always, was two steps ahead, working everything out in his own mind without sharing the details.

*

Night cast a blanket over the ocean, restricting visibility; danger from cargo ships ever present. In the vague distance, the lights of an imaginary town – a coastal resort like Mission Bay or San Diego with all its comforts. Easy to see how sailors were waylaid by such illusions and driven off course to their deaths.

She took over from Johnny at the helm, alone with the darkness, the familiar strains from *Indigo*'s passage. No wonder they called it the loneliest outpost; something about the night skies and the dark troughs all around that lent itself to serious contemplation.

Focussed on the uneven passage of the yacht, she fell into dull reflection. Distant waves broke out on the ocean, like voices calling from afar. The elements so much more powerful, a sense of majesty and nobility that no human could rival.

Henry came up, rubbing his eyes.

'Sleep?' she said.

'Not much.'

He took a seat beside her, adjusting to the new position, one level of discomfort swapped for another. *Indigo* bucked and heeled like a colt, always willing to test their powers of endurance.

'Nothing much to see out there,' he said. 'Seen one wave you've seen 'em all.'

'Wait till the wind picks up, they get bigger.'

He gave a nod, unsure of himself. 'Would you like me to take over?'

'I'm fine, thanks.'

'What happens if you fall asleep?'

'Then we all drown.' She smiled, unable to help a feeling of smugness. On land, Henry had been the host, showing them round and explaining the history of the island, the culture. Out here he was handicapped, reduced to the status of a cabin passenger, forced to earn his ticket to San Diego.

'How far can we cover in a day?' he said.

'Depends on the weather. With the wind behind us and no cross currents, maybe as much as forty miles – nautical miles, that is.' Part of her wanted to mock the pedestrian in him, suited only to dry land and fine food. But if he was to share the journey, he had to be aware of the dangers. Falling asleep at the helm was one thing, steering a wrong course another. They simply couldn't afford to take any chances.

'Did Johnny teach you to sail?' he said.

'He taught me the basics.'

'And who taught him?'

'Oh, I think he picked it up as he went along. Johnny's good like that. Turns his hand to pretty much anything.'

'Yes, so I gathered.'

Indigo heeled on the portside, spray lashing the deck. The moment gave her time to think, to re-establish the boundaries between them. Everything about Henry was designed to upset her equanimity in some way. Without him on-board it would have been easier. Just her and Johnny, alone against the sea. Henry was a stranger, someone she barely knew. Now she had to pay the price, for letting her guard slip and allowing herself to get drawn in.

'So quiet out here,' he said, breathing in the sea air. 'You'd think we were the only ones left in the whole world.'

'Until we get hit by a whale, then you'd know it.'

'Is that a possibility?'

'Well, I don't like to worry you, Henry. But yes, unfortunately, out here it is.'

'Christ.' He frowned at the darkness, this disturbing new revelation. 'Now I won't be able to sleep at all.'

Best not to encourage him, she decided. Play along in a spirit of politeness and general conversation; two people passing the time like they had done on the island. A chance meeting had brought them together, tossing them into the slipstream of events. She'd enjoyed his company, even sought out his friendship, his affections. Now it was different – too dangerous for both of them.

'Have you got family back home?' he said.

'I have, but I ain't seen 'em in a long while.'

'That's a shame.'

'Why is it?'

'I just meant … Well, sometimes it's good to have a sort of base. Somewhere to get back to if things don't work out.'

'Good if your folks have money, you mean?'

He laughed. 'I didn't mean that at all, but I like your way of thinking.'

She fixed her gaze on the horizon. Henry's presence so unsettling; the hushed and diffident tone that gave his words such sincerity; his warmth and attentiveness in place of Johnny's coarseness and aggression. Difficult not to respond with the same spontaneity, the same desire.

'People come and go,' she said. 'It's a fact of life.'

'Have you lost people you love?'

She recalled the night Randolph Carlson died. The crowds, the atmosphere. Cop cars and ambulances racing through the streets of LA. The papers called it the end of an era, and in many ways it was. Everything changed after that.

'You build your hopes around one person and they get taken away,' she said. 'That's why I've always learned to get along on my own.'

'What about Johnny? The two of you are very close aren't you?'

'That's different. We got kind of an understanding. We know how to help each other out.'

One day soon Henry would be gone, removed from her life like everything else. She would miss him, but inevitably – like most of the folk back home – she would forget him. That was the way it was and always had been.

'I should try to get some sleep,' she said. 'I'll come and wake you when it's your turn.'

He nodded, uncertain. 'I can't stop thinking about that whale.'

'Oh, I shouldn't worry too much about that. We get hit by one o' them, and all your problems will be over.'

The starlit night shone overhead, a glittering canopy increasing her sense of isolation. How absurd the notion of escape, that it could have taken root in her mind and become a real possibility. And yet there it was buried beneath the layers of trauma and intrigue: the primal need for comfort and security she'd left behind in California.

*

Johnny slept for six hours straight, an outcome that left him in remarkably good spirits. Henry stayed in his cabin, the door closed. She hoped he'd stay there a while longer so she didn't have to make polite conversation, or defend herself against his whispered insinuations. There could be no more friendly exchanges between them now. She had to distance herself, as much for his sake as hers. Soon they would reach the coast and the situation would change again, an outcome she feared as much as she willed it to happen.

She cooked up the last of the eggs and beans from the island, and carried the plates up to Johnny. He gave her his wolfish smile, a playful glint in his eye. 'Mighty fine spread, honey. Where's our cabin boy?'

'Still asleep. He didn't look too good when I last saw him.'

'Well that's a damn shame. Who's gonna trim the sails for me now?'

Since they'd left the island, Johnny had found a way to reassert his dominance and take control. She saw in him a spark of the qualities she'd always admired – his ability to recover from setbacks and eternal defiance of the odds so often stacked against him. Now he was the Johnny of old, smiling and confident, guiding them on towards Mexico.

'How far to San Diego?' she said.

'Few hours maybe.'

'Can't you be more precise than that?'

'Who put the bug up your ass?' He frowned at her, mock serious. 'Don't you have faith in Johnny Boy?'

'I just wanna get there, drop Henry off and move on.'

'And that's what we're gonna do, honey, but in God's time, not yours or mine. Ain't that what your old mammy used to say?'

She pretended to like him again, to find something agreeable or even desirable in his coarseness – his ridicule of her family's religion. His knowledge and experience would always outweigh hers, a fact he was always quick to remind her of – even his humour had an edge of superiority. Conversations with Henry were so much more satisfying; he listened to what she was saying and took a genuine interest in her opinions, didn't try to belittle her all the time. Johnny wasn't like that at all. For him it was all about what he wanted. Everything else came secondary.

An hour or so later, Henry emerged from his cabin. One look at his face confirmed the transformation. His playful smile had gone, in its place a sort of internalised suffering that only the sea could have brought on.

Johnny welcomed him on deck with an almost playful zest. 'Henry – we thought you'd expired in the night! How you feeling?'

Like a blind man, Henry pulled himself along on the guard wire, his gaze fixed ahead. Johnny watched with amusement.

'Why don't you shin-up the mast and give us directions! You think you could do that?'

She gave Johnny a warning nudge. 'Don't be so mean, let him be.'

Lurching forward, Henry emptied the contents of his stomach into the sea, retching until there was nothing left. Johnny noted the event with grim satisfaction, nodding to himself as if justice had been done.

Driven by a sense of duty, she went to Henry's side and, conscious of Johnny watching, put a comforting hand on his back. 'Why don't you go and lie down?'

His hands gripped the guard wire, knuckles white, his face ashen.

'I feel terrible.'

'Yeah, I know, but it will pass. You just have to give it time.'

Henry groped his way back to his cabin, mumbling apologies for his lack of participation. As soon as he'd gone, she targeted Johnny for his appalling lack of empathy. 'Did you have to be so hard on him when he's feeling like that?'

'He wanted to come along, didn't he? Ain't my fault he can't take it.'

'You got no heart, Johnny. No heart at all.'

'That's right. And the truth is, the best of him just went right over the side back there. So don't you go feeling sorry for him now.'

A wave rocked the yacht; she thought of Henry, suffering below in the forward cabin, feeling every lurch, every undulation. Johnny kept his eye on her, a baleful, uncompromising look that meant no good for anyone.

'Shame on you,' he said.

'Me? What the hell have I done?'

'All them fanciful stories he told you back on the island, like he was some kinda blue-eyed boy.'

'I don't know what you're talking about.'

'Yeah, you do. You know exactly what I'm talking about.' He stayed at the helm, resolute and determined, watching the angry waves break on the portside. She felt obliged to challenge him in some way, lest he saw her silence as a sign of her guilt.

'You think you know everything, Johnny, but you ain't always right.'

He flashed her a warning look. 'Listen to me now. I'm right 'cause I know a lotta things you don't. And you better remember that, or things'll get a whole lot worse around here.'

The wind dropped and the seas calmed. They changed sails, furling the genoa. She forgot Johnny's mean-spiritedness for a moment and focused on the task at hand. They worked quickly and efficiently together, knowing that the calmer seas only meant a brief respite. They'd been on the ocean less than twenty-four hours and already the onus was changing. Johnny had taken over, leaving no doubt as to who was giving the orders. And, like a dutiful servant, Laura-Mae stepped up to do his bidding.

A school of dolphins appeared alongside. She tried to count them as they leapt out of the water in a perfect synchronized dance, but gave up, there were so many. Their presence gave her hope, a sign they were on their way and nothing could stop them. And when they'd gone, the feeling remained; something pure and noble that couldn't be diminished by circumstance – or by Johnny's crude attempts to subdue her and keep her in fear.

The dolphins brought back other memories. When she was a child she used to call upon God to fill her heart with joy and take away the bad thoughts that came upon her in isolated moments. And God was sure to answer because He was in everything – the sun, the sky and the sea air. All she had to do to receive His blessing was open her heart and let the light in, then the darkness would be gone forever. That was what the reverend Calhoun used to say and she believed him. But so much time had passed between then and now and she was a different person. The child who had believed in God had grown up and become someone else, someone she didn't always recognise.

A wretched dry-heave came from the forward cabin, the desperate sound muted by the wind and waves. She glanced in that direction, her loyalties divided. She saw Henry, perhaps, as Johnny did – an inconvenience, a burden, someone they had to put up with for the rest of the journey.

'Perhaps I should check on Henry,' she said.

'Let him sleep it off. If he don't get over it soon it'll be a tough old passage, that's for sure.'

'You're so kind, Johnny, it just flows right outta you.'

'I ain't got time to look out for no one else, and neither should you.' His mean look put her in her place; how dare she harbour sympathies for Henry, or any similar weakness, unless it was an act, pre-planned and orchestrated by him. Difficult not to admire him under these conditions, to feel safe and secure in his presence like she used to. Everything could change at a moment's notice, from the serene to a maelstrom, and Johnny would be there, ready and eager to do battle.

Ignoring his advice, she went below and tapped lightly on Henry's door. He was laid on his bunk, eyes open, his face all pale and drained in the poor light.

'How you feeling?' she said.

'Terrible.'

'Can I get you a drink, a bite to eat?'

He grimaced. 'No thanks. I don't think I could keep anything down.'

The close confines of the cabin created an intimacy between them that was unavoidable. She had to resist the urge to go over and comfort him in some small way. Even in sickness he exerted a strong hold over her, an intense need she couldn't help but respond to. But just as Johnny's spirit had been restored by the adverse conditions, Henry's had been diminished. But this too was illuminating, perhaps the most realistic light to see him in.

'If it's any consolation we're over halfway there,' she said.

'Thanks, I wish you hadn't told me.'

She turned to go, conscious of the deepening shadows, the danger of staying alone with him too long. 'I'll be on deck. Let me know if you need anything.'

She got to the door and he called out, propped on his elbows, staring at her.

'I just wanted to say thanks.'

'Get some rest, Henry. Won't be much longer now.'

The closer they got to land, the more she thought about the implications of having him on board. His carelessness in the things he said. The way he sidled up to her whenever he thought Johnny wasn't looking, the whole thing creating an atmosphere that lay heavy upon the air. What if he told Johnny what had happened between them on the island in a moment's weakness? How could she defend herself against that?

Taking her place beside Johnny, she composed herself, looking for the right words.

'You were right,' she said. 'It ain't easy having a sick person on board.'

'Ain't that the truth.'

'We should never have asked him to come with us.'

'Well he's here now, honey. Just have to put up with it till we get to San Diego.'

Johnny steered *Indigo* through the next wave, lost in the simple task. She sensed his mind, turning over the same problems, the endless permutations that seemed to keep him going.

'Shouldn't we have got there by now?' she said.

'I don't see land yet, do you?'

'Just seems we been out here a long time.'

'Well I can't make us get there no faster.' He ginned at her, his amusement lighting up his whole face. 'I ever tell you about the time I rustled steers in Montana?'

'Johnny – '

'Two-thousand head of prime steak, all looking to do their own thing. Gotta know what you're doing with them sonsabitches. One wrong move you get trampled to death.'

'Will you listen to me, goddamit! What're we gonna do about Henry?'

Johnny shook his head, still back in Montana or some other mythical place he liked to recall. 'He's still puking his guts this time tomorrow, guess we'll have to throw him overboard. How 'bout that?'

A chill passed through her in spite of the heat. The certainty of the future up ahead; the fear of what she might be called upon to do; what she'd already done for Johnny.

Sensing her distance, he put an arm around her shoulders. 'We gotta stick together on this. Be me and you, just like it was before.'

She remembered why they were together. The thrill of being with him on such a wild quest where anything could happen. A lifetime craving excitement and meaning, finding nothing but the drudgery of work and dreams that seemed to fizzle out before they were realised. Johnny had given her all the things she wanted. But in return he demanded her obedience and loyalty, things she hadn't always given willingly.

But he knew how to spin the web, always testing her to see how much of the lesson she'd understood. How well they worked together, right from the early days – so well they were able to read each other's thoughts from a single look. Things had happened to change that understanding – the loss of all their finances in California; constant demands from the studios for her to give more of her time. Then meeting the Simpsons and getting involved with them. But essentially, the bond between them had always remained. Until Henry.

*

The rocking of the yacht induced a kind of trance, a narrow passage from which to view certain aspects of the past. Memories and faces. People who'd come and gone, finally disappearing for good as if they'd never existed. Hard to separate the real from the fiction when you'd told so many lies and spent so long covering your tracks. Each new destination an oasis, a colourful glimmer in the eye before it too was consigned to the same backwater.

Hearing voices, she sat up and listened. They seemed to come from the galley.

Still weary from lack of sleep, she went to investigate, overcome by a strange sense of foreboding.

They looked up when she came in, their conversation interrupted by an intruder. The dank, oily smell from the cabin made her feel queasy, the atmosphere heavy with some undisclosed menace.

'Ah – look who's arrived,' Henry said. 'Do come and join our little party.'

'Wine?' Johnny held up the bottle.

She froze, taking a moment to adjust to the scene.

'Why isn't someone at the helm?'

'That's all taken care of, honey. Thought we'd have us a little downtime.'

'Yes, that's right. Come and join us, Laura-Mae.'

Like conspirators in a stage play, they sparked off each other's lines. Henry looked on, ready to indulge Johnny's every whim. But the change in him was striking. Where before, he'd always been courteous and discreet, the drink had made him careless, no longer the man she thought she knew. Clearly, the seasickness had left him. He looked bright-eyed, playful even, having a good time.

Unwilling to commit, she stayed back by the door. Henry leaned forward, eyes all lit-up at some private amusement. 'Johnny's been telling me about your career in Hollywood. I didn't realise you'd worked with so many big names.'

'I think Johnny must have confused me with somebody else.'

'Oh, I don't think so. He told me how popular you were with the studio bosses. How they used to send for you in a limousine.'

Like two mischievous kids, each trying to outdo the other. Except there was an element of maliciousness to it that gave it an added edge. And all the while, Johnny looked on, the instigator of it all, controlling the way it went with a look of indulgence.

'Why don't you sit with us, honey?' he said. 'We're all friends here, after all.'

'Someone should be up there keeping watch. It's dangerous.'

'Just sit with us a while. Come on now.'

One look at Johnny and she knew. Anything said in the dark seclusion of the saloon would never get beyond *Indigo*'s walls. They could play out this little act for as long as they liked, but in the end it would cease to have any meaning.

Reluctantly, she took a seat. Johnny circled his glass on the table and stared at her with intent.

'Henry knows what we done.'

She stared back at him, not sure how to react.

'I told him,' Johnny said. 'Don't make no sense to hide it no more.'

The interior closed in, making it harder to think. They both looked at her, as if relying on her to come up with a solution – a denial, perhaps.

Henry broke the silence first. 'I knew you were in some kind of trouble when I first met you. But I'm here to help you both. That's what friends are for, isn't it?'

She stayed silent, afraid to implicate herself.

Johnny stirred from his lethargy. 'I think what Henry's trying to say, is that we're all in this together. Ain't that right, Henry?'

'Well, I wouldn't have quite put it like that, but – '

'We all have to pull together as a team, see? Help each other out.'

A feeling of dread grew inside her, that they'd worked all this out in advance to confuse her. Henry's sudden transformation into this drunken parody didn't seem right.

She turned to Johnny. 'Can I talk to you in private?'

'Well, I'm kinda comfortable here, honey.'

'Now – if you don't mind.'

Up on deck she tried to keep calm and think things through. Beyond the bow, the darkness of the ocean and the far-off horizon line.

Johnny came up, and stood behind her. The man she couldn't trust anymore, who'd thrown everything into such confusion.

'Why d'you do it?' she said. His silence taunted her. 'You leave us all in danger so you can get drunk with him and tell him things he shouldn't hear?'

'He's soused. I told him what he wanted to hear, that's all.'

'Why – I don't understand it?'

'Look – I was just buying time, OK?' He glanced behind him, as if expecting Henry to appear. 'Once we get to San Diego he's gone. It'll be just the two of us again.'

'What did you tell him?'

'Nothing he don't already know.'

'What does that mean?'

'He worked it all out while we were still on the island. That old coot Martinez saw a newspaper report about a couple who went missing and showed him.'

'And you went right ahead and said it was us?'

Johnny stepped up beside her, relaxed, almost agreeable. 'It'll work out, honey. All we gotta do is keep him sweet a while longer.'

'And what happens if he goes to the authorities? Then what?'

'Oh, I don't think that'll happen.'

'How can you be so sure?'

'Because ...' He grinned slyly. 'I think ole Henry boy's gotta thing for you. Thinks you're quite the cutest thing he's ever seen.

Who am I to make him think otherwise?'

She shrugged him off, confused and unsure of his motives. Worst of all, the feeling she'd been duped, that somehow the two of them had cooked it up together. And back of it all, the unnerving suspicion that this wasn't the first time. That day on the island, when she'd watched them, unobserved, at the café. An intuitive warning she'd tried to ignore.

'I wanna ask you something,' she said. And I want you to tell me the truth.'

'Sure, honey.'

'Have you got something on Henry? Something you ain't telling me about?

'Now what would I have on him?'

'So you never knew him before we got to the island? Is that what you're telling me?

He pursed his lips, eyes all agleam with the drink and that perverse humour of his that she could never understand.

'I swear to God, honey. I ain't never seen him before in my whole life.'

She knew then that he was lying. And that meant Henry was in on it too.

*

They pressed on in a southerly direction. *Indigo* responded well to the upsurge of wind, her sails stretched taut, bow rising and falling with each new swell. Laura-Mae willed the yacht onward, keeping an eye out for the first glimmer of land, hoping for and fearing its appearance at the same time.

Henry came up through the companionway, blinking at the sun's glare. Seeing her, he smiled weakly and ran his fingers through his hair – a night's alcohol-induced sleep and the haze of dreams soon forgotten.

'Did I miss something?' he said.

'Only your watch. But I covered for you, so I shouldn't worry.'

He sat by the butterfly hatch and exhaled, gazing at the swell as if it contained some great mystery.

'We must be nearly there.'

'About twenty-five miles, according to Johnny.'

'That's good – I suppose.' He rubbed his jaw, eyes narrowed against the sun. 'I can't remember too much about last night. Hope I didn't make a fool of myself.' They both recognised the lie at the same time. Her silence compelled him to go on. 'I shouldn't have drunk so much on an empty stomach. Stupid of me, really.'

His discomfort inspired a moment's pity, an urge to say something and make him feel better. But why shouldn't he suffer? He'd put her in an impossible position, then used it to manipulate the situation still further. There could be no going back.

Looking out at the rolling waves, he frowned. 'I don't think I could cope with a long voyage. I felt as if I was going to die.'

'You have to keep busy. Helps take your mind off things.'

He smiled weakly. 'I wish I had your fortitude. Don't you ever get sick?'

'Sometimes.'

Once, out in San Francisco bay with Johnny, they'd encountered a slow escalation of weather conditions, the wind up to thirty-five knots. Not easy to ignore the nausea that crept up and respond to the demands of the yacht. But that day she felt she'd passed some kind of test. Recalling the incident made her feel proud, a determined, tenacious side to her she hadn't known existed.

'You remember anything about last night?' she said.

'Not much, I'm afraid.' He looked to her for reassurance, but found only the barrier that had sprung up between them.

'You and Johnny looked like you were having a real good time.'

'Did I say something I shouldn't have?'

'Well that depends how you look at it, Henry.' For a moment, she forgot the warnings and believed the lie again. Henry was a friend, as he'd appeared to be on the island. All he wanted was to look out for her and ensure her safety.

Quiet for a long time, he seemed to draw inwardly. When he spoke, his tone had changed, a serious, almost accusing note that hadn't been there before.

'How did you meet them?'

'Who?'

'The couple who owned the yacht.'

Mention of the Simpsons changed everything. She took a breath and plunged in, knowing that out here on the ocean it didn't matter anyway.

'We met them in Los Angeles. Johnny got talking to them and they invited us on-board their yacht for dinner.' She gazed out at the ocean, recalling the detail. 'We got friendly with them over time. Went out on sailing trips along the coast. Johnny more so than me.'

He nodded, almost timidly, as if fearful of the outcome.

'Did you do it?'

'Do what?'

'Get rid of them?'

She shrugged. 'Sometimes things just happen. You don't particularly plan it that way.'

His frown deepened, an effort to take it all in. Tired of the game they were playing, she switched off mentally. They could sit here all night and she would never reveal what had really happened. The message Johnny had instilled in her when they first met: the value of keeping silent, of internalising all the things that couldn't be said.

'How do you feel?' he said.

'About what?'

'I don't know. I think a lot of things happened back there that you find hard to talk about.' He was baiting her now – that gently persuasive tone of his that never failed to elicit a response. She tried not to think, to block out his voice.

'It's too late to go back,' she said. 'I can't change what happened.'

'But you could give yourself up – have you thought about that?'

'What for? We'd be better off getting to Mexico where the law can't touch us.' She realised she'd gone too far. Henry gazed at her with something akin to genuine pity.

'Why don't you let me help you?'

'There's nothing you can do.'

'But there is. I have friends who have influence in these matters. All you'd have to do is make some sort of statement saying what happened. Absolve yourself of any wrongdoing.'

'I ain't making no statement.' She heard Johnny's defiance in her voice, his refusal to comply with anything that didn't fall in with his own will.

'But you can't keep running, can you?' Henry's voice had risen, a note of irritation. 'What's going to happen when you get to Mexico? Johnny will make some reckless mistake and you'll be found out.'

'Mexico will be different.'

'How will it?'

'We'll make some money. Find a place to settle down. The Colonel will help us out.'

Johnny's instructions had been to keep Henry talking. To keep up a kind of seduction routine, right up to the point she might need to physically turn him away. She'd done it in Hollywood with men who were far less deserving of her attentions – men who didn't have Henry's intelligence and style – nothing more to her than a meal ticket or the advancement of her career in some way. Henry was different. The longer she remained in his company, the less resistant she was to his advances.

'It must have been hard for you.' Henry said. 'Losing your career like that.'

'What do you mean?'

'Johnny told me … You know. The disagreement you had with a producer.'

She shook her head, mildly annoyed at Johnny's fabrication of the truth. 'I didn't lose my career at all. I walked away from certain people to get a better deal.'

On impulse, he took her hand and looked right at her. 'I don't care about any of that. I just want to help you.'

'Henry, I – '

'Please, just hear me out and I promise I won't mention it again.' He squeezed her hand, gazing at her with renewed intensity.

'Come to San Diego with me.'

She laughed. 'What?'

'I've got friends there. You'll be safe.'

'From what exactly?'

Easing her hand from his, she sat back. The rocking of the yacht stilled her thoughts. The way ahead didn't seem any clearer, clouded by the obstacles of doubt and uncertainty.

'You ever had dreams, Henry?'

'Yes, of course.'

She gazed out at the distant wave tips. 'I always wanted to ride the train from New York to Chicago. Sit in one of them luxury compartments and watch the world go by outside the window.'

'And that's something you can still do, isn't it?'

She heard his voice as an intrusion borne along on the wind. In her private fantasy she travelled alone, always in transition, seeking the next stop and the one after that. The only other passengers were the ghosts that lived in her head.

'I should wake Johnny,' she said.

'Stay with me a while – please?'

All the things she'd been through: the trauma, the indecision; arriving in California with little more than the clothes on her back and a few dollars in her pocket. Meeting Johnny and being carried off into a life that offered so much promise. What she had to put herself through to be with him. The suppression of her own drive and ambition. The gradual erosion of her values that made the wrong choices seem right.

'I was robbed once in LA,' she said. 'Someone grabbed my bag in the street. All the money I had in the world, gone in instant.' She didn't know why she was telling him: the memory of it had some obscure meaning. 'Kinda changes your view of people. But I got over it, didn't let it bother me none.'

Henry eyed her with pity, but he would never truly comprehend what she'd been through. The child, raised out in the farmlands, illiteracy and ignorance a birth right. How hard it was to leave all that behind and become someone else. To end up here on the ocean, trying to separate the lies from the truth.

'Johnny was on the island before, wasn't he?'

Henry opened his mouth to speak, and checked himself. She closed in, victorious.

'I knew it right from the beginning, soon as I saw the two of you at that café on the waterfront. Then Dr Martinez confirmed it for me later on.'

Still Henry said nothing, unable to look her in the eye.

'Why didn't you tell me?' she said.

'I don't know. It's all a bit … complicated.'

'So Johnny just turned up one day and that was it? You and him became the best of friends?'

Henry turned to her, seized with a look of desperation. 'Look – I only met him briefly when he sailed in to refuel. He spent a couple of days on the island then left.'

'You don't have to lie to me, Henry. It really don't matter no more.'

'I'm not lying to you, Laura-Mae, I'm telling you what I remember.'

'Who was he with?'

'I don't know who they were, he didn't tell me. It was – '

'Henry – just tell me the goddam truth!'

He shifted on the seat, trapped.

'I think it was the owners of the yacht.'

'The Simpsons?'

'I believe so.'

The longer she stayed with him the more uncomfortable she felt – the less able to tolerate his presence or put on an act for him. Part of her wanted to punish him, make him feel guilty for trying to upset the balance of hers and Johnny's relationship, as tenuous as that may be. And yet there was a need in her that his persistence fulfilled. The attention she got from him that she didn't get from Johnny. The certainty that he would do anything to be with her, and make any kind of sacrifice to make that happen.

Indigo heeled over in a trough, throwing them both clumsily together. Glancing at Henry she felt that same undercurrent that was hard to resist. In his eyes, a softness and kindness that was crying out for exploitation.

'I don't think you played a part in this at all,' she said. 'I think you're protecting Johnny.'

'From what?'

She stood, looking down at him with a tenderness she didn't feel.

'Goodnight, Henry. See you in the morning.'

*

She woke with a start to find Johnny standing over her.

'What's up?' she said.

About to go, he stopped, his gaze like an accusation. 'Maybe you should think again before you let Henry take the night watch.'

'What you talking about?'

'Forget about San Diego, we've drifted way off-course.'

She let him get to the doorway, confused.

'What we gonna do now?'

He shrugged. 'Guess he'll just have to come with us to Mexico.'

Johnny went up on deck; voices drifted back over the wind and the waves. She pictured him and Henry, engaged in some trivial conversation; Johnny's antenna for trouble, already up and working at twice its usual rate. And where did she figure in all this? Tired and under pressure, forced to mediate between the two of them.

There were other considerations now. Henry's knowledge of what had happened back in California and the uncertainty of what he might do with it. The likelihood that he would be with them until they got to Mexico. Too late, she told herself, it's already started. Like the anchor chain unravelling from its coil. Nothing you could do but wait for the impact when it hit the bottom.

To offset the anxiety, she kept herself busy on deck. But the bad thoughts kept coming back. What if Johnny and Henry were in collusion? Their whispered conversations leading them to dark plots against her. Alone and defenceless on the yacht she wouldn't have a chance. The cold and fathomless depths would swallow her up, just as they had the Simpsons.

*

Henry looked relaxed and comfortable when he emerged, no trace of the sickness that had troubled him earlier. She faced him with her newfound reserve, determined not to weaken.

'I guess you heard?' she said. 'Johnny says we've drifted off-course. Looks like you might be with us a bit longer.'

He sat beside her, and sighed. 'I don't know what to say. I must've lost concentration.'

She glanced up at the sails. 'If the wind doesn't pick up soon we're gonna drift with the current.'

'Can't we use the engine?'

'Not for long, we don't have that much fuel.'

Henry contented himself with his view from the stern, perhaps not fully aware of their predicament.

'The supplies ain't gonna last much longer either,' she said. 'Not with the three of us.'

'But surely, Mexico can't be that far away?'

'Let's hope so, for all our sakes.'

Easier to believe they were a tight little crew, sailing to some pre-planned destination where they would rest and refuel and continue their journey. And to go along with the pretence, all she had to do was maintain a certain image; days at sea with no makeup, looks sullied by the wind and ever-changing weather conditions left her unsure of herself and her feminine allure. But she must have done enough to warrant Henry's attentions, his eyes seemed to follow her everywhere she went.

'How do you feel about me coming with you to Mexico?' he said. The question seemed deliberate, intended to unsettle her in some way.

'I don't suppose we got much choice.'

'You don't sound too happy about it.'

'These things happen. We all have to adjust.'

'I thought that after our conversation last night you might

have – '

'Let's just leave it at that, Henry – OK?'

He gave a thoughtful nod and smiled faintly, humouring her, perhaps. The vastness of the ocean settled in around them, making all their problems small and unimportant by comparison.

'Johnny said you knew Margot Katz?'

She thought carefully before answering. 'I met her at the studios on Vine Street. The producer Barthez introduced me to her.'

'What was it like, meeting a movie star?'

'Not much different than meeting anybody else.' The lie didn't sit easily with her, especially given the strong memories attached. The house in Santa Monica. The smell of incense burning, photos on the wall of stars like Garbo and Jean Harlow.

Henry studied her in a new light, perhaps a little in awe of her as if she'd scaled some unassailable height. The real Margot Katz remained a mystery, hidden away behind the high stone walls of her mansion. But the gowns and the silk scarves Laura-Mae had inherited were authentic – still infused with Margot's perfume.

'Do you miss that life?' he said.

'Sometimes.'

How easy it had always been – this role she'd played most of her life, encouraged by her mother, who oversaw her every move and knew how to plan ahead. The smile and the right the tone of voice; the deliberate eye-contact to reel in the suckers. The entire purpose cosmetic, creating an image that didn't really exist. But this dual nature confused her. Sometimes she didn't know who she was supposed to be.

'You mentioned friends who might be able to help us?' she said, eager to move on.

'Yes, that's right. I can make some inquiries when we get to the coast. There's an attorney I know, who might be understanding.'

'Would he be able to get us papers?'

'Possibly.' He gazed at her, a glimmer of hope in his eyes. 'Will you come with me? We could find somewhere and start afresh.'

'What about Johnny?'

He looked away, unable to answer.

She felt strangely detached, the way she used to feel when a picture was finished and the cast and crew all packed up to go home. In spite of the sadness at such an ending there was always the necessity to move on, that something better might be waiting up ahead.

'I don't know what to do,' she said. 'My whole life's been this way, always waiting on someone else to make a decision.'

'But it doesn't have to be like that anymore. You'll be free to do as you please, go anywhere you like. You have to trust me, Laura-Mae. I can help you.'

Barthez used to say that a liar could never look you in the eye and tell an untruth; having known Johnny long enough she knew this wasn't always the case. But looking at Henry, she saw something she didn't like. His gaze held a genuine sadness – an undeniable yearning for her that he couldn't hide. But that made him unpredictable and dangerous, aspects she'd be foolish not to consider.

'Henry – I think we need to get something straight. You are not here to save me from Johnny.'

'No, of course not. I just meant – '

'I know what happened back there on the island, but that was a mistake. He gets to thinking anything's going on between us, it puts both our lives in danger. You understand that?'

'Yes, of course.'

'You don't know Johnny like I do … You don't know what he's capable of.'

*

His face looked pasty in the galley strip light. Maybe he was sickening again – a thought she found hard to suppress. No longer the tough and resilient Johnny of old, but a diminished version, determined to see it through to the end.

He asked about Henry, and whether she'd found out any new details about him they could use when they got to Mexico. Beneath his even tone was a note of caution. Henry might be treacherous somehow, not quite playing a straight game. They had to watch out for him lest he tried to come between them and break up the party.

Rocked by the motion of the yacht, she sat at the galley table. Shafts of sunlight glanced on the cabin walls. The relative calm of the ocean changeable, always prone to turbulent moods.

'Can't we turn back?' she said. 'Head for San Diego?'

'What the hell for?'

'We need fuel, supplies.'

'Too late for that. We got no choice, we gotta keep going.'

She didn't want to think about it. The prospect of running out of all the essentials with the three of them on-board.

Johnny sat up, his crooked smile gone. In its place that lingering, dispassionate look that suspected everyone and everything.

'So – what you got for me?' he said.

'What you talking about?'

'You think I'm a fool? You two lovebirds up there making all that sweet music while I'm down here trying to find us the way?'

She feigned shock. 'I'm sorry you think so little of me, Johnny.'

'Don't try to work that shit on me. I oughta drag your sorry ass into that cabin right now just to remind you of your priorities!'

'I wasn't the one who invited him along in the first place, remember?'

'And I didn't hear you complaining too much when I did.'

She sat through it, knowing his anger would pass. Whatever she'd done before, he'd always forgiven her – at least on the outside. The sickness made him unreasonable, took away his ability to think straight.

'Let's just take it easy,' he said. 'No sense getting all worked up for nothing.'

'Sure. Just as long as you know how I feel about it, Johnny.'

Soon they'd be in Mexico and it would all be over. They'd make contact with the Colonel and start their new life right away. Or maybe something would happen to change the course and take them in a different direction. Like it had the night they met the Simpsons in LA. A sequence of events that couldn't be prevented.

*

Henry stood at the guard wire, staring into the darkness. She fought the impulse to call out to him, and watched instead, wondering what he was thinking.

'Hi,' she said, finally, catching him by surprise.

He turned. 'Oh – I didn't see you there.' The look in his eyes startled her, an intensity she hadn't seen before. 'I can't believe how calm it is,' he said. 'A couple of days ago it was a maelstrom. I thought I was going to die.'

'Never a dull moment out on the ocean.'

Now they were back to the habit of being polite again, each statement containing a hint of something else.

'Johnny says we're nearly there,' he said.

'That's right. Won't be long now and we'll be eating tacos and drinking cold beer.' She didn't feel as optimistic. Supplies were running down; they'd used all the poultry and fish from the island, and most of the fresh vegetables. Cooking for three had been challenging – she had to constantly think up ways of being inventive without the choice.

Henry appeared in a different light, the qualities she'd first admired in him becoming harder to find. Now he was just a passenger, one more mouth to feed.

'I heard Johnny coughing again last night,' Henry said. 'Is he OK?'

'Johnny's fine. He just needs rest, that's all.'

Henry gazed at her steadily. 'And how about you? How are you bearing up?'

'I'm fine, Henry. You want coffee?'

Most people fell for appearances, the carefully worded lies and deceits, rehearsed so many times you came to believe them yourself. Johnny had taught her that and she'd learned the lesson well. The actress in her, playing each part with total conviction. But now it called for something else, a role she wasn't prepared for.

Henry sipped his coffee – the one thing they had in plentiful supply. Below, resting in the forepeak cabin, senses trained for the first signs of mutiny, lay Johnny.

'What will you do with *Indigo*?' Henry said.

'Sell her, probably.'

She knew what he was thinking, the Fourth of July event in California still preying on his mind. By telling him everything, Johnny had left it to her to make the denial.

'What were they like?' he said.

'Who?'

'The couple who owned the yacht.'

She took a moment to think, detached, as if asked to recall people she didn't know.

'Wealthy. Arrogant. Always talking about money.'

'You had some sort of disagreement with them?'

'Donald accused Johnny of something he didn't do. There was a fight. Johnny had to defend himself.'

'And where were you?'

'In the saloon, right there alongside Johnny.'

The details were hazy, like watching a grainy old two-reeler. At Johnny's insistence, she'd gone on deck and locked the door to the companionway, forced to listen to the struggle below. The whole thing had taken minutes, but seemed like an age. Time had ceased, in its place a strange vacuum that sealed all the events from the outside world.

Henry stared into the darkness, dazed and uncomprehending. She felt empty, purged somehow.

'We had no choice,' she said. 'They put us in an impossible position.'

The cries of a gull high above the mast, a sign they were nearing the coast, perhaps. Way off in some preordained future, a vision of happiness, held at arm's length and always unobtainable.

Henry nodded slowly. 'It must be a heavy burden to bear. I can't imagine what it must be like, having to live with it.'

'I told you. We didn't plan it, it just happened.'

The idea had been to sail around the bay and enjoy the lights along the shore. But at some point between the dessert and the after-dinner drinks it had all gone horribly wrong. She blamed

Donald's belligerence and loud, overbearing manner. If he hadn't have been so unreasonable their deaths might have been prevented.

'It doesn't change anything.' Henry gazed at her intensely. 'Doesn't make you any different in my eyes.'

'How's that?'

'The way I see it you were put in an impossible situation. A fight broke out between Johnny and this Donald chap, and you were caught in the middle of it.'

'It wasn't quite like that.'

'That's how it sounds to me.'

The world had changed that night, spun completely off its axis. She would never forget the look in Johnny's eyes when he came up on deck after it was over – a look she'd never seen before. Inevitability. Fate unravelling.

'So now you know,' she said.

'Yes, and I was just thinking how unfortunate it is for you.'

'Why – because I killed someone?'

'But that's just it. You didn't kill anyone, did you? You were just unlucky enough to be there when it happened.'

'Henry, that ain't – '

'You told me yourself. The whole thing was instigated by Johnny. If it hadn't been for him nothing would have happened.' He clasped her hand, with a look of desperation. 'Look – I'm sure we can find some way out of this mess together. Contact the authorities when we get to Mexico. Tell them what happened.'

She pulled back. 'What's the point? It won't change anything.'

'But he's the one who got you into all this, can't you see that? I just want to help you. Put an end to the dreadful situation you've found yourself in.'

The picture changed again. She saw a house in a wide, tree-lined street, dappled with sunshine. Children danced a joyful ring-a-roses in the front garden, smiling and trusting, never knowing anything but love before.

Tears filled her eyes. She wept silently, for all the things that could have been.

'I don't know what to do,' she said. 'I'm so, confused.'

Henry hugged her, trying to impart something of his quiet, calm strength, that at one point might have made a difference. She wiped her eyes, conscious of the way she might've looked in a close-up, how every emotion and every expression was caught in the frame for perpetuity.

'I'm so sorry,' she said. 'I should never have involved you in all this.'

'You haven't involved me in anything. I'm here for you because I want to be.. I told you that before and I meant it.'

The night closed in around them – a deep and impenetrable darkness that enclosed everything. And the lie still warm upon her lips. *I don't know what to do. I'm so, confused.* A line that could've been written by Van der Haas for one of his cheap novels.

Easing her hand from his, she stood. 'Goodnight, Henry. See you in the morning.'

'Don't go.'

'I have to sleep … We'll talk tomorrow.'

'Please be careful.'

His tone stopped her, the words heartfelt, urgent.

'What do you mean?'

'I just worry about you, Laura-Mae. I couldn't live with myself if anything happened to you.'

She left him there, an aura of loneliness around him framed by the ocean, the creaks and moans from the yacht's timbers. Johnny would be up soon, unable to trust him at the helm after the last time, when they'd somehow missed San Diego. That's all he'd been since they started out from the island. A cabin passenger, not much use for anything else.

But just maybe, Henry would be able to help her when they got to Mexico. He had contacts, money, the kind of prestige that opened doors when it was necessary. The thought gave her an odd thrill of hope. Maybe the time had come to break her ties with Johnny, and look somewhere else.

*

Dreams came intermittently: she was standing in a huge field, deep furrows forming narrow pathways between tall ears of corn. She couldn't work out which path to take, overcome by fear and indecision. When she woke, the pain had gone. Immobilised by fatigue and the 10-milligrams of codeine she'd taken earlier.

Lying in her bunk, she tried to focus. From the undulations of *Indigo*'s hull and the occasional sharp nudge from the current she guessed the wind had picked up in the night. The residue of the dream still lingered, like the effects of the codeine. An unnatural sleep, and an equally unnatural awakening.

Johnny was at the helm, focused on the rising bow, the spray thrown up with each lunge. Taking the seat opposite him, she searched the acres of empty ocean all around.

'Where are we?' she said.

'Straight to the promised land. Shouldn't be long now.'

'You OK?'

'I'm fine, honey. Never felt better.' He looked defiant and resolute, even with the hint of sickness in his waxy pallor, the peculiar brightness of his eyes.

'Have you had something to eat?' she said.

'Not yet. Thought I'd wait till you got up.'

'Want me to make you something?'

'Whatever you like, honey.' He looked right at her, a faint smile at his mouth.

'What's the matter?' she said.

'Nothing ... Nothing at all.'

The charts were still on the table where he'd left them. Supposedly, they were closer to the coast, having crossed the widest point of the ocean and left the worst straits behind. Soon, they would reach land, and step ashore for the last time, swapping the cramped conditions of the yacht for more mundane luxury: a hot shower and a cool bed, the sheets starched and white, turned back by the maid; food prepared in a proper kitchen and brought to them by waiters. She looked forward to these things, but in a cautious, distracted way, knowing that they weren't yet real.

She took his coffee up, and lingered, unsettled by his quiet demeanour.

'Henry still asleep?' she said.

'Guess he must be.'

'I'll go check.'

'You do what you gotta do, honey.'

The door to the forepeak cabin was closed. She stood outside, listening to the yacht's creaking hull, the gentle rhythm of the water against the sides.

She tapped lightly.

'Henry?'

Nothing stirred.

'I was gonna make some breakfast. You want anything?'

An impulse stirred, irrational but compelling. She gripped the handle and turned it, opening the door a fraction.

Inside, it was gloomy, the light filtered through the porthole curtains. She made out the twin bunks at the front, both empty.

A sense of unreality pervaded. The dreamlike persistence of her earlier waking state where nothing made sense anymore.

Hurrying out, she checked the saloon. Then the closet, the stern cabin. By now an inkling, a conclusion that was hard to avoid. Johnny's strange manner. The look on his face. It all made perfect sense.

Johnny glanced up, the same quizzical smile to greet her. The sounds of the ocean filled in, lyrical, almost peaceful, the bow rising and falling in a trough. For a moment she almost forgot. The past an empty space. Nothing left in it to worry her anymore. Johnny had taken care of everything.

'What have you done!'

'It's over,' he said, flatly.

Reality flooded in, a surge of adrenalin that infused her whole body. She stared at him, uncomprehending.

'You can't have! ... Please! ... Tell me what you've – '

'Quit yelling! I told him how dangerous it was up here. He must've slipped and fallen overboard in the night.'

She slumped on the seat in shock.

Johnny watched her, cautiously, eyes narrowed. 'Everything's gonna be fine, honey. Just like it used to be. You ain't gotta worry 'bout a thing.'

She wept quietly, a hollow ache that started somewhere deep inside and numbed the exterior. But somehow the tears weren't real. At the back of her mind, the awful conclusion that it was somehow inevitable, perhaps even necessary. Henry had been a problem, a threat. He got in the way and had to be removed.

'I can't believe he's gone,' she said.

'You can't let it trouble you none. It's over. Gotta put it out of your mind.'

'You lied to me, didn't you? You had no intention of stopping at San Diego at all, that was part of your plan.'

'It don't matter now. It's finished. Nothing's gonna bring him back.' His even tone disguised all the things he didn't want her to know. Now he was the kind and compassionate Johnny, doing his best to console her and keep her from harm, protecting her from the bad old world.

Drained and unable to think, she sank back. And still he kept talking – all the things they would do when they hit Mexico, a perverse optimism in his voice he no longer tried to hide. Gazing out at the ocean, she filtered out his voice; no more than a backdrop to her thoughts.

'What about his things?' she said.

'We'll get rid of 'em soon enough.'

'But what about the people on the island? They knew he left with us.'

'Honey … It's over. Ain't nobody gonna come looking for us out here.'

And there it was, the unmistakeable note of victory. Once again, Johnny was in control and wanted her to know it. Everything else appeared so normal: *Indigo*'s effortless roll with the swell; the waves breaking against the beam. Even his solitary place on deck – only the previous day she'd watched him climb the mast to free the spreader and thought how strong he looked, in spite of his illness. How he must have enjoyed the final act, seeing it all unfold before him. Doing away with Henry meant nothing to him, little more than ridding himself of a minor inconvenience. Now it was the two of them, just like it always had been.

*

Everything changed from that moment on. Alone and left without options, she had to think and somehow plan ahead. The safest way to get from here to Mexico was to align herself with Johnny's views. Convince him they were still in it together.

Joining him on deck, she took a seat, and composed herself.

'You were right,' she said. 'We should never have brought him along.'

Johnny looked at her gently, a tenderness she hadn't seen in a long time.

'That's right, honey. Fella like that gct no place out here on the ocean.'

'He asked too many questions.'

'He did too.'

'Musta lost his footing and slipped in the night.'

'That's how I reckon it happened. Lost his footing and pitched right over the side.'

The closest she'd get to a confession from him, this absurd conversation where they both avoided the truth and teased out a more acceptable version. But the more she thought about it the more plausible it sounded. People disappeared all the time; fell overboard and drowned. Even experienced sailors. For all his charm, Henry had been a liability; she'd known that all along, right from their first meeting on the island. Now that he was gone they could focus on the rest of the journey. Get to Mexico and make contact with the Colonel. One thing she'd always been good at, adapting and changing her plans to suit the situation.

Right there, she resolved to put her memories of Henry in a locked room, where thoughts of him wouldn't be able to affect her. And if at any point she found herself weaken, she would strengthen her resolve by recalling what had really happened. How close she'd come to being taken in by him.

No sooner had she made the decision it started to come apart. The fallout from Johnny's actions created a sense of unreality. Now there was just the two of them, as it had been before the storm washed them up on the island. The cabin that had housed Henry for such a brief and tragic passage was now out of bounds to her, a place she was fearful to visit.

A loneliness settled in such as she had never experienced. She felt at times as if her soul had been cleaved in two. And the person responsible for it – who had blithely and wilfully reconstructed her life without any consultation – now manned the helm, oblivious to the pain he'd caused her.

Henry's last words came back to her. His warning, 'Please be careful.' The thought arose as a natural progression. If Johnny could rid himself of one obstacle so casually, he could rid himself of her too.

*

The wind increased their speed and made the passage smoother. She kept an eye out for land – that electrifying moment when the first strip of grey appeared on the horizon. Now and then an unwanted thought would come along to spoil the anticipation; a poignant reminder of what might have been. Henry's promise to take her away somewhere that would never transpire. The thoughts came and went, released into the wind. Reality flooded back in. *Indigo*'s passage taking them ever onward, to a future she no longer desired or understood.

The last effects of the codeine had worn off. In its place, a headache, the sun's glare harsh to her light-sensitive eyes. The last few days came back in snatches, like the memory of a dream. Their stay on the island. The dancers on the beach at the festival. The monastery with its frescoed walls and deep, cloistered silence. Henry's disruptive presence that aroused in her a strange yearning every time she saw him. How he'd changed the mood and the tone of the conversation, bringing her a happiness she knew couldn't last. And yet he was still there in her head and in her heart – the essence of him, refusing to be diminished.

Muted coughing below deck brought her back to reality. Johnny came up, his eyes red and watery.

'You all right?' she said.

'I'm fine.'

'You want me to get you anything?'

He shook his head, irritably, and settled back at the helm. In the long silence that followed, she fancied she could hear his thoughts, weaving together some new conspiracy.

'Were you in love with him?'

Startled, she looked up.

'What?'

'You don't have to answer.' He fixed his gaze ahead. 'I just thought that now might be the right time to talk about it.'

She took his plate, and walked away.

'Where you going?' he said.

'Below.'

'I asked you a question, didn't I?'

'And I got nothing to say right now.'

She left him at the helm to brood on whatever iniquity his mind had seized upon. Of course, it wouldn't end there. This was only the beginning, a subtle testing of her composure to see how long she could hold out. The perverse pleasure he seemed to get from it all. The taunting and the baiting. Seeing her with other men – even manipulating the circumstances that caused those assignations to happen, then demanding she share the details with him and accusing her of being a whore.

She took over from him at the helm while he went below to study the charts, sliding into his vacant seat with a feeling of unease. Time passed with its usual indolence. *Indigo*'s passage took on a new urgency – like trying to control a wild horse. The yacht had a similar wilfulness, a spirit that needed careful handling, resisting her attempts to bring it under control.

A school of dolphins appeared, moving swiftly portside. The sight raised her spirits: a good omen, a sign they might be near land. They've come to guide us, she thought. Like an escort, leading the way home. As quickly as they'd arrived, they were gone, leaving only the wave-tips and the ocean. She felt forlorn, and unusually downcast. The sighting had given her hope, temporarily blanking out the current situation – the lack of sleep and cramped conditions. And most of all, the empty space inside her that couldn't be filled. A strange and persistent longing for Henry.

*

Johnny came up on deck, an unlit cigarette in his mouth.

'Where d'you get that?' she said.

'I found a packet in the hold – want one?'

She stared at him in disbelief. 'I can't believe you've done that. Don't you have any respect at all?'

'It's just a goddam cigarette. He ain't gonna need 'em where he is.'

The cigarette was intentional; one more test to see how she reacted. If she pressed the point he'd want to know why, opening up the subject for discussion again.

Sitting beside her, he made himself comfortable. 'Soon as we hit land, I'm gonna buy me a big cigar. Just like the ones Barthez used to smoke, remember them?'

'Never mind that. What we gonna do if a storm comes in?'

He looked up at the mast, and shrugged. 'Looks like the wind's picking up. Might have to change sails.'

'There's something else,' she said. 'If we don't hit land soon we're gonna run outta food.'

'How much we got left?'

'A day or two maybe.'

'How 'bout water?'

'Pretty much the same.'

The lack of supplies didn't seem to faze him. He had that unshakeable confidence that things would work out – at least to his way of thinking. *Indigo* would take them wherever, and that would be that. If they survived they would surely live out his plan in some strange foreign territory, with her in a daze, unable to think or make plans for herself. Mexico seemed distant and unthinkable, about as far from home as she could imagine. She would surely suffocate in the heat and the dust, unused to the language, the customs, forever lamenting what she'd left behind.

Watching Johnny's movements on deck, she felt a hostility towards him she hadn't felt before. It was all his fault. He was the one who'd involved her in this, from their earliest liaison to their disastrous time in Hollywood, where he'd ruined her chances of developing a career. If she hadn't met him none of this would have happened. She'd have gone on to a life of passion and fulfilment, untouched by any of the troubles he seemed to bring along.

He came over, his face flushed and tense. 'I've done all I can. We'll just have to ride it out.'

'What's the latest forecast?'

'I don't know, I can't get through on the goddam radio.'

Even with the best preparation in the world they still had to face whatever was up ahead. Having been through rough waters before, she knew what to expect. But the unknown factor made it hard to gauge. The darkening skies prepared them for the worst.

The mainsail thrashed in the wind – the repairs made by the local on the island looking to come undone. Even under half-sail, the pressure could be felt, tugging at the fixtures and threatening to cause even more damage. Maintenance took time and ingenuity, difficult enough in calm waters. During a storm everything was harder, sometimes impossible, as conditions became increasingly unstable; she'd lost her footing once before, barely able to hang on as the yacht keeled over and the waves crashed in. The fear of being washed overboard never left her from that moment on.

'We can't be far from the coast,' he said. 'Get through this, we're home and dry.'

'You been saying that since we left the island.'

He grinned at her. 'You should have more faith, Laura-Mae.'

'I don't have faith in nothing no more.'

'Well, shame on you. What would the good ole reverend Calhoun have to say about that?'

Every time she was alone the thoughts came back. The shock of finding the cabin empty. Johnny's smug indifference to Henry's plight. Easy to convince herself he'd slipped in the night and fallen overboard, just like Johnny said. It was an accident. If they could have prevented it they would have done and Henry would still be there with them now, sailing to Mexico.

Now they had other things to think about. The darkening skies up ahead.

*

Clouds rolled in on the flanks like auxiliaries for the main thrust. Waves that had been choppy before were now a foot higher, driven by an unseen force. Now that the waiting was over, she welcomed the start. The familiar blend of fear and excitement, of being up against something so powerful it made all other concerns obsolete.

Working in tandem, they yelled warnings across the deck as each new wave broke the bows. *Indigo* rolled with every successive assault – always the fear they might find themselves caught side on and tipped into a trough; the possibility of snapping the mast or capsizing. The waves came on, taller than the mast itself at their peak, their sheer height and volume overwhelming. Each one should have been the last. But then came the next and the next. Survival seemed a vague hope; an equally hopeless prayer that should the unthinkable happen they would be snatched from the seas and rescued, whisked away to a safe place.

Hours passed in the same state of uncertainty; at times, *Indigo* looked like she might break up and go under. Then, like an army in retreat, the waves lost their momentum, the troughs not so deep, so inescapable. They worked together to bring the yacht under control – the two of them now battered and drained, in an even worse state of disrepair. High above, the clouds parted to reveal a milky sun, the test finally over.

Johnny surveyed the scene, his eyes dull with fatigue. 'You better go below, see how much damage has been done.'

She opened the hatch, almost afraid to look inside. Several

inches of sea water lay in the bottom, and floating in it, pieces of debris loosened by the storm. An air of gloom existed in the saloon, complete with a soundtrack of running water. Wading through it, she rescued familiar pieces of hardware and laid them on the table. The top lockers had been forced open, emptying most of their contents; thankfully, the flashlight and flares were still sealed in their packaging, alongside the toolkit Johnny used to make adjustments to the engine. Even the lights flickered on and off, the storm having affected the electrical system.

The light from a porthole filtered down. Floating on the water were hundreds of grains of rice; the last packet they had, torn from the hold during the storm and scattered throughout. She stared at the debris with a huge sense of loss. Their meagre supplies reduced even further.

Johnny appeared behind her. 'How does it look?'

'The rice is gone.'

Wading through to the master cabin, he stood in the doorway and shook his head.

'Better get all the bedding up on deck. This'll take some time to dry out.'

'Great.'

He turned, frowning. 'What's your problem – we're still alive, aren't we?'

'Right now that ain't much of a consolation.'

'Well you better hang onto it 'cause it's about all we got.'

When he'd gone, she made her way to the forepeak cabin, ignoring the stab of anxiety that tried to warn her off. The door was shut. Reaching out to open it, she paused, half expecting Johnny to come up behind her and ask what the hell she was doing.

The cabin was quiet, untouched by the storm. Standing inside, she breathed in the faint smell of damp, the more unpleasant stink from the bilge. Henry's bunk lay as he'd left it, the blanket turned back to one side. No outward sign that he'd been there at all, just as Johnny would've wanted.

On impulse, she opened the locker above the bunk. Life jackets and wet weather clothing, packed diligently by the previous owners. She opened the next locker. Henry's travelling bag lay inside.

How wrong it seemed at first, as if the very act of touching it might violate his memory. Spurred on by curiosity, she dumped the bag on the bunk, and opened it. Clearly, Henry had intended to travel light. The two pairs of shirts and single pair of pants hardly seemed adequate for a voyage of any duration. Beneath the clothing was a book, *Coming of Age in Samoa* by Margaret Mead, a faded check marking the page at 122.

In a side pocket, she found a tin of Nembutal, lots of little yellow capsules inside – the type Margot Katz used to take to help her to sleep. Henry didn't seem the pill-popping kind, but then you never could tell. People hid a whole bunch of things beneath a convincing veneer.

The thought struck her that Johnny had been in there too. How else would he have come by Henry's cigarettes? Maybe he'd been through the bag already, and taken anything of value. Where was Henry's wallet, and any papers he might've been carrying?

Closing the cabin door, she went up on deck, preparing herself to deal with Johnny, and the aftermath of the storm.

They cleared the debris, drying off anything worth saving. Sodden clothing went up on deck to dry in the sun. Everything had a damp, washed-out feel – spun through a giant tumbler and spat out over *Indigo*'s interior. In her head, a kind of hollowness at having to deal with it at all, a switching off of any emotional response.

The fortune-teller in Los Angeles had predicted a trial up ahead, the loss of something of great value. Looking back it was easy to see how the elements had all conspired to make that prediction come true. The awful fate that had befallen Henry. The fact that she'd slept through it all, sedated and exhausted, waking to find it was all over and the deed had been done. Then the storm – surely a sign of God's displeasure.

'We brought this on ourselves,' she said, quietly.

'What's that?'

'Nothing.'

Johnny seemed more morose than ever, brooding on his own problems. His cough barked intermittently, a harsh and aggressive sound that seemed to convulse his entire body. She could only wonder at his state of mind – he, who'd been the driving force behind them all along, inspiring her with his plans to get to Mexico and start a new life. Whatever they had left between them wasn't enough; the storm itself symbolic of a personal unravelling, forcing her to reassess everything she'd previously accepted without question. She didn't belong to him anymore. His embrace used to offer security and a feeling of being cared for. During the course of the journey something had happened to change all that. The loss of Henry, perhaps. A precious lifeline torn from her that could never be recovered.

*

The afternoon sun dipped low on the western horizon. They might have been out here for eons, ravaged by the forces of nature and somehow put back together again. The sea was calm once more, but it didn't make any difference. To her it seemed a kind of wasteland, pitiless and barren, in which nothing could possibly survive for long. Adrift on all this, her poor dispossessed soul, with no anchor and no direction. All the things that might have offered comfort and reassurance, abandoned and left behind.

Now, more than ever, she had to be especially careful. Sat up front with a grey blanket round his shoulders, was the source of it all, the cause of all her troubles. He looked reduced in some way, as if the storm had used up most of his resources. But she knew this to be illusory. Whenever Johnny Boy was hurt or wounded he was at his most dangerous, ready to manipulate the situation to his own advantage.

'How you feeling?' she said.

'I'm fine.'

'You don't look too good.'

'Well, looks are deceiving, honey. You of all people oughta know that.' He pulled the blanket closer and turned away from her. She felt nothing, no pity, no tenderness. Any reoccurrence of his illness would mean double the work for her. But still the need to look after him persisted. Even after all that had happened, their roles were still clearly defined.

'Why don't you go below and rest?' she said. 'I'll take over here.'

He turned to her, a glassy, hooded look in his eyes. 'You know what, Laura-Mae? I wish, just for once, you would leave me the fuck alone. Is that too much to ask?'

'I'm just trying to be helpful.'

'Well sorry to disappoint you, missy. You ain't being helpful at all.'

She kept herself busy below, sorting out the cupboards and repacking some of the stores. Johnny stayed up on deck under his blanket, meditating in the sun like a native Indian. She tried to feel compassion and empathy, but found only her own battered psyche, forced to cope with him and everything else that came along.

The sweet tea she brought him seemed to restore some of his earlier humour. He sipped it, hunched over, the blanket around his shoulders, a murmur of approval for the simple pleasure it gave him.

'You know what I could never make out?' he said. 'All those hallucinations I had back in Chicago when I had the fever. They seemed so real.'

'What made you think of that?'

'I don't know. I just did.'

'You were pretty unwell. You thought the doctor was trying to kill you.'

He looked at her with a glint of wild humour. 'The doctor? Hell, I thought it was *you* trying to kill me, Laura-Mae!'

Perhaps he was delusional, a symptom of the same fever. More likely another one of his tests, a way of amusing himself at her expense by grilling her about some aspect of the past she could barely remember.

He looked at her sidelong, with the same warped smile.

'You ever think about doing me in?'

'All the time.'

'Be serious now. Supplies are running low, water level's down. Pitch me over the side you get to keep it all to yourself.'

'I might just do that, Johnny.'

He fell quiet, a brooding silence that didn't bode well. When he spoke, his tone had changed, a note of sadness there. 'I keep thinking 'bout the time we met. The fun we had.'

'Is that what it was?'

'Don't be like that, honey. I saved you from them two-bit westerns ole man Barthez wanted you in. If it weren't for me you'd have ended your days in Arizona, getting sunburned and saddle sore.'

'I did what I had to do.'

'You sure did. And there ain't no shame in that. No shame at all.'

She tried to laugh along with him, but the sound came out brittle and harsh. There were things he didn't know. Secrets she'd kept, that would've shocked him if he'd found out. Other places and other men; hotels and bars that offered the same opportunity. The old guy who bought her a meal and gave her money when she ran away from home. In return she slept in his bed and made empty promises that didn't mean a thing, a transaction she considered perfectly reasonable at the time.

Barthez had promised to take her to Paris, with its cobbled streets and luxurious hotels, the little cliques of artists and intellectuals who'd left their homelands to settle there. If nothing else, Barthez had introduced her to culture. She'd enjoyed their conversations about art and literature, and other highbrow subjects, even if most of it did go right over her head. She was uneducated and naïve. Barthez had an understanding of the world that she found enlightening. People were pretty much the same all over, he once said. Like a river flowing to and from the same source, all trying to escape the same demons. You had to know how to treat them to get the best out of them, make them feel they were an indispensable part of the whole. And that's what she'd been working on her whole life. The same tricks she'd picked up from watching her mother with the menfolk back home.

'You think we're gonna die out here?' she said, thinking aloud.

Johnny sniffed and shrugged the blanket higher on his shoulders. 'I sure hope not, Got me a nice fat steak lined up in Mexico.'

She didn't care much for his levity, and took her mind off somewhere else. But wherever she went there could be no escape. She was a prisoner, vulnerable to his every whim.

'My mammy always said I had the devil in me,' she said.

'Well your mammy was a pretty good judge of character, Laura-Mae.'

'I hated them for what they did to me.'

'Well, yeah, I can understand that. Working you all day in the fields till your fingers were raw. What kinda life is that for a sweet little girl?'

'Wasn't that at all.'

He watched her, intrigued. 'What was it then? That brother of yours, tried to drown you in a water butt when you were five?'

'I hated him, too.'

'Sure you did. And the best move you ever made was to get away. Leave all them cornhole fuckers behind.'

The memory stirred deep within, cold and hard like something she'd been forced to swallow. The nurse's abortive fingers and soothing cadence drifting through the laudanum with a dreamlike quality. 'Now you just lie still and you won't feel a thing.' The physical alteration was real and clearly evident in the dull pain she felt the next morning. But on a conscious level she might not have been there at all.

'What's up?' Johnny said. 'You ain't talking to me no more?'

'You wouldn't understand.'

'Oh – so you think ole Johnny ain't been through shit too?'

What happened had been the province of the same adult authority that had taken charge of her life ever since she'd been born. She had no say in any of it, just as she had no say in the schools she went to, or the church she had to attend every Sunday, where the women sat stiffly with their hands in their laps, observing the rank and file with the same pious disapproval. It was done, and it would never be talked about again. Proof of her sinful nature. The seed of a man inside her, and the shame she must surely carry with her wherever she went.

'I'll get your medicine,' she said.

'Well praise be I got someone like you looking out for me.'

She stepped back, seeing him from a different perspective.

'You really don't care about me at all, do you, Johnny?'

'What you talking 'bout? You forgetting all the things I did for you back in California. I'm the best thing that ever happened to you, and you know it.'

She hated him almost as much as she hated the folks back home. Always those closest to you who caused you the most pain and expected to get away with it.

'One day you'll understand,' she said, leaving him there to ponder. Being Johnny, he had to have the last word, and called out behind her.

'It's *you* gotta understand a few things. Make no mistake about that!'

Searching the contents of the medicine box she found the small bottle of codeine he relied upon. In Chicago, his temperature had risen dramatically. She hadn't known what to do and panicked, forced to leave the hotel room to seek advice. Now, the thought of his being ill didn't have the same sense of urgency. Whatever happened, it would take its course.

She handed him two tablets and a glass of water. He stared at them indignantly.

'What's that?'

'Codeine. It's all there is.'

He swallowed the tablets and a slug of water, and returned to his previous state of moroseness, gazing out over the water as if she wasn't there.

'Will you eat something?' she said.

'I ain't hungry.'

'I think you should.'

'What are you a goddam doctor?'

She stayed with him, unmoved. The scene felt strangely comfortable, familiar, something they'd acted out many times before in different guises.

'You can't just give in to this,' she said. 'You've gotta fight it.'

'I gotta fight what exactly? Being stuck out here with you telling me what I should and shouldn't be doing?'

'I'm just trying to help, Johnny.'

'Well you ain't helping at all, missy. Not one little bit.'

He drank the mushroom soup she made for him, spilling droplets on his beard. She couldn't bear the noises he made, his laboured breathing as he bent to the next spoonful. He'd been the same in Chicago. Every time she tramped up the stairs to their room on the fifth floor she felt a new level of anxiety, a dread of what she might find when she opened the door; the shades drawn and the fan on, its whirring blades inadequate against the August heat. But it was the look in his eyes she remembered most of all. A sudden and inexplicable terror, as if the devil himself had just walked in.

'Remember how we used to go dancing in Encino?' he said. 'They were good times, don't you think?'

'Why don't you get some rest? I'll take over here.'

'You think we'll ever dance again?'

'Maybe.'

'Well I sure hope we will. 'Cause when ole Johnny Boy's with you, honey, he don't ever want the night to end.'

His mood changed like the wind in the sails. One minute quiet, the next animated and full of good humour. But where before she could share in those memories and take the same pleasures of recall, now they seemed empty and without substance.

She heard him coughing again later, a worrying rattle in his chest that went on and on. She tried to ignore it and searched the horizon instead, hoping for a glimpse of land. Nothing but the endless blue sea. Now that she'd adopted the nursemaid role, Johnny had settled in as the patient, almost without realising it. And, sure as night followed day, he would abuse her accordingly, resisting all her attempts to help until it drained her spirit.

The wind dropped, and with it their speed. She tried to busy herself with things to do below, sloshing around in the two inches or so of water that lay in the bottom. Most of the storage lockers had been repacked, the loose items scooped up and dried off, anything perishable thrown out. The split bag of rice had been a bad sign, a depletion of their food supply that could have made the difference between life and death, but at least she'd managed to salvage some of it. Then there were the endless questions. How far were they from the mainland? What if they drifted off course and ended up thousands of miles away in the middle of the ocean? The prospect haunted her. She only had to look at the far horizon to fear its depth, its infinity.

Indigo's undulations soothed her. She allowed her mind to drift back. The past, like a garishly-decorated room where people she'd forgotten wandered in and out. She saw them all clearly, the events that had taken place passing before her eyes like the scenes from a movie. Her meeting with Johnny. Events that would turn the innocent little girl from Cooke County into someone else, someone she didn't particularly want to be.

*

The train pulled in at the station. Carriage doors slammed and whistles blew. People swarmed around. And there waiting to greet her, wearing a sports jacket, shirt, and grey flannels was the boy she hadn't seen for ten whole years. They embraced on the platform, his hug rather formal and quickly withdrawn. Later, she would learn that his reticence wasn't due to rudeness or a lack of feeling, but more an aversion to any public display of affection. She found it amusing, an aspect of his character she quite liked. But he wasn't anything like the boy she remembered from home, who wore the uniform of the farmhand, the raggedy-assed pants and the flat cap. This was someone of taste and outward sophistication, who'd learned the ways of city folk and knew how to emulate them too.

'How was the journey?' he said.

'A bit cramped, but I got here alright.'

'You most certainly did. And may I say you look like a million dollars.'

Taking her arm, he steered her through the crowds – more people than she'd ever seen in one place at any one time. The case she'd brought seemed inadequate for her needs, and the clothes she'd packed so obviously inferior to the fashionable garb of the women around her. But the sense of excitement drove her on. This was true freedom, to be away from home at last, and all the restrictions it had placed upon her. She wanted more than anything to be a part of this pioneering community, who'd come from different parts of the world looking for the same thing.

They sat in a coffee bar, alive with music and chatter, quite the glitziest place, with its juke box and photos of movie stars on the walls. Johnny talked and she listened, enthralled at his exploits. He worked for a renowned producer, Barthez, who was contracted to a big studio on Vine Street. Part of his job was to find new talent and introduce them to Barthez, who might put them in one of his pictures if he thought they were good enough.

'Is it hard to get work out here?' she said.

'Not if you know the right people.'

'Could you get me a job?'

'Maybe. What else can you do besides look pretty?'

'I can sing and dance a little?'

He laughed at her childlike response, but not in a cruel way. This was California, he said, where all the movies were made. Everything was controlled by the studio bosses, who ran things like a military exercise. To get ahead in this town you had to adopt a different outlook, a whole new way of seeing things.

Little by little her defences came down. She found herself taken in by him completely, comfortable with him and protected by his aura of sophistication. The stories he told were fascinating. Famous actors and actresses he'd met. The mansions he'd been to on Fremont Place. This was Hollywood, the same place Margot Katz got her famous start, paid $200 a week, which even back then seemed a huge amount of money. In less than two years,

Katz was earning $1000 a week, her salary renegotiated by studio bosses who saw the earning potential of their famous product. That's what actors and actresses were, Johnny said. Just like commodities bought and sold on the New York Stock Exchange.

Pausing to light a cigarette, he observed her intensely. 'You gotta hustle to make it here, same as anywhere else.'

'I ain't afraid of work.'

'I ain't talking 'bout work, honey. I'm talking 'bout using this.' He tapped his temple. Her uncertain frown seemed to amuse him even more. 'What would the good folks back home think if they could see you now – taking up with ole Johnny Boy?'

'I don't care what they'd think. I came out here to get away from all that.'

His grin widened. 'Welcome to California, honey. I think we're gonna get along just fine.'

The music and the colourful people made her feel awkward and unrefined. And to add to her unease, Johnny kept right on staring at her like she was the most unusual creature he'd ever seen. But he did have charm to go with it. And the stories she'd heard about him back home only seemed to add to his air of mystery. Out here he was somebody. He'd made a name for himself. Back in Cooke County he'd been a gas station attendant for a while. There was even talk he'd gone to prison for stealing a car and crossing the state line. The rumours gave him an added attraction, an element of danger that was hard to resist.

'Did you find me a room?' she said.

'I did, but there's a bit of a problem. They had some kinda gas explosion and had to evacuate the top floor.'

'Where am I gonna stay?'

'Oh, I'm sure we can work something out, honey.'

The undertones of a seduction she willingly played into; a veil drawn around them both that no one else could see through. She couldn't concentrate on anything else: his smile, his mannerisms; the sensual way his mouth moved when he was talking. She found herself being drawn in, taken along a path she hadn't intended going. And later, walking out with him along Sunset Strip, she surrendered – a decision she reached without any prompting on his part. She couldn't wait to be alone with him, away from the traffic and the crowds.

His room was on the fourth floor of a large, brick building off Main Street. Up a wide staircase, and along a hushed corridor, every footstep amplified on the bare boards. At last, he put the key in the lock, and they were inside. The door closed behind them. Without a word, they embraced, seized with the same urgency, the same need. She broke away, reminded of her promise to herself to remain chaste – at least for the time being.

The bedroom contained a single bed and a rug to cover some of the bare boards. Johnny was insistent that the bed was hers to sleep in. He would put up on the couch in the front room. 'But that ain't fair on you,' she said, but he waved away her concerns in his usual easy-going style. 'Don't you worry 'bout me, honey, I've slept on dirt floors and cattle ranges before. This here's luxury.'

Lying in the soft bed, her face oiled, makeup removed, she heard him undress. Shadows fell through the open door; boards creaked as he moved from one side of the room to the other. Then silence. Only the lamplight that cast the room in a soft glow.

'Shall I turn out the light?' he said.

'If you want to.'

A click, and then darkness. The tension built in her a delicious expectation of what could be, a test of her powers of restraint. No body heat or accidental touch between them to spark off an embrace like the one when they'd first entered the room. This was torture – but an exquisite form with many layers still to unfold.

'You comfortable in there?' he called out.

'I'm fine, thanks.'

'Seems funny, me in here and you in there.'

'I thought that was the arrangement?'

'It don't have to be …'

She knew she couldn't hold out much longer. Besides, it was his bed and she had no right to it.

'Maybe I should find a hotel,' she said.

'What for?'

'Then you can have your bed back and I won't take up no more room.'

She heard movement, and there he was in the doorway, his body lean and hard in the soft light.

'I gotta better idea.'

He was more than she'd dreamed of. In his arms she became someone else, stripped of her inhibitions and worries. His primal nature allowed hers to surface. They were made to be together. Whatever fears she had earlier were unfounded. And after, he talked of such wonderful things. Luminaries she'd read about in magazines and would never have dreamed of meeting. His promise to get her a job at the studio as an extra, under the tutelage of the great producer Barthez, who'd created so many of the stars she'd seen up on the screen. Little did she know how much that would demand of her and how much she would eventually lose. But that would come later.

*

Days and nights on-board *Indigo* hadn't done much for her feminine side. She studied herself in the vanity mirror. The sunburned face that stared back looked blank and jaded, the mouth down turned and set firmly in a stubborn jaw. The hairbrush freed the strands damaged by the heat and extreme weather conditions, but it couldn't revive the part of her that was so obviously missing. She didn't feel attractive in the least – not like she did back in California, catching the eyes of strangers in the dance halls and bars. Any appeal she might have possessed had been eroded, worn down by the rigors of the journey; the poor diet and lack of sleep. Now, when she opened her eyes to the new day, it came with the realisation that she was alone – truly alone and without help. The man whose love she'd known only briefly was gone, never to return. Snuffed out and destroyed by a monster.

The wind speed dropped, turning minutes into hours. Johnny stayed on deck, still wrapped in the grey blanket, sweat coating his forehead. Every time she went up to see how he was, he grunted a confirmation, refusing to look at her. All she could do was endure it, praying they would soon reach the coast where she would be able to make suitable arrangements – get him to a doctor and find a place to recover. Then work out the next step, whatever that might be.

Descending the steps to the galley, she heard him call out, his voice harsh and indistinct. She went back on deck, and stood a few feet away, waiting.

'I called you twice,' he said.

'I heard you the first time. What do you want?'

'What do I want? I'll tell you what I want, missy. I want you to stop treating me like a piece of shit and start remembering who I am around here!'

'Why don't you calm down, you'll make yourself feel worse.'

'Don't tell me what to do, I ain't a goddam kid no more!'

He wasn't well, she told herself. She had to take that into consideration and not get drawn into a fight with him. Whatever it was that was driving him, it must have been a huge burden to shoulder all on his own. The strange, heroic things he did on her behalf – pledging himself to her in such a way that it humbled her to think of it. But her silence wouldn't work either. She had to find a way to stand up to him. Stop him from taking over completely.

'Where you going?' he said.

She stopped, forced herself to look at him. 'Below. I got things to do.'

He looked at her, mute and unseeing. The defiance in him seemed to waver, an odd vulnerability setting in.

'What's the matter?' she said.

He stared out at the water. 'I'm all in. I ain't slept for three days trying to keep us on course.' He sounded diminished, lacking conviction.

'Well rest then. I told you I could take over.'

He shook his head at some inner frustration. 'Make me a drink, will you?'

'What would you like?'

'How 'bout a drop of ole Mrs Winslow's Soothing Syrup.

Remember that? Ma used to give it to us when we was kids. Sleep like a goddam baby.'

'Sorry to disappoint you, Johnny.'

'Just brandy, then – and put some of that baptismal fire in it, the kind reverend Calhoun used to drink before he faced the congregation.'

Now they were on opposite sides. Nothing she could do for him would be enough. He'd find fault with everything, sniping and criticising until it became unbearable. The weariness in his tone implied he no longer cared anymore, but that could just as easily be a ruse to bring her guard down.

'Please don't take it out on me,' she said quietly.

'Take what out on you?'

'Whatever it is you're thinking. It ain't my fault.'

He stared ahead, one hand on the helm. 'Quit talking and get me the drink.'

She found the brandy in the locker – a donation from Henry when they'd first arrived on the island. Reminders of him everywhere. Images of the two of them at the monastery and the café on the harbour front, memories that gave her no comfort. Perhaps his spirit was out there on the ocean and in the wind, whispering words of encouragement, willing her to go on. But no matter how hard she listened, she couldn't hear a goddam thing.

Johnny barely looked up when she brought him his drink, too absorbed in his feverish state to take much notice.

'Drink this,' she said, 'it'll make you feel better.'

'What is it?'

'Brandy, like you asked.'

He stared at the glass. 'What else you put in it?'

'Strychnine - what do you think?'

He took a sip and swallowed, nodding his head with grim approval.

'Anything else you want?' she said.

He settled back and half-closed his eyes. 'Why don't you sit with me a while. I think we should talk.'

She sat, dutifully, waiting for him to speak. He appeared to collect his thoughts, in no great hurry.

'I always did like Barthez,' he said. 'Thought he had a good head for business.'

She stiffened, knowing what was coming next.

'But he turned on me, see. Threatened my livelihood. And I couldn't have that now, could I?'

'None of that matters out here, does it?'

'Well that depends which way you look at it.' He gazed at her with a strange longing. 'I only ever wanted you, Laura-Mae. You know that, don't you?'

'Sure, Johnny.'

'Never wanted them cheap whores on Sunset Strip. The kind you could ply with booze and take down some alleyway. I never wanted that at all.'

She learned a lot from Barthez. He taught her the essential rules of conduct for both the actors and the crew. Those who understood the system became part of a large family and got all the benefits from that closed fraternity. Those that didn't were sent on their way, driven out by their inability to conform. Over time, she learned how to play along, at least outwardly; that basically it was an act you put on – and she was always as good an actor as the next. Barthez singled her out for special attention. He was preparing her for something better, he said, something more worthy of her natural ability.

'It all seems such a long time ago,' she said. 'Like it never happened.'

'Oh, it happened all right. I seen it with my own two eyes.'

Certain moments in life that defined the future. The first time she saw Margot Katz on a reel of film. The consummate performer, using the same techniques she'd acquired on one of the vast studio sets: the flash of the eyes for the camera; the sad, vulnerable look that men seemed to find irresistible. The sense of power she must have got when she walked in a room and all the eyes turned in her direction. In the days before sound, the face conveyed everything on the screen, all the turbulence and passion of one's existence. Margot's face – such depth and allure that inspired the newshounds and held audiences in a trance. The advent of sound stripped away the mystery and replaced it with something else. Talking pictures – a little too much of real life intruding upon the filmmaker's vision. Margot's greatest asset soon became obsolete.

Johnny sipped his drink and stared out over the ocean. 'There's an old saying I heard on the farm in Texas. Three can keep a secret if two are dead.'

'I don't care much for that right now, Johnny.'

'Why not? We got us the best kept secret right here on this yacht. Between the moon and the stars ain't nobody gonna hear what happened.' The fever shone in his eyes, sweat tacky on his forehead. The words weren't his, but the work of whatever force had taken him over. The reverend Calhoun said some folk opened themselves up to become instruments of the devil. When that happened they were done for and only God could help them. Looking at Johnny, she wondered if that hadn't happened already.

They got drunk one time in Chicago and played a game. Each had to ask a question and the other had to answer truthfully. When it was her turn, she asked Johnny if he'd ever killed anybody. Where the question came from she had no idea. Intuition, maybe. A hunch rising from her subconscious, and stirred up by all the late night conversations they'd had. Sly and evasive at first, he became more candid, talking real low and monotone-like so she had to strain to hear. There had been an incident once, he said. A fight in a bar that went out into the street. The other fella somehow ended up with a knife in his belly, but Johnny couldn't remember how it happened. There were other times, he said, but only ever out of self-defence. When she questioned him further he wouldn't answer. The game ended there.

She often wondered why she hadn't run away back then. Something about him that night scared her, but she stayed out of loyalty. That and the truth she discovered later on. Just how far he was willing to go to get his own way.

*

The wind picked up late in the afternoon. She busied herself with maintenance, the jobs Johnny could no longer do now that his fever had taken hold. Now and then he took to his bunk, giving her ample time to think, to plan their course without his constant interference. Strangely, the prospect of sailing *Indigo* single-handed didn't faze her. By her estimation they were fairly close to the coastline now, perhaps as little as ten-miles away. She'd even looked at the chart and managed a little rudimentary navigation of her own. Having been through rough weather, and a whole range of adverse conditions, she was confident of pulling through without his help. She'd acquired certain skills, discovered she had good sea-legs and rarely got sick. The whole thing had become a challenge, a way of proving to herself that she could do it alone.

A few times she heard the radio burst into life, a disjointed conversation in Spanish between the coastguard and an anonymous vessel out there on the water somewhere. Johnny's claim that the radio didn't work could have been a ruse, one more trick to keep her unsettled. But the voices gave her hope, an undeniable link to the mainland that even he couldn't dismiss.

She took him soup in the stern cabin, and put a pillow behind his back, helping him sit up. He seemed weaker and more disoriented than before.

'What's this?' he said.

'Chicken soup. You gotta eat to keep your strength up.'

'I ain't hungry.'

'Please, just eat, you'll feel better.'

Like a child, he gave in and opened his mouth for the spoon. After a few mouthfuls he sank back, exhausted.

'I need to get up,' he said.

'No you don't. You need to stay here and rest. We're not far from the coast now. As soon as we anchor I'll get you a doctor.'

'I don't want a doctor – why can't you get that through your goddam head?'

She touched his forehead, repelled by the sticky heat, the skin hard as marble. 'Get some rest. I'll come back and see you in a while.'

'Laura-Mae?' he called as she walked away. 'You ain't gonna sell me out now, are you?'

'Rest, Johnny.'

'I got the power to destroy you … You hear me?'

She made herself a small bowl of salvaged rice, and sat on deck, not enjoying it but forcing it down anyway. With the stores slowly dwindling, the coming hours would prove critical. She would need all her strength to sail the yacht and make any adjustments to their course, forced to get by on a minimum of sleep. Johnny's condition would make it harder, but provided she kept the right focus she would cope. There was no other option.

*

Sunset came and still no sign of land. Thoughts she'd pushed to the back of her mind during the day crowded in – images of Henry on the beach during the festival, or standing at the bow with the wind in his hair, a teasing half-smile that lit up his features. Awful to think of him missing, his body washed up on some lonely shore. And the inescapable fact that in her own way, she had somehow been the cause of it.

She took Johnny a cold drink during a lull in the wind. He lay on his back in the dank cabin, covers off, his bare chest glistening with sweat,

'Here,' she said. 'This will help you cool down.'

'Where are we?'

'About ten-miles off the coast, I think.'

'I meant where exactly? What are the co-ordinates?'

'I'm not sure, I'd have to check … Here, sit up and drink.'

He did as she asked, taking the mug in both hands like a chalice. His hair was coarse and thick, his beard even longer. The poor light from the cabin gave him a wild, almost feral look.

'How do you feel?' she said.

'Like I'm on fire. Hot and cold at the same time.'

'You want more blankets?'

'No.' He laid back, and stared at the bulkhead. 'I just want to get off this thing. Lay up somewhere cool and quiet.'

You'll get your wish, she wanted to say. You can spend as long as you like on your own, because I won't be there to comfort you.

He gazed up at her as if he knew – that strange, almost telepathic insight they'd developed from their earliest meetings.

'You hate me for what I did, don't you?' He flashed his grimace of a smile, as if the thought gave him pleasure.

'I don't hate you at all.'

'He had to go. You knew that as well as I did.'

She sensed a confession, deliberately staged to sound out her real feelings.

'I think you'd better rest,' she said quietly.

'I've rested enough. There's things you need to hear.'

'I don't want to hear anything right now. I'm tired and I – '

'You're damn well gonna hear!' He sat up, eyes bulging. 'You think I didn't know what you were up to? You and that smooth-talking parasite up there in that goddam monastery? I oughta taken care of him long ago – you as well!'

She turned to go, resolute, hardened.

'Don't you turn your back on me now. You hear me out.'

She stopped, and turned. 'You don't know what you're saying, Johnny. It's the fever talking.'

'Oh no you don't!' He struggled to sit up, almost jubilant. 'You ain't gonna squirm your way out of it that easily. I know the truth, I saw it in your eyes. You had no intention of staying with me at all, did you? You had it all planned out. You were gonna wait till we got to Mexico then run off with him.'

'That's a bunch o' crap and you know it.'

He swayed there, resting on his elbows, with a look of pure victory. 'Damn shame you weren't there to see it happen.'

'Johnny, I – '

'How I got him up on deck while you were asleep, offered him a cigar.'

'I don't wanna hear it.'

'That was his downfall, see? Thought he was too clever to avoid what was coming by taking me for a fool. You think I ain't seen his type before? All them fancy clothes and fancy talk? Didn't help him none, did it?'

She took a few steps towards the doorway, desperate to block out his voice.

'Don't you walk away from me now. I got more for you, honey-pie!'

Compelled to stay, she turned to face him. He kept nodding to himself, as if at some irrefutable truth.

'You know what he said to me before he took his tragic tumble?'

'I don't care what he said.'

'Come on now, Laura-Mae. You can do better'n that. Why, you could even act as his defence council, seeing as poor ole Henry ain't around to talk for his-self.'

'I think you're delirious, you don't know what you're saying.'

'Really?' He propped himself upright for maximum effect. 'Well there weren't much wrong with me that night, I can assure you. I made sure ole Henry boy knew exactly what was coming to him before I did it. How 'bout that?'

She held his gaze, unable to move. He smiled his ghastly smile, knowing he'd got to her in the worst possible way.

'Ain't you gonna say something?'

'I'm tired, Johnny.'

'Well, I'm sorry it had to end that way. I guess he just kinda overstayed his welcome.' He grinned, goading her further. 'Don't you wanna know what he said?'

'I think you need to rest, Johnny.'

'Well seeing as we're all friends around here, I'm gonna tell you anyway.'

She readied herself for whatever was coming. Johnny's grin stayed fixed, his face obscured in the dim light of the cabin.

'He said you was a real mystery to him. Try as he might, he just couldn't seem to get a handle on you. I said, hell, I been feeling the same way since I set eyes on the girl when she was fourteen.'

'I'm tired o' talking, Johnny.'

'Talking's good. Helps clear your mind of all the crap that's in it. And I'll tell you something else. Ole Henry thought he could save you. Thought he could ride on in like Randolph Carlson and carry you off. How 'bout that?'

She took a step back, determined to block out his voice.

'But there was one little detail he forgot, see? ... Henry didn't know you like I do. He never saw the things I seen.'

'I gotta go,' she said. 'Get some rest, I'll come and see you later.'

'Yeah, you do that, honey. But don't ever think you're better than me ...'

Standing at the guard rail she felt a shudder, forced to relive Henry's final moments. The awful surprise he must have felt when he realised Johnny's intentions. Easier to believe he'd just disappeared, washed overboard during the height of the storm.

Now she knew the truth there was nowhere she could go with it, nowhere to hide. She was as guilty in his death as Johnny, almost as if she'd been standing alongside him when it happened.

She stayed on deck for what seemed like hours, unable to bear his stricken face, or hear any more of his murderous recollections. Lost in a past that no longer existed, she wondered how she'd come to end up this way. In the beginning it had been hard to adapt. Every time Johnny asked her to do something she knew wasn't right, it nagged at her conscience – all the things she'd been taught not to do as a child, in case she offended God and went straight to hell along with all the bad folk she knew. For convenience sake it just seemed easier to go along with it, rather than argue and cause a scene. She'd been an actress most of her life, even before Barthez and Hollywood came along. Able to put on a smile and go through the motions, knowing that if she played it right, most folk would fall for it and believe anything she said.

Hollywood, the perfect place to lose yourself, a strange new world where the privileged few gathered to act out their fantasies. She'd never seen anything quite like it. Barthez's mansion on West Adams Boulevard, with its spacious rooms and high ceilings, hallways decorated with framed paintings and bronze statuettes. The music and the drinking. The beautiful people. She only had to close her eyes and she was back there as if it were yesterday.

But there were things she could never tell Johnny. The night there was a different kind of party at the Barthez mansion. Ecstatic faces and semi-naked bodies caught in the lamplight; gasps of pleasure from shadowy corners. Wandering along the hallways, she was hardly able to believe what she was seeing. In one room, two women and a man on a big bed, their limbs entwined like snakes. As she passed by, the man glanced up and beckoned her to join them. Horrified, she hurried on to a darkened room at the top of the stairs, where she sat in nervous contemplation. Two men in evening dress entered, and stood for a moment watching her. Emboldened, they took a few steps towards her, silently seeking her consent. And, without a word uttered between them, she gave in, seduced by their presence, the atmosphere in the house. The first touch was electric, a tentative hand on her waist, the face of one so close she could taste the wine on his breath. The most natural thing in the world to add to her pleasure in this way. In their arms she became transcendent, lifted to some other place.

When it was over, they slipped away as quietly and anonymously as they'd appeared. Alone on the chaise longe, she smoked a cigarette, struck with the enormity of what she'd just done. She would never see them again, forbidden by the strict protocol of the system that guarded its stars so carefully. But she knew who they were because she'd seen them on the studio lot and in the movie houses. They had wives and a public image to uphold. She had nothing, except the potential Barthez talked about. That, and the mysterious something she'd just given away without thinking.

*

Johnny came up on deck, the grey blanket around his shoulders now a permanent fixture. The virus, or fever, whatever it was, seemed to have retreated, an illness in remission. But that same bright light shone in his eyes, wild and unnatural, suggesting it could always return.

'You're up?' she said, trying to hide her disappointment.

'Thought I'd get me some air. Suffocate in that goddam cabin.'

Taking a seat by the helm, he eased himself gently down as if his joints still ached. He'd lost weight, his once powerful and masculine frame now reduced and lacking in vitality. And yet still an air of danger surrounded him, the sense that he was saving his energy for whatever trials lay ahead.

'How you feeling?' she said.

'Fine.'

His stock answer to everything. She didn't believe him, the answer there in his drawn features and hooded eyes.

'Did you manage to sleep?' she said.

'Couple hours maybe.'

Indigo's bow slammed into a wave. He winced at the shock, and shifted his position on the seat.

'You hurting?' she said.

'Every bone in my goddam body.' He sniffed, and wiped his nose with the back of his hand, staring out at the water. The wilful child, refusing all offers of help and being all the more difficult because of it. He once told her how he used to lie in bed for days, administered to by the housemistress of the home he was in, who'd bring cool flannels for his forehead. Bed, for him, had been a place of safety, a legitimate place to hide from the master's heavy hand, or the schoolwork he didn't want to do. Perhaps there was still a little of that in him now, the urge to escape responsibility, to be pampered and looked after. Laura-Mae, the kindly housemistress, taking care of his every need.

'What we gonna do?' she said.

''Bout what?'

'There's still no sign of land, and we got nothing left to eat.'

'Where's your faith, Laura-Mae?' He flashed a wry smile. 'Ain't that what you been telling me all this time?'

Some of his old belligerence had come back, even if he didn't have the physical strength to back it up. Too much disturbance might bring on another coughing fit and he'd have to lie down again. Consoling herself with this thought, she turned her mind to the coast. They couldn't be that far away. All they had to do was keep going long enough to sight land.

Johnny pulled his knees up to his chest and breathed a long sigh. 'We have a little falling out while I was unwell?'

'What do you mean?'

'Well, I seem to recall getting a bit carried away. Saying things I shouldn't have.'

She looked out at the endless blue sea and thought about Henry.

'It don't matter what you said. It's over now.'

'Well whatever it was, I didn't mean to cause you no discomfort.'

'You ain't caused me nothing, Johnny.'

'That's good then. I'd hate to think a little thing like that might come between us after all we've been through.' He took a deep breath and settled back, the lord of his realm once more. She wished to be far away, walking city streets, surrounded by ordinary people. Back in California, perhaps, where each new day offered promise and excitement.

A wave nudged the port side, intruding on her thoughts. The action reminded her of their plight, that they were still adrift on the ocean with no real idea of where they were – the terror of a storm breaking out and all that entailed. Fear that the yacht would capsize and they'd drown, and no one would know what had happened to them.

She said a silent prayer to whatever force might be looking over them. A strong faith in something might have helped during these times, but she couldn't fake it, it simply wasn't there. Johnny was right. After what they'd done, it seemed absurd to even consider such a thing. God didn't help sinners. Once you'd abandoned Him there was no hope for you. All you had left was the devil, and he made sure there was nowhere left to turn, no happy endings like there were in the movies.

'I think we should send out a distress signal,' she said.

'What for?'

She stared at him, appalled by his lack of concern. 'We're running out of food and water. We don't even know where we are.'

'You do what you gotta do.'

'What else is there? We can't go on like this, we're gonna die out here.'

She tried the radio, turning the dial through the various channels: nothing but foreign voices and static; discordant jazz music that sounded so out of place. Sending a distress signal over the airwaves would mean giving up the idea of getting to Mexico. But even capture by the authorities was a better option than perishing alone.

Something stopped her. Johnny's wrath, perhaps. The accusation that she'd betrayed him after all they'd been through. Switching the radio off, she settled back in defeat. The silence contained a multitude of background noises – the lapping water and slight wind in the sails, the occasional rattling of cleats in the rigging. Like the ocean itself, the stillness had a depth to it. So many different variations depending on your mood. Loneliness, or yearning – then at other times an intense feeling of well-being that had no particular cause. This time there was no escaping the sense of isolation, of being trapped out there with no one to help. Johnny's presence made it worse; the added stress of dividing her time between him and sailing *Indigo*. The real test would be how much longer she could cope.

*

Survival in its rawest form – watching the stores dwindle each day knowing there was no means of replenishing them. Every time she opened the locker she got a sinking feeling. No more potatoes and tinned soup, no more wine and brandy. Nothing left that could remotely be called a luxury. An abundance of fish swam in the sea, but they had no way of catching them; the rudimentary method of trailing a line behind the boat seemed only to work in theory. Soon they might be forced to use that method again in order to stave off hunger. Fish were a bountiful source of nutrition and energy. One good haul could mean the difference between health and starvation, life and death.

She cooked up the last of the salvaged rice and they ate in solitude to the undulations of the sea. When he'd finished, Johnny put the plate down and settled back, lost in his thoughts. The loneliness she felt deepened, even extending to them as a couple, and what they'd lost. How inseparable they'd been in California before they were forced to leave and go on the run. She'd have done anything for him then, her dreams bound up in his, no matter what their basis in reality. Now there was nothing left. Not even a paltry cracker to keep them going.

'That's it,' she said. 'We're all outta food.'

'You sure 'bout that?'

'What – you think I'm lying to you now?'

He lapsed into resentment, muttering curse words and frustration against the elements that were lost on the wind.

'What about the fishing lines?' she said.

'What about 'em?'

'I thought maybe we could catch something.'

He stared hard at her, a glint of his crazed humour back. 'How you gonna do that?'

'We gotta do something. Can't just sit around waiting.'

She found the fishing line, a handheld device with a green line wound around a wooden framework. Small grey weights hung at one end, like mini cannonballs, plus a vicious-looking hook.

Johnny watched her prepare the device, his stupid grin firmly in place. 'Let me know if you need a hand, honey?'

'I don't need nothing from you.'

'Want me to go below and oil up the skillet, ready for when you haul something in?'

'You ain't funny at all, Johnny.'

'Hey, I'm just trying to help. I really think you could be onto something here.'

Careful not to tangle the hook and the weights, she unwound the line, securing the frame on the seat by her knee. Beyond the stern lay the wake, the undertow churning over the water. Enough fish out there to feed them for weeks, and all she needed was one. She visualised the catch, a moment of pure jubilation as she hauled it on-board, its fat, scaly body flapping around on the deck. Johnny's face would be a picture, silenced at last by her skill and ingenuity.

Something was missing. The bait, obviously – but something else, too. She didn't know the remotest thing about fishing, her efforts born from necessity, the possibility of starving to death on-board the yacht. And all Johnny could do was sit there and mock her, exercising his right to be an asshole.

The fish she'd anticipated didn't come. Johnny watched with his languid smile, secure in the knowledge he'd proved her wrong again. 'Maybe the fish've taken a vacation, honey. They all got tired waiting around for you.'

'And maybe I'm tired of listening to your bullshit. Ever think about that?'

An idea came to mind. She went below and searched the hold, finding a few pieces of dried fruit on the bottom. The last of their supplies. A symbol of hope that something else might be waiting out there.

Careful not to let Johnny see, she put the plan into action. With the tiniest piece of dried fruit attached to the hook, she fed the line out from the stern, and sat back to watch.

'Good luck with that,' Johnny said.

'Whatever I catch is for me. You ain't getting a damn thing!'

The waiting game set in. Bored with the novelty, she looked around for something else to do. This was all there was, an endless search of the water beyond the stern. Nothing to do but sit and think. Endless speculation on events that had been and gone.

Closing her eyes in the heat, she let the past filter in. They were all there: Barthez, Margot Katz, the heads of the studios. And always Johnny there too, refusing to allow her to be alone, even with her memories.

'Strange what happened to Van der Haas,' she said.

'What made you think of that out here?'

'I just did.'

He scratched his neck, and pondered. 'Van der Haas was another one, couldn't hold his liquor. Goddam hacks are all the same.'

'But to just disappear like that, with one of his pictures about to go into production. It don't seem right.'

'Maybe he got tired of ole man Barthez criticizing his work.'

'But he would've said something, surely?'

'Guess we'll never know, honey. People do strange things.'

Van der Haas, the 'enigma', as he liked to call himself. One more aspect of her life that had come and gone. Someone else who'd offered her the world, then left with so many empty promises. And just to make it worse, he was married. One more complication to add to her problems.

*

They booked in under the name Harper – Mr and Mrs. She had no idea where the name came from: whether he'd dreamt it up then and there, or if it had come from one of his novels. When she asked him, he shrugged, claiming not to know. By then it didn't matter anyhow. She was used to the subterfuge.

From reception, they carried their bags along a narrow corridor to their room. Little did she know it would be this way from there on in, a succession of hotel rooms and guest houses, avoiding the newshounds and anyone who might discover their true identity. It didn't strike her that she was taking part in anything illegal – that she might, in fact, be labelled a criminal if they were apprehended. The sense of inevitability about the whole thing made it hard to resist. Van der Haas was adamant. Whatever happened, they had to keep it quiet lest the wrong people found out and ruined his career. A scandal such as this would destroy his reputation, he kept telling her. Never once did he stop to think what it might do to hers.

The room was small, but comfortable, the bed cover immaculate, pillows plump and clean. Questions naturally arose that demanded answers. Would she change her mind at the last minute and want to leave? Did she care enough about him to risk her own career in a venture that could only have one outcome?

Unpacking his case, he dropped a revolver on the bed – black and mean-looking with a short barrel. She stared at it with mild consternation.

'What's that for?'

'It's a safety precaution.'

'For what?'

'I don't know. I just like to have it with me.'

She picked it up and turned it over in her hand, surprised at the way it felt; a small thrill of pleasure at the power it held. The two seemed to go together: Van der Haas's status in Hollywood and the snub-nosed weapon he carried as an extension of that.

'Have you ever used one?' he said.

'I shot my daddy's rifle once on the farm.'

'I'll teach you how to use it one day. You never know when you might need it.'

Van der Haas had an interesting past before he came out to California. He told her he'd been in an automobile accident that left him hospitalised for three days, barely conscious. The injuries he'd sustained caused headaches and blurred vision, an inability to process time. He even thought he might have to give up writing, possibly the worse fate that could befall someone like him, who made his living turning out film scripts for the studios. She felt sorry for him, and more than a little guilty at the way she'd treated him when they first met. But when she asked him about it he shrugged it off, saying it was one of those things that happened to people all the time. 'The driver lost control and we turned over. Doctors said I had a fifty-fifty chance of pulling through. But here I am, still breathing. How lucky you are to have me, Laura-Mae.'

She didn't care much for his sense of humour, or the meticulous way he arranged his clothing whenever they booked in somewhere; folding his pants and checking the creases, making sure they were perfectly aligned. But he did at least treat her with some courtesy when they were alone, and even wrote tender love poems that she kept in her case. He was a hopeless romantic, he said, and lived his whole life that way, dreaming up characters who took up residence in his head, running amok like delinquent children and ruining his equanimity for days.

The hotel rooms and guest houses they frequented soon became a kind of prison. Nothing to do but make love and sleep, listening out for cars on the forecourt below, the raised voices and doors slamming along the corridor. She wondered if the neighbours could hear them through the thin walls, just as they could hear muted conversation and the blare of a radio on the other side. The thought of being overheard gave their vigorous lovemaking a more illicit feel, raising her excitement to an almost unbearable level. Van der Haas didn't share her lack of inhibition and clamped a hand over her mouth to stop her from crying out. The couple might call the manager, he said, and have them ejected. Then what would they do? She reminded him that he was to blame, that it was his idea in the first place, complaining half-jokingly that he'd corrupted her and ruined her for life. He didn't like to talk about such things, embarrassed by the attention it might bring upon him. Always his reputation to think about and never hers, which didn't seem to mean a great deal to him anyway. But she did have her own reasons to keep it quiet. Not least, her turbulent relationship with Johnny, already known as a hothead at the studio, and someone who liked nothing more than to get his own way.

For a while she enjoyed the feeling of control it gave her, of knowing how easily she could manipulate the situation, getting him to comply. Van der Haas had influence. He knew people. With a little coaxing from her, he might pass on her details to one of the studio heads, who would see her potential and open up the books, giving her the opportunity she was looking for. But somehow it never happened. Whenever she mentioned it, Van der Haas would get angry and say she was trying to manipulate him, using him for what she could get.

Sometimes, during the height of their passion, she looked into his eyes and a profound fear set in. It couldn't possibly last. She was the latest in a long line of girls he would inevitably grow tired of and move on. He had his wife and family to think about, and they had to come first. In order to prevent that happening she needed a plan. Some kind of hook, or bargaining tool. A means of reeling him in.

Then Johnny turned up after a brief hiatus in Frisco, and she took up with him again. Events moved of their own accord, a natural progression with its own rhythm, its own momentum. She kissed Van der Haas in the studio parking lot one night and never saw him again. Strange how she accepted his loss philosophically, without too much crying or lamentation. People came and went. That was the way her life had always been. And now she had someone who filled the void completely. Now she had Johnny.

*

Shadows gave way to murky light, the grainy fog of dawn before the sun came up. Confused, she went to the porthole and looked out. *Indigo* appeared to drift in the channel, a listlessness about her that didn't seem real.

A sense of panic grew.

Dressing quickly, she went up on deck, relieved to find Johnny at the helm.

'Why didn't you wake me?' she said.

He turned, smiling. 'Thought I'd let you sleep a bit longer. Looked like you needed it.'

Gazing out at the ocean she felt daunted, crushed by its infinity.

'Where are we?' she said.

'Can't be more than a few miles from the coast.'

She wanted to believe him. If his calculations were right they had to be closer now. But she no longer trusted his judgement, or his mental state – to let him take over the helm again would be to invite trouble. Everything depended on *Indigo* reaching the coast within the next couple of days. After that, the water supply would have dwindled to the critical stage, and any hope of making a successful transition fading with it.

The sun came up on another day. Her stomach tightened, an intense pressure in her head, the way she often felt when she was developing a migraine. And no one around to blame, nothing but the rolling seas and devilish winds to rattle the sails and cleats, further disturbing the balance of her mind. Visions of hotel fronts set in lush grounds came and went; white-coated

waiters bringing food and drink. Tantalising fantasies that grew in her mind, impossible to resist.

Taking the helm, she steered into the waves, keeping an eye on the horizon. Johnny sat with her, unusually quiet. He didn't look too good; the skin had peeled from his chapped lips, the sunburn on his forehead more pronounced. The last thing she wanted was to fight with him with so few miles left to cover. But the sense of responsibility remained. Even after all he'd done to her, she still felt obligated to look after him, to ensure he got the treatment he needed. The inescapable conclusion that it was somehow her fault. Because of her they'd ended up this way.

Standing, she made to pass him. He put out a hand to stop her.

'Where you going?'

'Get you some cream for your face.'

'Well that's real thoughtful of you, honey. Real thoughtful indeed.'

Ignoring his sarcasm, she went below. The codeine tablets were in the first-aid box with the quinine and the antiseptic solution; the one thing they had plenty of when they left California. And she still had the little Nembutal tin she'd found in Henry's bag, if she needed a temporary solution.

A thought crossed her mind – so powerful and unexpected she couldn't shake it off. How much better life would be without Johnny, without his constant sniping and black moods. She'd be free to sail into Mexico alone and it would all be over. No more struggling to please him. No more soothing his nightmares when he woke from a fevered sleep. The hold he'd had over her for the last few years would finally be broken.

The thought faded, became a part of the backdrop, just waiting to surface again and spoil her peace of mind. If anything happened to him she'd be lost, directionless. And how would she make contact with the Colonel, the only person left who could help them?

Applying the cream to Johnny's forehead, she put all these thoughts behind her. He sat there looking dumb and unusually passive, the act bringing them temporarily closer. The nursemaid and the patient. Perhaps the most intimate they'd been in days.

An illusion, she knew, like the thin grey spit of land she kept seeing on the horizon, a figment of her imagination that made the burden a little easier.

'I been thinking 'bout Van der Haas,' he said. 'How he disappeared like that with no warning.'

'Maybe he went back to New York, he had family there.'

'You in love with him, too?'

She read his look and checked herself. 'I was only ever in love with you, Johnny.'

'Well that's good, honey. Kinda helps me get things clear in my head.'

Barthez had a Spanish-style villa in Hollywood. The few times she'd been there had opened her eyes to luxury in the truest sense of the word. California seemed to offer such boundless opportunities. Blue skies and heat, sunshine in every room. The drive along Wiltshire with the windows down and the warm breeze coming in, a view of all the big houses to the right. Then later, passing through the small coastal roads on their way to the place Van der Haas had rented out. Like tourists, freed from the burden of demoralising hard work and conformity – all the things she associated with life back home. For a moment she could pretend they were a real couple, that he wasn't married to someone else.

You in love with him too? The question confused her, like a riddle she had no answer to. She couldn't be sure of her feelings for anyone anymore – especially her feelings for Johnny. They would always be different – outsiders trying to find a way in to the select clubs and cliques that made up Hollywood. Even the waiters in the diners and bars treated them with a certain coolness she found disconcerting. Johnny's casual attitude didn't help. He didn't care what anybody thought about him, and would often joke about it to make her feel worse. 'Me – I'm a good ole southern boy, make no mistake. They don't like it that's their problem.'

His casual references to violence frightened her sometimes. The smug pleasure he took in describing the suffering he'd inflicted, especially when he thought the victim deserved it. She was learning new things about him all the time. How his moods could change quickly, almost without her noticing. The rage that would suddenly take him over, making him frightening and unpredictable.

The first time he yelled at her she'd been taken by surprise, unprepared for the level of anger that erupted within him. He apologised soon after, filled with a remorse that seemed genuine. But the confusion remained, the sense that he was two different people. Although he never raised a hand to her, the threat was always there, an undercurrent to keep her on guard for as long as he wanted.

She checked the fishing line, feeling its tautness. The set up gave her a strange feeling of satisfaction, that here was something she'd thought of on her own, without his say so.

'Caught anything yet?' he said.

'Not yet.'

'You could be waiting a long time, honey.'

'Well you ain't gotta worry about that, have you?'

His smile was fixed and unnatural, a facet of his illness she recognised from their time in Chicago. This insistence of his on getting up and carrying on as normal, just to prove he could. To counter her feelings of hostility towards him, she tried reminding herself that he was still sick and didn't know what he was doing or saying. But it was hard, almost impossible to maintain with the two of them in such close proximity.

Later, he grew morose, a distant quality to his voice that made her wary. He talked of his own end somewhere up ahead, as if he almost looked forward to it.

'You afraid of dying, Laura-Mae?'

'I don't wanna talk about it.'

'Why not?'

'Because it ain't right to talk about such things out here … Why don't you go below and rest?'

'Rest when I'm dead – didn't I tell you that before?' He watched her from his seat at the helm. 'Most folk are afraid of it, see. And that's what makes 'em stupid.'

'Maybe they ain't got God in their lives.'

'Well that's where you're wrong, honey. All them righteous folk back home, putting money in the church collection. What good it ever do them? All they get's a hole in the ground like everyone else.'

She tried not to listen, to close her mind to the things he was saying. He nodded smugly to himself, keeping her under surveillance.

'You know what I admired about you most of all? Your ability to keep your mouth shut. I could take you anywhere and not have to worry you'd say the wrong thing.'

'I'm glad you valued my performance so much.'

'Oh, I did, believe me. Couldn't have done it without you. And all that stuff you did back there in California. That was a helluva thing.'

'What stuff?'

'Meeting up with the Simpsons. Keeping them sweet all that time. You were always one step ahead of the game, honey. Had it all figured out before I did.'

'That ain't true at all.'

He laughed softly, shaking his head. 'You really are something, you know that? I watched you, Laura-Mae. I know what you're capable of.'

She focused on the green line in the water. He kept on at her in the same needling tone, knowing he had the advantage. She couldn't block out his voice, or the insinuation. The idea that some of the claims he made contained an element of truth.

'Maybe we should get married when we get to Mexico,' he said. 'Seal the goddam deal that way.'

She stared at him in disbelief.

'I'm serious,' he said. 'Maybe that's what's been missing all this time. We could even take the honeymoon suite at one of the best hotels.'

'I don't think so.'

'Why not? Don't you think ole Johnny Boy'd make a good catch? Or maybe you were looking to get hitched to someone else.'

Once again, she knew what was coming; a costly mistake

she'd have to pay for. Johnny would never allow her to forget, never let it go. Stupid to think she could get away with it, with him watching her every move. But she couldn't help herself. Henry had begun to feature in her daydreams more often. She fantasised about the two of them up at the monastery, the clothes he was wearing, the smoothness of his tan. The warm smile he always greeted her with that made her feel happy, even if only at odd moments. Strange to think that the image she carried of him in her head meant more to her now than it did when he was alive.

Johnny cocked his head, mockingly. 'Have I upset you, honey? Talking 'bout things you don't wanna hear?'

'I got nothing to say about it. Far as I'm concerned it's over and done.'

'And I can understand how you feel. I mean, after all, Henry ain't likely to come back and pay us a visit anytime soon, is he? No more than ole Van der Haas. They're gone, nothing more than a memory blowin' on the wind.'

She sat quietly, biting back the urge to respond. Johnny had that perverse look on his face, like he was just warming up and couldn't be contained.

'Everybody's hiding from something, see? And that's your trump card, if you know what to look for. Watch someone long enough, you can find out what makes 'em tick, what their hopes and fears are. Then you can make a move. Take whatever you want.'

'Is that what you did with me?'

'Oh, now you were in a class all on your own, Laura-Mae. Hell, there were times I thought I was the pupil and you were the teacher. Look at how you played ole man Barthez, sat up in that office o' his, pulling the head off the turkey every chance he could get, wishing it were you instead.'

'He had a picture lined up for me. He was gonna make me a star like Margot Katz.'

'Come on now, honey. Barthez was about as much use to you as Van der Haas, full of bullshit and empty promises.' He shook his head, disappointed somehow. 'You ain't smiled once in days,

Laura-Mae. What's the matter – lost your sense of humour?' His eyes were red-rimmed, sweat beads on his forehead. In spite of his attempts to disguise it, his fever was back; he had that stoned look of indignation, eyes burning bright.

'I'm too tired for all this,' she said, more to herself than to him.

'Yeah, well I wanted to come clean. Tell you a few things you oughta know.' He narrowed his eyes, his smile fixed. 'I'd liked to have done it in a more civilised way, but we just don't have the time or the inclination.'

Gazing out over the water, she hoped for an end to it. But something in his tone made her curious, overcame her resistance.

'What things?'

He relaxed and stretched out his legs. 'That good ole Barthez who helped you get your first break. Rumour has it he liked young boys, too, but we won't get started on that.' He flashed her a skewed smile. 'What he did have was a contract all made out for one Laura-Mae Ellis – which I wouldn't have believed if I hadn't seen it with my own eyes.'

She looked for a sign he was baiting her.

'What're you talking about?'

'A contract. I saw it right there on his desk waiting to be signed.'

'You're lying.'

'Why would I lie about a thing like that? He told me his-self. Even showed me the paperwork.' Sensing her confusion he honed in. 'Course, he would've expected you to do something for him in return, or you'd wind up playing chorus girls and two-bit whores for the next seven years – and all for 200 dollars a week. Only one thing stopped him getting what he wanted, and that was good ole Johnny Boy.'

She guarded her reaction, trying to take it all in. He nodded, watching her closely.

'I figured you'd be grateful one day. Knowing I'd stepped in and saved you from that hook-nosed piece of shit. Just like you were grateful I saved you from Van der Haas, that other snake in human form.'

She didn't know whether to believe him. Even if it were true,

and not some twisted part of his imagination, it wouldn't make much difference to their current plight. But the thought of him deliberately sabotaging her career was too much to bear.

'What's the matter?' he said. 'You got nothing you wanna say to me?'

'Why didn't you tell me before?'

'Because it weren't the right thing to do. I just didn't want it on my conscience no more. Wanted you to know everything.'

She read his look, the unmistakable flicker of amusement in his eyes. The only way he could get back at her. Take away the very thing that might have brought her lasting happiness. And all she could do was put up with it, just as she'd always done, absorbing everything he'd thrown at her over the years without retaliation.

'Well, I hope you're happy now,' she said. 'You got what you wanted.'

'What I wanted? Jesus Christ. I did it all for you, Laura-Mae.'

'That ain't true and you know it.'

'Really? I think you gotta selective memory when it comes to the truth. Like the night we met the Simpsons at Ventura Beach. Remember that, do you?'

'Johnny – '

'I figured you might wanna talk about that too, see? Maybe clear up some of the discrepancies in your account of what happened.'

'I know what happened.'

'You sure about that?'

She refused to look at him, to engage in the stupid game he was playing. But he'd opened the lid of the box, and she knew just what was inside.

*

They parked by the Hotel Continental and sat for a while watching the people. Even in the late evening, the heat bore down, relentless and uncomfortable. To the right, the scalloped balconies of the new apartments, the large, colonial-style building that looked out over the bay.

Strolling towards the diners by the water's edge, she was struck with the tranquillity, the soporific effect of the heat that drained the energy and made everyone head for the shade. Small groups of tourists strolled by, the men in shorts and polo shirts, the women in short dresses, their shoulders sunburned red. Here they could blend in without fear of being noticed, a couple like any other, enjoying the backdrop of waves on the beach and the open-fronted diners, candle-light flickering on the tables.

Waiters in black pants and starched white shirts loitered out on the roadside touting for business. One of them gestured to the open table area, with a well-rehearsed invitation. 'My very good friends – this table you would like?' She smiled at the comic timing, the amiable versatility of these people who didn't need to break a sweat for anyone.

They sat at the back, to the music of waves breaking on the shore. The sound touched on her loneliness, a sense of being so far from her home she might never return. The talk was always about money. They'd done all they could, cutting back on spending and eating out less often. But over the last few days Johnny had become more and more intense, snapping at her for the most trivial things. At times she couldn't bear the tension.

'What we gonna do?' she said.

'I gotta plan, honey. Just you wait and see.'

The waiter brought wine; at least they could enjoy one last night out, even if they were down to their last few dollars. Johnny's fault for instilling in her an expectation for the best of everything, a desire she was happy to indulge no matter what they had to do to make it happen. But now they were paying the price for his recklessness – the trouble he'd caused, first with Van der Haas, then with Barthez at the studio. The day Barthez fired Johnny, most of their troubles had started.

He told her his plan, the one he'd been brooding over for days. They would head along the coast for the Gulf of Mexico, far enough away from federal jurisdiction and the likelihood of being apprehended for the felonies he'd committed in California. He knew people who could help them start a new life. This would mean cutting ties with the past, and everything associated with it, but they would be free.

But what would we do?' she said. 'We'd have to start all over?'

'I know a guy who operates a gun-running business over the border. They call him the Colonel. He could help us.'

'Why would he help us if we ain't got no money?'

'He's a friend of mine. We go back aways.'

She didn't know anything about this Colonel he talked about, but the name figured more and more in their conversation. Johnny's faith in this man's ability to help them was contagious. She came to see the Colonel as a kind of ally, a guarantor for their safety when they got to the other side.

Johnny took her hand in his, on his face that special intensity that demanded her compliance. 'I need you with me, honey. You're the only thing in this world I got that means anything.'

She couldn't answer. The stretch of blue water beyond the restaurant looked endless; the thought of leaving such an idyllic spot for the unknown so daunting. Thousands of miles from home with nothing to fall back on. No comfort, no security. Only Johnny, with his crazy schemes.

He sat back, focussed again. 'All we gotta do is stay cool and relaxed. Something will come along soon, it always does.'

And sure enough, Johnny was right. Just as they were thinking of leaving, a couple turned up. The couple's arrival changed the ambience, the mood created by the fact that, up until now, the diner had been almost empty. The man had a loud voice, his bulk conspicuous in an equally loud green jacket and open-necked shirt. The woman was younger, heavily adorned with makeup and jewellery.

Johnny raised a hand in greeting. 'How y'all doing?' He turned to Laura-Mae, and said under his breath, 'Just smile and let me do the talking.'

The couple joined them at the table, and conversation started. They were landowners from mid-west, who'd retired and moved to California for the clean air and miles of beaches. The man's name was Donald Simpson, his plump cheeks flushed with good living. His wife, Sheri, looked on with a bemused smile; at least ten years younger, she acted as his foil, the butt of an occasional cruel joke which she took without her expression ever changing. Her motivation seemed entirely based around money and acquisition, her conversation made up of little else – her clothes all made by top designers like Madeleine Vionnet and Coco Chanel. After months sailing the coast and eating too much rich food, they were looking for a place to retire so they could better monitor Donald's heart condition.

Sheri leaned forward eagerly. 'And what do you do?'

'Well – '

'We're in the picture business,' Johnny said. 'Laura-Mae's about to sign a lucrative contract with one of the big studios, but we can't say too much about it for legal reasons, if you know what I mean?'

'Oh, that's so exciting!' Sheri gazed at Laura-Mae with a new admiration. 'Have you been in anything we might know?'

'Let's order the drinks,' Johnny said quickly, 'then Laura-Mae can tell you all about it.'

Soon they were part of the scenery. Donald's interaction with Johnny was fascinating to watch, a jarring mix of jokes and crude observations that only they seemed to find amusing. She couldn't help a grudging admiration, amazed at how quickly Johnny could adapt his character to fit the situation. Taking his cue, she joined in, smiling and agreeable, doing her best to follow the conversation.

They had a yacht moored in the bay, Sheri said. Wouldn't it be nice if Laura-Mae and Johnny came over and had a look. So they made plans there and then. The start of a friendship she already had her doubts about. But Johnny made it look so easy it was hard to resist. And the bottom line as always. The Simpsons had money, they didn't.

*

'You remember that night?' Johnny said.

'How could I forget?'

'Well, I was real proud o' you, honey. Made me realise just how far you'd come.'

'I only did what you wanted me to do.'

'Sure you did. And they never suspected a goddam thing.'

In spite of her protests, he stayed at the helm, steering them in a south-easterly direction. Increasingly morose and uncommunicative, he preferred his own company and the wide open space beyond the bow. Whenever he spoke, it seemed intended to undermine her in some way, or to reinforce the differences between them.

Hunger set in; her last meal had been a handful of rice and a salty cracker, snapped in two so she could savour the taste. After that, the supplies were gone, finished. Johnny's appetite had diminished because of his fever – a fact she was grateful for. But she still had to deal with the frightening prospect of having no food. If they didn't sight land soon, they would have to accept the unthinkable. They were lost. Stranded out on the ocean with no supplies and no contact with the mainland.

Johnny's revelation about Barthez troubled her. The thought of a contract lying there on his desk ready for her to sign. So many unanswered questions. Van der Haas's disappearance in Hollywood that had barely made the papers. Then the girl the detectives had questioned her about, and the fateful crash in Johnny's car. Johnny had always denied that the incident had anything to do with him, but its aftermath had left a shadow.

Whenever she mentioned it he got belligerent, accusing her of being naïve. But out here on the ocean with nothing else to do, these minor spats became serious altercations, with neither side willing to back down.

'Trouble with you is you trusted too many people,' he said. 'Couldn't see what was plain in front of your eyes.'

'I only trusted the people who helped me.'

'Is that right? Old man Barthez helped you too, did he? Dressing you up as a whore in one of his lousy goddam cowboy pictures?'

'That role was good for my career. I even got a mention in the Ed Sullivan column.'

'You never had a goddam career until I came along!'

His jealousy gave her the advantage, a kind of victory to think she could defeat him so easily. Perhaps that was all they had left. The final round in the unresolved battle that had been running ever since they'd met.

'There are things I've wanted to tell you as well,' she said. 'Things that don't sit right with me no more.'

'Oh, yeah?'

Feeling his gaze, she chose her words with caution. 'You were right. Henry did want me to leave you and go off with him when we got to Mexico. He was obsessed with me, wouldn't leave me alone.' She waited for his response, but nothing came back. 'But I never once thought about going, even though it would've been the easiest thing in the world to do.'

He stared at her, puzzled. 'He asked you to go off with him?'

'That's right.' An odd calmness came over her, the need to punish him further. 'I guess he was in love with me. Wanted to take me to a better life.'

Johnny shook his head, seeing her in a new light. 'You disappoint me, Laura-Mae. First you got taken in by Barthez and Van der Haas, then you got taken in by Henry. But the biggest mistake you made was thinking I didn't know about it.' He paused for effect. 'I saw the look on your face when you came back from that monastery. The guilt and the shame of it was written all over you.'

'Well that's where you're wrong, Johnny. I didn't feel no shame at all. Why should I when I'd done nothing wrong?'

'Oh, my poor innocent child. There's me, accusing you o' things you ain't done, when all along your heart was right here with Johnny.'

That uncanny knack he had of guessing her motivation before she even knew herself. All the things they'd been through: the trek from one state to another, making money whenever they could; the time they'd spent in Chicago, where he'd fallen ill and she had to look after him. None of the hardship or sacrifice mattered anymore. All it had done was reduce them to this.

'Ole Henry boy wouldn't a been no good for you anyhow,' he said. 'You'd have gotten bored of him soon as you set foot in Mexico.'

'Well I guess we'll never know now, will we?'

'That's right, honey. Guess we never will.'

Whatever 'truth' she tried to reveal, Johnny would somehow turn it around to match his own version. Worse still, some of the things he said were true; she couldn't deny it to herself any longer. All the things she'd done with him had been of her own volition. Her deliberate cultivation of Barthez to further her career. The affair she had with Van der Haas that ended in tragedy. Even the act she put on the night they met the Simpsons, knowing what was going to happen. How the four of them had become friends, going out on sailing excursions along the coast. Donald's increasing reliance on Johnny on-board the yacht, and how quickly Johnny learned the rudiments of sailing.

She'd pushed all these things to the back of her mind. But Johnny had made her take a peek in that darkened room, and she didn't like what she saw.

*

The drinking and storytelling went on around the galley table while they were still moored in the bay. Donald did most of the talking, his voice getting louder and his observations more obscene. Johnny encouraged him, sharing tales of his own — variations of incidents she'd heard before that he made bigger and bolder to create the desired impression. Sheri listened, only interrupting occasionally to confirm something Donald had said.

Then Donald insisted that Sheri show them the handgun he'd bought especially for her — a small, pearl-handled revolver that fit neatly into her shoulder bag. They all remarked on what a fine piece of craftsmanship it was, perfectly made for the palm of a woman's hand. Laura-Mae asked if she could take a look, and Sheri said, yes, of course, and handed it over. Holding the revolver in her right hand, she felt its weight, the cool contours of the metal against her skin. Johnny told how he'd once seen a man play Russian Roulette in a bar in Chicago, drunkenly spinning the chamber and pointing it at his head. The story resonated with her for some reason, perhaps because of the theatrical element, the drama such a scene would cause. And while Donald poured more wine and they talked some more, she examined Sheri's revolver in more detail, thinking how snugly it fit and how tempting it felt with her finger on the trigger.

Gripped by some strange impulse, she looked up.

'Why don't we play right now?'

Johnny stared at her across the galley table. 'Play what, honey?'

'You know. A little game, like the guy in the bar.' She put the revolver to her head and held it there. Donald froze, his jaw hanging open. Sheri put a hand to her mouth in horrified anticipation.

'Put the gun down, honey,' Johnny said with forced calm.

'What do you think would happen if I pulled the trigger?'

'Just put it down now.'

She held the gun there, defying him, conscious of the electric atmosphere in the room, the eyes of them all upon her.

Reaching over, he grabbed her wrist, and snatched the gun from her hand. 'I said put it down! Hell's the matter with you?'

No one said a word, the congenial atmosphere broken.

Unable to take the silent reproach, she got up and fled – up on deck, where the lights of the bay had an instant calming effect. She thought about what she'd done. The strained looks on everyone's faces. For the few seconds she'd held the gun to her head she had their complete attention, the sense that she was in complete control.

Johnny came up, and took hold of her arm. 'Hell's the matter with you! You trying to ruin everything?'

'I was just fooling around.'

'What – by putting a loaded gun to your head and acting the goddam fool? How'd you think that makes me look in front of people?'

'Sorry to ruin your evening, Johnny.'

He shook her roughly. 'Now you listen to me. We gotta good thing going on here, and I ain't having you louse it up.' He let her go, and looked out over the water, composing himself to face her. 'Now come back down with me. We'll make out it was the wine made you do it.'

'I don't like the way Donald keeps looking at me.'

'Yeah, well just stick with it a while longer like I told you. That's all you gotta do.'

She went below, and the incident was forgotten. But she knew instinctively that it wouldn't end there. Donald kept right on staring at her in that sleazy, hooded way men had when they were drink-taken. And she detested him more and more for what he represented, the comments he made to her when Johnny wasn't there. He reminded her of all the mean and loathsome opportunists who'd gone before, determined to take from her the only thing she had to give, that sometimes they were prepared to take by force if necessary. She had her own way of dealing with people like that.

When Johnny gave the signal later, she was ready. Everything just naturally fell into place.

*

Pale dawn gave way to the rising sun, an infusion of colour across a murky grey sky. Like sailing into a furnace, the entire horizon lit-up. She felt an overwhelming sense of smallness, the sheer insignificance of her existence in the face of all this. And yet somehow she was a part of it too, forced to endure the unendurable.

The wind dropped. *Indigo*'s speed decreased; the mainsail, once full and stretched tight, now flapped listlessly. Thoughts of food converged – plates of salad and sardines, baskets of fresh bread, a hog roasting on a spit. Hopes of seeing the coastline materialise had come to nothing. In front of them the same expanse of sea, stretching into infinity.

Sunhat on, and cream smeared over her shoulders, she sat on deck. Johnny lounged in the stern by the helm, gazing out at the horizon.

'How long before the wind picks up?' she said.

He shrugged. 'Who knows? I ain't privy to that information.'

The warm breeze dropped away to a whisper, and a new source of anxiety set in. The flat seas had simply switched off, even the wave tips falling away in apathy. *Indigo* simply sat there on the glassy surface, abandoned, lacking energy and motion.

'Can't we start the engine?' she said.

'We could, but we'd run out of fuel. We'll just have to sit it out and hope our luck changes.'

She had the eerie feeling that time had stopped. Even the odd gull that circled above them seemed affected, falling on the air current and struggling to rise back up again. Perhaps it had always been this way. Nothing moving beneath the surface; no signs of life out there on the ocean. Without any wind, the heat bore down, making it awkward to move around. They were stuck here, the two of them, forced to make the best of it until conditions changed and something happened.

By mid-afternoon there was still no wind. Johnny tried to downplay the seriousness, claiming they were closer to land than she thought. Incensed at his stupidity she lost her temper. 'How can you come out with such crap! You don't even know where we are, for Chrissake!'

He gazed back at her, sullen and vindictive. 'I know more 'n you, you hear?'

She sensed his lack of conviction, his inability to change a thing. The locker space that once contained the tinned produce, dried meat, and powdered milk was now empty; all that remained was a depleted jar of coffee. To maintain the strength needed to sail the yacht they would need sustenance of some kind. A squall like the last one would mean a concerted effort to store things away and whip in the mainsail, attend to all the myriad jobs on deck. Without the necessary energy they wouldn't be able to cope.

Tired and hungry, she took over at the helm. Johnny looked diminished, like the fight had all but drained out of him.

'Sorry,' she said.

'For what?'

'Yelling at you earlier … I said a prayer we'd make it to the coast.'

'Well, that's good to know, honey – maybe that'll do the trick.'
'How you feeling?'
'Oh, I've had worse than this.' Something in his smile chilled her, a little too hard to be sincere. She knew then that the game wasn't over. She would have to watch him all the time. Try to anticipate what he might do next.

*

She woke to the sound of the engine coughing to life. The guttural, diesel sound reassured her in some way, a sense they were finally moving.

Johnny emerged from the saloon, his face sombre, a look that said he'd done it for her and she ought to be grateful.

'How much fuel we got?' she yelled above the engine.

'Not much.'

'Enough to make it?'

He shrugged. 'Who knows? What choice we got?'

Scanning the horizon from the bow, she looked for the slightest outline, a smudge of distant grey that might signal land. The same desperate hope sailors must have had from the earliest voyages. All she saw was the sea, miles of desolate ocean stretching around them.

Twenty-minutes later they were no better off. Johnny reduced the speed to conserve whatever fuel was left, conscious of the distance ahead. The hope she'd felt earlier turned to a numbness, a feeling of unreality.

Finally, after heading pointlessly at the horizon for as long as he could bear it, Johnny gave up and turned off the engine. *Indigo* settled into the wash, and the heat bore down again.

'That's it,' he said. 'Nothing else we can do.'

'What about the radio? Can't we try that again?'

'There's no signal. I tried it earlier when you were sleeping.'

She sank down onto the deck, drained and unable to speak. The prayers she offered up sounded weak and ineffectual, even in her own head. Johnny was right. The God she prayed to didn't listen, probably didn't exist, except as a vague notion of comfort to hang onto. Now all they had was each other, and the thoughts of what might've been had it turned out different. All this and the stillness that bound them to *Indigo*. The glassy indifference of the water lapping, the depths beyond.

*

'Hey – come over here and see this!'

Looking up, she saw Johnny peering over the portside. Joining him, she stared down at the water and froze. A black dorsal fin broke the surface, cutting back and forth in a scything motion, a display put on for their benefit. A chill went through her at the thought of how close they were, only *Indigo*'s flimsy hull to separate them from the dark shadow.

'How 'bout a swim?' Johnny said.

'Don't even joke about it.'

The shark stayed with them, diving beneath the hull and resurfacing. Its streamline grace made it perfect for the environment, a deliberate show of menace to anyone watching. What were the chances of survival in the water? she wondered. How long before you were torn to pieces and left to the elements?

As silently as it had appeared, the shark slipped away into the depths of the ocean. Like a portent of disaster it stayed in her mind. Stuck in this barren place with no respite, no human hand to reach out and offer comfort. And out there were these silent predators, taking their time, waiting for the moment to strike.

The last splutter of the engine had long faded away. Exhausted, she lay on her bunk and tried not to think. An overwhelming despair set in. All around her a boundless silence; no wind to stir the sails. Nothing but the sour, resigned look on Johnny's face every time she passed him on deck, as if he'd been waiting for just this moment to test her resolve and see how far she would go without breaking.

When she went on deck later, Johnny avoided her gaze. She stood looking down at him, doing her best to stay calm.

'Did you try the radio?'

'Still no signal.'

'But you'll keep trying, won't you?'

'Sure, honey.' His voice sounded unusually remote. She tried to bring an authority to her own, to challenge his mood of despondency.

'We're gonna make it. The wind'll pick up soon, I been praying for it.'

'Well you keep right on praying, 'cause that's about all we got.'

His solemn declaration unsettled her more than she could show. But more than that it was the look he gave her, a kind of glassy-eyed acceptance of the whole thing. This is it, he seemed to say. We've gone about as far as we can go under our own steam, now it's down to fate to decide the rest.

*

They made contact late that afternoon. Johnny sent their coordinates to a man who spoke in faltering broken English, his voice repeatedly cutting out over the airwaves. She couldn't help thinking how unlikely it was that anyone would find them out here; they hadn't seen another ship for days.

Johnny kept repeating the same details, an urgency in his voice that hadn't been there before. Couldn't they send someone out to meet them? Bring fresh supplies? 'We've run out of food and water,' he said, with a note of desperation. 'We can't last out much longer.' The foreigner rambled on in his confused English, lapsing into a dialect she didn't recognise.

Frustrated, Johnny gave up, and sat glaring at the radio. 'Goddam foreigner, couldn't understand a single word I said.'

The whole thing seemed so unfair, a ridiculous joke being played on them from above. Who would find them out here? Even a plane would have trouble spotting them on such a vast tract of ocean.

'We can't just give up,' she said. 'There must be something else we can do.'

'Like what?'

'What about the flares – can't we use them?'

'Maybe later, when it's dark.'

The idea grew in her mind. Firing off a flare would light up the night sky and signal their position to any ships within a certain radius. It might be all they needed.

She sensed Johnny's reticence, that same hesitation he'd shown when she asked him to try the radio.

'You don't want to, do you?' she said.

'What?'

'Use the flares. You don't want to, I can tell.'

'I said we'll try later, didn't I? Now quit hassling me like it's my fault we're stuck out here.'

His attitude bothered her, but she understood the reasoning behind it. He always said he'd rather die than face the chair, or years on the farm – and under Californian State law the former was always an option. And, if captured, she too would have to take her chances, relying on the fairness of a trial and a merciful judge. Better they were apprehended by the Mexican authorities, if at all.

But it was no longer just the prospect of prison they were facing. The likelihood of starving to death out here on the water had become a real possibility. Long hours stretched before them, an unbearable void that could only be offset by distraction. The last meal they'd eaten seemed like a banquet – a pitiful handful of rice and a strip of dried meat.

To take her mind off food, she focused on abstractions instead: pleasant fantasies of home life that surprised and amused her as if they were real; walking back through the alleyways of her childhood that added a touch of nostalgia. Innocent daydreams that weaved in and out of her consciousness like a reel of film. Her mother, standing in the doorway, calling her in. Six hungry kids sat around the kitchen table, all jostling for position, the older boys snatching hunks of bread right out of the little ones' hands.

Images of Henry, too. In one such fantasy she lived with him in a beautiful house on a hilltop with spectacular views. At night they danced to classical music, alone in a spacious ballroom filled with oil paintings and grand furniture. Soothing images, so real they helped release a small part of the dread and anxiety she felt. If *Indigo* was to become her prison, she had to find a way to deal with it, to cope with the trauma of so many hours on-board with nothing to do.

Johnny came down later and sat at the chart table. She prepared herself to confront him, hoping he would listen to reason.

'We're gonna have to cut down on the water,' she said. 'Make what we got last.'

'Whatever you say, honey.'

'Don't say it like that.'

'Like what?'

'Like it's my fault or something. I'm just trying to think ahead.'

In odd moments she thought about jumping overboard to escape, an impulse she'd had once before when seasickness took hold. But the sharks were out there waiting, patrolling the depths like sentinels. Nature, it seemed, had worked it all out beforehand, cutting off all the escape routes and leaving a paltry hope as consolation. More evidence that the God she believed in didn't exist, the prayers she offered up little more than empty whispers.

Johnny's eyes shone with an unnatural brightness, his pupils dilated; on his face the same sickly grin. She got the feeling he was enjoying the situation, pitting his ability to suffer against hers. In many ways she was still his pupil, waiting for him to show her the way. The test was to see how far she could go under her own direction, without needing him to instigate the next move.

'Why don't you try to get some rest,' she said.

'What – and miss all this? I got me a front row seat and that's where I'm staying.'

Nothing stirred but a gentle lapping against *Indigo*'s hull and the creaking of her timbers, the sounds that encapsulated life on the water. Dark thoughts arose. Troublesome links to the past that lingered in spite of her efforts to get rid of them. The unsigned contract lying on Barthez's desk in his book-lined office. The telegram Van der Haas had sent her from Encino before he disappeared. She'd lost so much, a life rich with possibility and glamour. And all for what? So she could travel all this way and end up with nothing?

*

Footsteps in the saloon. An intrusion into her thoughts; a reminder Johnny was still there in the background and not just laid on his bunk staring at the cabin walls. Maybe he'd fall ill again and not make it through the night; the fever would catch hold of him for good this time and not let up. The thought gave her an odd thrill, a glimpse of freedom. No more bringing him drinks and whatever medicine she could find to improve his condition. No more listening to his constant abuse. Sick people often turned on the nursemaid as a way of getting even. She'd seen it before with her granddaddy, who snapped and growled his way to the end from cholera, refusing help from anybody, including members of his own family.

Now the food supplies were gone, Johnny's sickness would be even harder to cope with. The water supply wouldn't last. She'd seen the markings on the tank and realised how low they were, but had chosen not to tell him. All these elements drained the vital energy needed to survive.

A burst of static from the saloon – he must have been trying the radio again. She heard him turning the dial, the crackle of voices breaking out. Shards from the outer world that had given up on them. Then music – a symphony, loud and distinctly out of place.

She found him at the galley table, staring into the void; sweat lined his forehead, his eyes glassy and unnatural. Discordant jazz music pounded the saloon walls, violins like devils, screeching out across the still water.

'What're you doing!' she yelled.

'Sending out a distress signal like you asked. Is that OK?'

The music jarred, an insane parody of their situation that overwhelmed her completely. She switched the radio off, and turned to face him.

'What the hell's the matter with you?'

'I was just trying to make contact with the outside world, honey. Ain't that what you wanted?'

She sank down onto the seat opposite his, and took a breath. The warm air caught at the back of her throat. He smiled at her, unperturbed.

'You know you really shouldn't get so worked up about all this, Laura-Mae. It don't help none.'

Some other time she might've shared the joke with him. One of the things she'd first found so attractive about him, this ability he had of making her laugh when she was trying to be angry.

'I'm all in, Johnny.'

'Me too, honey. Guess all the prayers in the world ain't gonna help us now.'

Easing himself from the seat, he stood, and headed for the steps.

'Where you going?' she said.

'All hands on deck. There's work to be done.'

The view from the deck added to her despair, an endless succession of white-tipped wavelets, so small they barely disturbed the surface. The only place on earth where the wind had dried up, leaving them floundering. And bearing down from its highest point, the noonday sun, as indifferent to their plight as the sea.

She couldn't rely on Johnny anymore, that much was certain. Something in him had become unhinged, affected by the heat, his illness, the worsening conditions. A practical plan, that was what was needed: an inventory of the situation that would establish their true position and how close they were to the coast; a look at the charts might help pinpoint their location and the distance remaining.

Hunger took hold with renewed intensity. In a desperate bid to find sustenance, she ransacked the locker spaces looking for supplies she might have missed. Nothing but a few stale crumbs at the bottom to taunt her – she ate them up anyway, grateful for the find, a trace of guilt lingering because she hadn't shared them with Johnny. The longer it went on, the worse the situation became; the constant gnawing in her stomach and the dull ache in her head a continual reminder. The likelihood that the water would also run out. A single glance at the ocean confirmed the injustice – volumes of undrinkable seawater that couldn't be touched without risking nightmarish hallucinations and even death. They had nowhere else to go. No option other than to endure and hope that relief would come from somewhere.

Night fell. The stars shone in the firmament, almost touching the black horizon line where the two met. Out here, a peace that might have transcended the hardship they were going through had there been some end to it in sight.

Johnny sat with her, scratching his beard, withdrawn to a place she couldn't reach. She felt compelled to speak, to establish some form of communication between them no matter how hard it might be.

'How you feeling?' she said.

'You asked me that before. I can't make the wind blow.'

'Johnny, I think we oughta – '

'Remember that song they used to play in Ventura? Went something like, "If I had wings like an angel, over these prison walls I would fly. And I'd fly to the arms of my poor darlin', and there I'd be willing to die." '

'Look – we can't just sit here. We gotta do something.'

He stood abruptly. 'You wanna do something? That's fine by me. Let's do something.'

She heard him below, banging cupboard doors and pulling out the contents. He came back and stood at the guard wire holding a flare gun.

'You realise what'll happen if they find us out here?' he said.

'What choice we got?'

He fired the gun. Brilliant streaks of orange and red exploded high above *Indigo*'s mast, lighting-up the night sky. A surge of hope rose within her. Out here, they were the only ones to bear witness, but maybe a passing ship's crew member would see the warning lights, and alert the captain. The ship would change course and come to their rescue.

The sparks died out, the last traces falling over the ocean, then blackness.

'Do you think anyone saw it?' she said.

'Who knows? A thousand miles of ocean, and we're right in the goddam middle.'

A familiar fear set in: the feeling of being alone and abandoned in such a hostile place. Beyond *Indigo*'s bows, the same vastness that stretched in all directions, east to west. The sensation she had sailing out in the bay for the first time, when the coastline disappeared and all that was left was the sea.

'How many flares we got?' she said.

'Two more. We'll save them until later. Increase the chances of someone seeing us.'

'Please don't blame me for this.'

He fixed her with his fevered gaze and smiled. 'Guess it all had to end somewhere. Why not out here with you?'

Now he was composed and amenable, as if his earlier behaviour had been a one-off. Perhaps it was the reality of the situation, weakening his resolve and making him more vulnerable. Whatever it was, they were now united in one respect. An acknowledgement of what was happening and how little they could do to change it.

'I think we should … ' She turned, thinking he was still there, but he'd gone below.

Alone on deck, she surveyed the dark wilderness, an idea of what it would be like if something happened to Johnny and she was left on her own. Would she be able to find the necessary strength to carry on? Reach the safety of the coast without him, and somehow make contact with the Colonel?

*

Looking in on him from the cabin doorway, she knew at once. He was laid on his bunk, face up, eyes closed, breathing unevenly.

'Johnny?'

He didn't stir. She tried again.

'Johnny – are you? – '

'Let me alone. Can't you see I'm resting?'

She took a step inside the cabin. He looked weak and somehow reduced on the white under sheet, his body glistening with sweat.

'Can I get you anything?'

'Just leave me to die in peace, ship my bones back to Texas.'

'Please don't talk like that.'

'Talk any goddam way I please.'

Leaving him there, she tried the radio again, tuning in to several frequencies without success.

'Mayday! Mayday! Mayday! … This is the yacht *Indigo*. We're somewhere off the Mexican coast, co-ordinates unknown. We've run out of food and we have very little water. Please help us!'

A burst of static in reply.

'Hello? … Is anybody there?' She sank back, exhausted. The onus now on her to take control. Johnny had nothing left to contribute. Any hope of them reaching safety would be down to her.

She took a swig from the water bottle, and checked the level. Enough, perhaps to last for one more day at the most. Johnny would have his quota. She'd see to it, measuring out the remainder so that they each had an equal share.

Something stopped her. The precious liquid meant life or death. The more she gave to Johnny, the less there was for her. And yet to deny him would be unforgivable, a betrayal of the worse kind.

*

The cabin was dark by the time she went in. She stopped by the door, a palpable distaste at the sight of him lying there, so reduced in all his faculties. The fever had given him a strange aura, as if his whole body had been lit-up somehow.

'I've brought you some water,' she said.

He tried to sit up, his breathing ragged.

'Here, let me help you.' She put her arm under his head, noting how cracked and parched his lips were. An involuntary revulsion went through her, quickly suppressed. Already he was becoming a burden to her: a duty, a responsibility, something she had no real connection to.

She put the glass to his mouth. He drank, droplets of precious liquid catching in his beard. She took the cup away, and held it at arm's length.

'Take it easy, it's got to last.'

As she went to get up, he gripped her arm, raising his head from the pillow by an act of will. She tried to pull away.

He tightened his hold, his eyes wild and fearful. 'You gotta help me.'

'Johnny, please!'

She managed to break away, his grip leaving a red mark on her wrist. He sank back on the bunk, exhausted. Gazing down at him, she felt sadness. The essence of whatever life had possessed him was no longer there. He seemed closer to the end now than at any other time.

His eyes locked onto hers, desperate to impart something she couldn't understand.

'There's things you should know.'

'You already told me that.' She spoke softly, nursemaid to a sick child. 'Now I'm going on deck. I'll come back later and see how you are.'

'I did what I could, Laura-Mae.'

She stopped at the door, barely able to look at him. Something in his voice made her pause, an edge of desperation, perhaps.

'She didn't mean nothing to me. Nothing at all.'

A confession of some kind; a reference to the fateful night in California, perhaps.

'I only ever wanted you, honey. That's all I ever wanted.'

'Johnny, if you've got something to – '

'Everything I did I did for you … But she kept on at me, see? … Wouldn't leave me alone.'

'Who?'

He stared back at her, the driving force that was once so strong now diminished.

'Thought they were better than us,' he said. 'All that money

… Didn't mean a goddam thing.'

'Who you talking about? … Sheri?'

He nodded slowly, watching her reaction as the realisation sank in.

*

She sat with the journal on her lap. Tucked inside the back pocket was the faded dollar bill, various receipts and postcards from places they'd stayed at – all with some sentimental attachment long since forgotten. Reading through the earlier entries she felt the same discomfort, the words of someone no longer around. But the need to know persisted, making her read on.

She didn't mean nothing to me. Nothing at all.

Johnny's statement didn't make sense. Could've been the fever talking. And yet he meant for her to hear it, the intent clear in his eyes.

Turning the pages, she looked for a word, a clue. The entries were written in Sheri's meticulous hand – neat blue lines on rich, crème paper. Descriptions of parties and invitations, the leisurely pursuits of the privileged. All the things she herself had read about and scorned, thinking them brash and boastful, the recollections of someone who'd never known what it was like to have nothing.

Then the first reference:

May 15 – "Johnny came over to talk about a real estate deal with Donald. They seem to get on well together. I can't help thinking that Johnny's like the son Donald always wanted."

Gripped by a sense of urgency, she read on, scanning later entries for any further mention of Johnny. The tone changed. An element of doubt and uncertainty crept into the writing.

May 29 – "Johnny came over while Donald was out. I like his company and we have a lot of fun. Wish he was around more often."

June 3 – "Donald's arranged for us to go sailing again with Johnny and Laura-Mae. I'm so confused. Not sure how I'm going to feel, seeing Johnny with her, knowing what she put us through the last time."

June 7 – "We sailed to an island yesterday, just me and Johnny. Donald's away for a week, so it won't bother him none. Sometimes I don't think he cares what I do. But being with Johnny is so exciting, he makes everything such fun."

June 9 – "We had such a good time I didn't want to leave. Johnny is everything Donald is not, and I suppose being with him so intimately brought it home to me. It's all happened so fast I'm not sure what to do."

June 10 – "My head's all over the place. Johnny came over when Donald was out and we fooled around by the pool. I don't know what to do. I think I'm falling in love with him."

Closing the journal, she sat there, numb with shock. Johnny's lies and deceit finally exposed between the pages. Everything else made sense now. All the denials he'd made on the island to cover himself. Dr Martinez' insistence that he'd seen Johnny before. Henry's subdued behaviour whenever they were all together.

She went back to the cabin, and tossed the journal on the bed.

'I hope she was worth it.'

He stayed mute, his silence a deliberate provocation.

'What's up – you got nothing to say?'

A strange pity arose in her, an understanding of what it must have been like to carry this secret around for so long, after all the other lies he'd told her.

His flat, uncompromising look gave it away; one more aspect of him to deal with. Something else dawned. A sense of betrayal. Of having lived and performed in his shadow for the better part of five years, during which time she'd suppressed all her hopes and desires to become his plaything. He knew everything there was to know about her. All the details of her childhood. The abortion she'd had. How her daddy had run off and left her when she was a kid. And yet he'd denied her the one piece of him that might have made a difference.

'I guess I never knew you at all,' she said. 'The promises you made me. All them heartfelt pledges of love when we were in California. You were making them to her too.'

He stirred, agitated, breathing heavily. She looked for some connection, some significance. All she got back was his mute stare, the watery-eyed look of sickness that still beheld an element of insolence towards her, as if everything he did was intended to get back at her in some way.

'Do you hate me now?' he said.

'I don't hate you at all. I feel sorry for you, 'cause you can't help being the way you are.'

She felt lost, a sense of confusion on the one hand and a reluctant understanding on the other. The man she'd known for so long as Johnny Boy was really someone else. His whole life a kind of fraud, a pointless deception.

'You planned the whole thing, didn't you?' she said. 'The argument you had with Donald, making out it was all his fault … Then you drew me in to help get rid of Sheri so she wouldn't be a problem to you no more.'

Fourth of July – fireworks exploding in the night sky, a mood of celebration in all the towns and all the cities across America. *Indigo* moored out in the bay. The meeting with the Simpsons and the intended trip on the yacht. It all made perfect sense from Johnny's perspective. His needing her to know was a kind of reaching out, an attempt to make up for all the trouble he'd caused.

The past flooded in, a door opening to another room. Things she'd never connected before. The night Van der Haas went missing, and Johnny claimed he'd been in Ventura. She'd always felt that something was missing.

'You killed Van der Haas too, didn't you?'

He made no attempt to speak. His look said it all.

'You killed him because he'd been with me, and you couldn't

take it.'

The door opened a little wider. The night she'd found him at the galley table with Henry, the two of them drinking, their conversation and laughter, excluding her from joining in. Johnny had let it play out then, dictating every move as he saw fit. Henry must've known about Sheri, one more betrayal from someone she thought she knew.

She lay a hand on Johnny's forehead, soothing him, just like Margot Katz did to Randolph Carlson in *The Barbary Pirates*. 'Rest up. Won't be long. When we get to Mexico, we'll make contact with the Colonel, get you some help.'

He shook his head slowly, his turn to pity her now.

'What?' she said.

'I thought you was cleverer than that, Laura-Mae. Thought you had it all worked out.'

'What're you talking about?'

'There ain't no Colonel. Never was … How 'bout that?'

*

Alone on deck, she played out the film of their time together: like one of Barthez's cheap tragedies, where the poor innocent female was completely subdued by the leading male. How close they'd once been. The sheer joy and exhilaration of being with him, sharing his passion and energy. She'd given everything up to be with him, leaving her job at the studio, the security of a system that always took care of its own. Now all she had was this. The shell of a man who wanted only to possess her, who'd destroyed every opportunity she had for happiness and left her with nothing.

*

She went to him when evening fell, unwilling to venture too close. In the gloom, his chest heaved, his mouth locked in a permanent grimace. He didn't seem aware that she was there, his gaze fixed on the ceiling.

'Johnny – can you hear me?'

His breathless answer, ragged and indistinct. The voice of someone she no longer knew or understood.

She forced herself to speak. 'I want you to know it don't matter no more. Whatever you've done.'

He raised his head slightly.

'Water!'

Holding the glass to his parched lips, she watched him drink. When he'd finished, she stood back, unmoved, detached from his suffering.

'Were you in love with her, or was it just a casual affair?'

'Honey, listen – '

'I need to know. You owe it to me.'

He lay back, an effort to speak. 'I told you. She meant nothing to me. Nothing at all.'

She took a few steps towards the door, the empty glass in her hand. A few grains of sediment lay in the bottom, where the powder from the Nembutal capsules hadn't fully dissolved.

'Rest,' she said. 'Won't be long now.'

She settled in the stern and waited. The move gave her mental as well as physical freedom, allowing her to think and plan the next stage without Johnny getting in the way. Now they lived apart, even if the act was little more than a token. She could find ways to move around without disturbing him, forget he was even there.

The charts took her mind off things. She tried to work out where they were in relation to the course he'd set; they could have drifted off by miles now without knowing. All she had were the coordinates of an unfamiliar sea, and the instruments that baffled her because she'd never fully learned how to use them. On top of all this, her own weakened physical condition. The all-consuming hunger that never went away.

Without radio contact, they had no chance. With no other vessels in the area, there was no way of letting anyone know of *Indigo*'s position. The one flare they had left would illuminate the night sky for miles around, but in these waters there might be no one around to see it. If they didn't get picked up soon, she'd end her days with Johnny, their corpses drifting in the sun.

*

Alone with her thoughts, she gazed out at the water.

Everything seemed logical now. All her previous uncertainty had gone. And in her head, the voices of those she'd loved and lost willing her on. Her mother, talking to her when she was still a child, instilling in her the need to be the best you can be at all times. That if you looked hard enough, there was always a solution to every problem, a way out of any adverse situation you happened to find yourself in.

She knew what she had to do. Like closing the lid on a box of bad memories so you could start all over.

*

The gloom inside the cabin settled, pale light from the saloon relieving the shadows. She took a step inside, drawn to the still figure on the bunk and all he represented. For a moment she thought he'd stopped breathing, the creaking of *Indigo*'s timbers and the lapping of water the only sound.

'Johnny?' she said, little more than a whisper.

The unmistakeable turn of his head in the direction of her voice. The odd glint of defiance that summarised an entire lifetime.

'I feel kinda weird,' he said. 'Like the lights keep going out.'

She stood over him, out of reach, hands behind her back where he couldn't see them.

'I had to make a decision,' she said.

The blink of his eyes, a flicker of uncertainty, perhaps. The Nembutal, working its way through his system.

'Had to work out the best thing to do.'

His top lip curled in a lazy grin, all part of the game he'd been playing ever since she could remember.

'I always did what you wanted me to do,' she said. 'But somehow that was never enough.' She stepped closer. He lay still, compliant almost, as if this too was expected. 'But that's OK, 'cause it's over now … You're going home, Johnny.'

Whipping the cushion from behind her, she clamped it down over his face, and held it there until he stopped moving.

When it was over, she stepped back and looked at his still form.

All around, the sound of water gently lapping.

*

She stayed on deck until the sun came up. Spectacular as they were, the colours didn't mean much to her. She'd be quite happy never to see another sunrise again.

The fishing handle lay on the seat where she'd left it, the green line suspended over the stern and into the water. Next to it, the small paring knife she'd used to trim the tangled excess. Perhaps a fish might come and she'd find the strength to haul it on board. Except now it didn't matter. Nothing mattered except the story she had planned in her head.

*

A speck on the horizon, like a mirage at first. Soon she could make out the bow cleaving the water, the sound of the engine disturbing the tranquillity. There were men on board; she could sense their interest, their keen anticipation, even from a distance.

On it came, the engine growing louder, the bow wave getting bigger. Now she could see them, the upright figures of the federales in their dark green uniforms, guns by their sides. And in that moment she imagined Barthez, standing behind them with a bullhorn, ready to yell 'Cut!' when the scene was over.

All she had to do was step aboard the vessel and into the custody of strangers. And there she would tell them exactly what had happened. How she'd been held prisoner all this time, coerced into doing all those terrible things. God alone knew what she'd been through and He would surely forgive her. And forgiveness would mean a return to the life she'd abandoned. A big house with servants, just like the one Barthez had in Beverley Hills. There she would sit by the pool and drink gin cocktails, reading about her comeback in the trade papers. Life would be good again. Just like it had been before she met Johnny.

FICTION

<u>The Butterfly Collector</u>

What happens when everything you have is not enough?

Restless property developer, Peter Calliet meets a sullen young woman at a party and an obsession begins that links past and present in a deepening tragedy.

Peter has everything in terms of material success and security. The obligatory fast car, lucrative contracts with his powerfully connected father's property empire and a plush renovated flat. Devoted fiancée, Claudia, expects to move in and marriage is imminent. But Peter has a dark past that taints his movements. Meeting Natalie, a volatile artist with an equally disturbed background, can only lead to more heartache. If Claudia discovers that Peter has been seeing Natalie, her dream world will be destroyed, adding to his burden of guilt. But even that can't stop him. The secure and rewarding life he has worked so hard to achieve begins to unravel.

'Peter Calliet is very believable, with that mix of liberal thinking and callousness that's essentially human.'
Nikki Copleston

'Dickson has a talent for expressing emotional anguish perfectly in prose and it makes the characters feel even more believable.'
The Kindle Book Review

FICTION

<u>Drowning by Numbers</u>

It's 1994. Blur and Oasis are in the charts. New Labour are on the horizon. Ladbroke Grove is the place, a thriving hub of art, music and cultural diversity.

Emerging from the wreckage of another lost weekend, Indie Guitarist of the Year, Joe E Byron, hurries home on the Tube to face the consequences of his actions. Ten years on the road has taken its toll. He should be spending more time with Justine and the kids. Instead, he's restless, angry, and in conflict with his manager and the rest of the band. Dark habits threaten his marriage and his career. The curse of addiction which will rob him of everything. And at the heart of it all, a yearning to be free, to take off and never come back.

But that can't happen.
There's too much at stake.
Besides,
He's a god.
He's a legend.
And the only thing worse than dying
is the prospect of fading away.

'If you're looking for a happy ever after ending, this book is probably not for you, but if you're looking for an excellent read with a hopeful ending, you will love Drowning by Numbers.'
Pamela Fudge

FICTION

<u>Billy Riley</u>

Fresh out of prison after five years, debt collector and one-time enforcer Billy Riley heads back to his council estate home with wife Eileen.

But things have changed since he's been away. The local kids run round in gangs, terrorising the neighbours with drive-by shootings and random drug deals. Respect for the old criminal hierarchy is gone. And turning 40 inside hasn't helped. His best years are behind him, future opportunities slipping away.

'Riveting... This begs to be adapted for the big screen!'
Jonathan Evans

'Hooked from the start, fascinating characters and a compelling storyline.'
EM Flattery

NON-FICTION

<u>Surfing The Edge</u>
A Survivor's Guide To Bipolar Disorder
The TV's on
The computer's on
The stereo's on
Sleep is a waste of time

Welcome to the world of Bipolar Disorder, a journey to the outer edges of the mind. A series of conversations told with humour, honesty and insight by Adam, Faye and Alastair, three survivors who have experienced the illness first hand. With contributions from Mental Health professional, Chris Kelly.

'Couldn't put this down, it rang so many bells for me. I recommend this to sufferers and recoverers or even just the nosey parkers.'
Angela Warren